Melissa nodde
was serious.

"Aren't we talking now?"

Bryan's tone teased, bringing another blush to her cheeks. "Before I consider taking on this job, I think we need to get some things straight. Important things."

Bryan stared at Melissa. She had that look. The look women got when they were determined to put a guy in his place. "Like what?"

"Well… I want a job, Bryan, nothing else. And the effort you're putting into being…nice and– and flirtatious isn't needed, because it's wasted on me."

"Is that right?" She was giving him hell because he was *nice*?

"Don't take it personally. I'm just asking you not to bother. There's no pressure for you to be…you know, Bang 'em Booker. That's the last thing I want. Just be my friend again. My *boss*," she stressed. "If you can do that, we can work together." Melissa held out her hand. "Deal?"

He took her trembling hand in his. She'd taken the lead and said everything he'd wanted to say to her. Well, not quite the same things, but close enough. The no-flirting rule, keeping things professional. It was all good. "Deal," he murmured, ignoring the slight punch in the gut he felt because she looked so relieved.

Dear Reader,

Melissa first appeared in *Man with a Past* as a secondary character battling a disease that has touched us all in some way. Breast cancer has taken mothers, daughters, aunts, friends. With Melissa, I wanted to portray the happy ending every cancer patient deserves. Melissa has had a tough time of it, and she deserved a hero who'd appreciate all she's gone through. That man is Dr. Bryan Booker.

Getting them together wasn't easy, because Bryan is perfect in so many ways. Too perfect. Tall, gorgeous, Taylorsville's most eligible bachelor. While she's... scarred, a woman who considers herself cancer postponed, not cancer-free. Can you put yourself in her world? How would you feel? I found myself digging deep, examining my life in ways I hadn't before, and finding things, both good and bad, that I needed to reevaluate.

I'm a firm believer that life and all its gifts, problems, struggles and moments boil down to what we believe, what we believe *in,* and how it's all too easy to let our fears rule our lives. It's easy for someone else to say don't do this or that, but when it's you, well, things are different, aren't they? Melissa is afraid and she has every right to be. But Bryan is a hero of heroes, and he proves to her that her worth isn't based on her cup size, her scars or the length of her hair.

I hope you enjoy Melissa and Bryan's story. Write to me at P.O. Box 232, Minford, Ohio 45653, or e-mail me at kay@kaystockham.com. For more information on my books, blog and monthly contests, check out my Web site at www.kaystockham.com.

God bless,

Kay

HIS PERFECT WOMAN
Kay Stockham

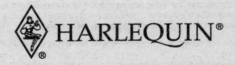

HARLEQUIN®

TORONTO • NEW YORK • LONDON
AMSTERDAM • PARIS • SYDNEY • HAMBURG
STOCKHOLM • ATHENS • TOKYO • MILAN • MADRID
PRAGUE • WARSAW • BUDAPEST • AUCKLAND

ISBN-13: 978-0-373-71424-7
ISBN-10: 0-373-71424-6

HIS PERFECT WOMAN

www.eHarlequin.com

Printed in U.S.A.

ABOUT THE AUTHOR

Kay Stockham has always wanted to be a writer, ever since she copied the pictures out of a Charlie Brown book and rewrote the story because she didn't like the plot. Formerly a secretary/office manager for a large commercial real estate development company, she's now a full-time writer and stay-at-home mom who firmly believes being a mom/wife/homemaker is the hardest job of all. Happily married for fifteen years and the somewhat frazzled mother of two, she's sold four books to Harlequin Superromance. Her first release, *Montana Secrets*, hit the Waldenbooks bestseller list and was chosen as a Holt Medallion finalist for Best First Book. Kay has garnered praise from reviewers for her emotional, heart-wrenching stories and looks forward to a long career writing a genre she loves.

Books by Kay Stockham

HARLEQUIN SUPERROMANCE
1307–MONTANA SECRETS
1347–MAN WITH A PAST
1395–MONTANA SKIES

Don't miss any of our special offers. Write to us at the following address for information on our newest releases.

Harlequin Reader Service
U.S.: 3010 Walden Ave., P.O. Box 1325, Buffalo, NY 14269
Canadian: P.O. Box 609, Fort Erie, Ont. L2A 5X3

To cancer survivors the world over,
most especially my mom, who showed me
a real woman's strength.

To Bill and Jessica—may you live happily ever after.

And to my family for all the smiles, the love
and the laughter. I am blessed.

CHAPTER ONE

"WANNA PLAY DOCTOR?"

Bryan Booker looked up from his computer and froze. Now that the latest agency temp had his attention, the woman gave him a smile impossible to misinterpret and sashayed over to his desk. She perched on the edge, fingering the stapler with suggestive strokes while she gave him another come-get-me glance.

"I thought maybe I'd stay and keep you company this evening. I'm sure we could...get some things done." She leaned closer, until her top gaped and he got an in-your-face view down the V-necked smock to her Victoria's Secret bra.

He swallowed a sigh. The fact he knew what brand of underwear she wore by sight alone was certainly indication that he knew too much about women's lingerie—and not enough about hiring employees. "Tricia—"

"You're not looking up porn sites, are you?" Her tone chided, but her salacious expression stated all too clearly she wished he were.

Bryan forced a tired smile. "Just e-mailing my parents. They're touring Europe for their fortieth anniversary."

"How romantic." Tricia leaned over even more and began to caress his arm. "Bryan, I was wondering...would you like to have dinner with me? I know you said we had to keep it all business during office hours, and I understand because of what a stick-in-the-mud Janice is, but she's not here, we're officially closed—" she almost purred the words "—and I bought something special today at lunch that I would love to show you."

Frowning, Bryan carefully plucked her hand from his arm and got to his feet. In response, Tricia lowered the leg she had crossed, leaving him plenty of room to step between if he so chose, but instead he grasped her wrist and tugged her off the desk.

After the invitation she'd just tossed out, she probably thought he was about to lead her upstairs to his apartment. He turned down the hall toward the reception area and waiting room, stopping in his tracks once he spotted the mess Tricia had neglected to clean up. A desk was under there somewhere.

"You didn't get the filing done?" he asked needlessly, pained at the sight of all the work he'd have to sort through before reopening his doors on Monday. He'd wanted to spend the weekend with his granddad, maybe take him out for a drive in the convertible since the weather was supposed to be mild. That wouldn't be happening now.

"No, not exactly. Between the patients and phones, and those horribly written notes you expect me to transcribe, I didn't have time. But…how about you let me make it up to you another way?" Her palms found his shoulders and she pressed her ample breasts against his chest. "I promise you'll like what I have in mind."

"You took a two-hour lunch." The results of which were contained in a pink Victoria's Secret bag sitting beside her purse. The knowledge that the nearest store was an hour away brought to mind his hellish afternoon of trying to keep up with patients, files and phones instead of the sensual pleasures advertised so prettily.

"You missed me?" Her smile widened, and seconds later she held a handful of gauzy fluff. "It wasn't easy making a decision in such a rush," she murmured before holding it up in front of her. She bit her lower lip before sliding him a coy glance. "Come on, Bryan, say something. Do you like it?"

He frowned again. "Tricia, I meant what I said about keeping relationships professional in this office."

Tricia's otherwise pretty features pinched into a series of lines and grooves. "That wasn't just for Janice's benefit?"

"No. You left me high and dry while you shopped, and you didn't return when you were supposed to, knowing Janice wasn't here to pitch in and cover for you."

His full-time R.N. had become a grandmother as of two o'clock that morning. A preacher's wife, Janice had been married nearly as long as he'd been alive, but she was feisty and fun, and he didn't have to worry about her coming on to him—or flashing him her lingerie. Janice's timing sucked, though, because she'd requested two full weeks of vacation to help her daughter get back on her feet after giving birth. Vacation that had begun this morning.

"I'm sorry about today, Bryan. Really." She wet her lips. "Forgive me?"

Firming his hold on Tricia's elbow, he grabbed her belongings from atop the mess and headed for the door. "Tricia, I appreciate the, uh, effort, but I don't think you're quite right for the job as my office manager."

"Oh, but—"

"I'll call Sierra and let her know I won't be needing your services any longer, but thank you for your time and hard work this week."

She placed a hand on his chest and dug in her heels, stopping their progress. "But, Bryan, I can make you feel *soooo* much better about your breakup with Holly."

She was attractive, no doubt about it, but he wasn't interested. *Because he needed help with filing?* Bryan bit back the curses on the tip of his tongue and escorted her the last two steps. "For the record, there was no breakup. Holly and I never dated exclusively." He shoved the items he held at Tricia before opening the door and gently but firmly pressing a hand between her shoulder blades to urge her outside.

Tricia blinked as if she'd only just realized her surroundings. On her face disappointment warred with fury, and her pink-coated lips peeled back in a grimace. "You mean...that's *it?*"

"'Fraid so. Take care of yourself and be careful driving home."

Her mouth dropped open, and her chest rose and lowered rapidly in agitation. "You're firing me *and* turning me down?"

He couldn't quite believe it himself. Bryan eyed the negligee in her hand, but not a single flicker of desire stirred within him. "Don't take it personally."

Tricia stood for a moment, huffing and puffing and visibly shocked that he'd said no to her considerable charms. Her mouth snapped closed, opened again and then she released an outraged shriek that rivaled any child who didn't want a needle before she stalked off toward her car. Bryan watched her go. How had life come down to scenes such as these?

He shook his head and was about to return to his computer when he noticed his neighbor standing on her porch not fifteen feet away. She snickered behind the hand covering her mouth.

That was the problem with his practice. Located between two occupied homes, his patients didn't have any privacy.

And neither did he. "Glad I could add a little amusement to your day, Ellen."

Tricia left the lot, tires squealing, and the act incited another round of laughter from the Taylorsville social worker, this one louder than the first since she no longer made an effort to disguise her amusement. Tears trickled from Ellen's eyes, and she nearly dropped the box she held clutched to her front in her bid to wipe them away.

Reluctant, Bryan jogged down the wheelchair ramp and over to her porch to take it from her. "Where to?"

"There." She waved a hand to where her car was parked, trunk open. "Oh, my. Bryan, I needed that so badly."

With a smile on her face and eyes sparking, Ellen looked to be around his age of thirty-two rather than the six or eight years his senior he knew her to be. "Bad day?"

She waved a hand in front of her as if she wanted to shoo away the question. "Nothing that time and patience won't solve," she murmured mysteriously. "But right now I've got some errands to run before heading over to the toy drive and barbecue at the police station. You'll be there, won't you?"

Her tone suggested he'd better put in an appearance. "I've got a ton of work to do, but maybe I'll drop by later."

Her brows rose in surprise. "You're working on a Friday night? Again? What happened to Crystal? Or Lisa? Or—" her tone lowered a notch "—Holly?"

"You know Holly and I never dated exclusively," he repeated for what had to be the thousandth time. He promised himself there and then that he'd be more discreet in his hookups.

"So she was another one hoping to change your wayward ways?"

Bryan lowered the box into the trunk. "All I can say is that you women have a vengeful streak."

"Looked to me like she was more than willing to comfort you this weekend," she murmured, gesturing to where Tricia's car had been parked.

He glanced at the blackened tire marks left behind. "My office is a disaster, and all Holly's sister will send me from the temp agency are marriage-minded women too afraid to break a nail unless there's a chance it might involve rough sex."

Ellen chuckled at his complaint, her expression telling him she didn't sympathize much. "I take it you haven't had any luck coming up with a fund-raiser then?"

He closed the trunk with a scowl. "When have I had time? Besides, people will gladly donate toys and food, but when it comes to cold, hard cash, they still look at me like the new guy just waiting to take their money and run. It's been three years and I'm still the outsider. I'm beginning to think the clinic will never happen."

Ellen clucked her tongue, the sound motherly. "Think positive—you'll come up with something. And I'll give some thought to your office manager dilemma. In the meantime, go lock up and come to the station for dinner. The work will still be there tomorrow."

"That's the problem." He glared at his office door and wondered how he'd be prepared for Monday morning the way things were now. If anything, Tricia had made more of a mess.

"No," Ellen corrected, "the *problem* is you pick the wrong women—something you've done as long as I've known you. If you want to change the way people see you, then you need to figure out why you're keeping yourself from finding happiness."

"They won't donate because they think I'm not happy?"

He tilted his head in pretended interest. "Ellen, that's far-fetched even for you."

"Fine, make fun, but the next time you find yourself in the mood, pick a woman, *not* a girl, who makes your blood heat just thinking about her."

"Makes my blood heat. What *have* you been reading?"

The woman gave him a good-natured swat. "You're not listening to a word I say, are you? Be that way, but if you ask me, you've brought this on yourself."

Bryan held up his hands in surrender, walking backward until he felt the asphalt end and the grass begin. Three steps more and he grabbed the door of his practice. "I didn't ask. Besides," he added with a teasing grin, "if you'd agree to date a younger man, I wouldn't *have* a problem." He yanked open the door but didn't make it far. Ellen's laughter stopped him again, and even though he told himself to keep going, his body refused to obey his brain. "What?" he demanded darkly.

Ellen shook her head at him, a patiently tolerant expression on her face. "Bryan, Bryan…oh, I feel for you. The moment you decide you've found the perfect woman, she's going to treat you *exactly* the way you've treated all those women whose hearts you've broken. You wait and see."

MELISSA YORK DROVE around the back of the house she shared with her father and parked, her thoughts a chaotic mess filled with snatches of conversation listing all the reasons she wouldn't be hired by the companies supposedly looking for employees.

Groaning, she opened the car door and the August heat practically melted her in the five seconds it took to grab the bag of groceries from the backseat and hurry inside. After her checkup with her oncologist in Baxter, she'd spent the day making cold calls to the few businesses at which she hadn't already left her résumé, then driven back to Taylorsville to do the same. Now she kicked off her heels, inordinately glad to be home.

Heaven knows she wasn't in the mood to cook, but since she was now well enough to help out, she figured healthy meals and a clean house would go a long way to repay her dad for the way he'd cared for her during the worst moments of her life.

Organic chicken awaited in the fridge. Maybe a salad? Lots of veggies, anyway. Cancer supposedly hated vegetables. *But loved her.* She wrinkled her nose, relishing the memory of good, old-fashioned, high-fat junk food, and set the bag of fruit and vegetables on the counter before reaching into the refrigerator for the chicken she'd left marinating overnight. In her haste she managed to drop the hard plastic container on her unprotected toes. "Ow! Oh, *shoot!*"

She hopped on one foot and held the other with her hand, rubbing hard and squeezing. Frustrated tears blurred her vision. Nothing had gone right today! Grabbing hold of the countertop for balance, she wriggled her brightly painted toes and glared at the Rubbermaid container on the floor. At least the lid had stayed on. She picked it up and slammed the large rectangle on the counter.

"Must've been some day," a voice murmured from behind her. "Anything you need to tell me?"

She started at the sound of her father's voice. So much for having dinner ready on time. She noticed her dad's hair was messed up. "Why are you home so early? Are you sick?"

Ruddy color filled his face. "Hello to you, too. No, I'm fine. I, uh, decided to come and get some paperwork done before a meeting."

"Oh."

"Well?"

Remembering what he'd asked, she shook her head. "You know I would've called you if anything showed up. I'm fine."

"Doesn't look like it. Bad day?" he asked, holding out his hand to keep the door between the living room and kitchen from swinging back and forth the way it normally did.

She nodded and washed her hands in the sink before moving back to take off the container lid. "You could say that."

Heavily callused hands settled on her shoulders and turned her to face him. "It can't be all that bad."

"No?" She reached up and smoothed his mussed hair, noting his cheeks got a little red again. "I think I'm wearing a big scarlet *C* on my forehead. I put applications in all over Taylorsville and Baxter, but *suddenly* the job market has disappeared." She shook her head in annoyance. "All they see is a walking cancer ad."

He pulled her hand away and held it, kissing her knuckles. "You'll find something, give it time. But why are you fixing dinner? Did you forget about the barbecue?"

The barbecue? She *had* forgotten. But only because she hadn't been asked to get involved. "Yeah, I...I guess I did. What was I supposed to bring?"

Her dad chuckled. "Just yourself. Everything's done. Came together smooth as silk. Ellen—remember me introducing you a while back at the station?—she's done a great job. She's, uh, in the living room now. We were going over some last-minute details when you got home."

For an event that would take place someplace else? Melissa eyed her father again. Was that lipstick on his mouth?

He let go of her hand and rubbed the spot, making it redder.

Just an itch. She shook her head at her imaginings, no doubt the aftereffects of paranoia brought on by being stared at like a leper during her job hunt. If she didn't find a job soon, she'd climb the walls. A house could only be so clean.

"Hal?" Ellen called from the other room. "I think I'll head over to the station now."

Melissa wondered why the woman didn't come into the kitchen to say her goodbyes. The brief meeting a few months back had left her with the impression of a well put-together woman with a warm smile, but little else.

"I won't be long! Tell Nathan to get the grill fired up before the mayor gets there and complains about the smoke."

"You need to go," she murmured. "I'm sorry for interrupting your meeting."

Her dad lifted his hand and smoothed it gently over her too-short hair. Barely an inch and a half long because it was taking forever to grow, she'd recently had the fuzzy ends trimmed and the overall style looked very Peter Panish. Not exactly a style most women would pick, but better than no hair at all.

"You vent anytime. Better out than in, you know that. Besides, taking your frustration out on a plastic container is a lot better than taking it out on a person like some people do."

Smiling at the truth of his statement, Melissa wrapped her arms around him and gave him a big hug. "I know," she said, resting her head against his chest with a sigh. The steady beat of his heart soothed her frazzled nerves; the scent of him calmed. Her dad was the one person who'd never let her down.

"You sure you're okay?"

She nodded again. "Yeah. But thanks for listening. I don't know what I'd do without you."

He squeezed her tight. "You'd do fine, Mel. You'd do just fine."

"I HAVE AN IDEA."

Bryan held the phone to his ear and leaned his head back against the desk chair. "Hey, Ellen. Shouldn't you be at the barbecue setting things up?"

"I'm on my way now," she informed him, "but I had to talk to you. There's no time to waste."

"Sounds urgent. What's up?"

"I know the perfect woman to be your office manager."

"Who?" Bryan sat forward, Ellen's excitement rubbing off on him. As a caseworker for the county, Ellen knew a lot of people wanting to better themselves, find work. Had she thought of one of them?

"Well, you know the, um, police chief?"

Bryan stilled, his racing thoughts skidding to a stop. "Hal York has a job," he murmured, deliberately misinterpreting and not commenting on the fact that he knew Hal York, mainly because the man parked his police cruiser behind his practice—and Ellen's home—about every night.

"I meant his *daughter*. Do you know Melissa?"

Bryan pinched the bridge of his nose. "Yeah, I know her," he murmured, his mind locking on an image of Melissa York, her bald, turban-wrapped head bent, her shoulders shaking while she sobbed after learning the truth of her infant daughter's death. He stood and paced around his desk. No way could he hire Melissa. "Does this mean you're ready to 'fess up and admit you and Chief York are an item?"

"Will it help? Hal loves me, but his daughter comes first. At least until she can focus on something else and stand on her own two feet."

Unease tightened his stomach. "Ellen—"

"You need help," she said, her voice taking on a pleading quality.

"I can't hire Melissa York." She hadn't talked to him after that day at her house. A glance here and there when they happened to meet up in town, a shaky smile before she quickly averted her eyes. He thought he'd done a good thing by telling her the baby she'd buried not long after birth hadn't been shaken to death, but instead his research into the incident had left Melissa blaming herself.

"Why not? She's *perfect!*"

Pulled from his thoughts, Bryan asked the obvious question. "Have you discussed this with her?"

"Bryan, she needs a job to get back on her feet, and it's always best to hire someone hungry for work. They make better employees, something you could use right now."

"I take it that means no?"

Ellen paused long enough for a healthy dose of guilt to settle in. He'd caused Melissa pain, however unintentionally, and she obviously felt awkward around him now. Way different than when they were little kids spending their summers playing together on the street corner downtown while her dad and his grandfather worked. But that was a long time ago, and Melissa wouldn't *want* to work for him any more than he wanted her to.

"Bryan, please? Will you give her a chance? For me?"

He hedged, trying desperately to think of a way out. "What does she know about running an office?"

"I know she's a smart, capable young woman who used to work as a teacher's aid while taking night classes at college. Hal said she loved her job, loved being busy. An office would be a breeze for her. And, Bryan—" her voice lowered "—Hal also told me that she used to handle the fund-raisers for the station. I feel badly when I think of that. I wouldn't have taken over the Christmas toy drive if I'd known. Especially since…"

"Since what?"

A weary sigh came over the line. "Well, Hal's asked to marry me—"

"Congratulations."

"—but I don't want our marriage to begin with tension between us. Which means we can't get married until Melissa is able to support herself again. She's put in applications all around, but she's had trouble getting hired because of...well, I think too many people know her medical history."

Yet something else for him to consider. Bryan fought his frustration. He hated being put on the spot like this. "You mean her cancer."

"Bryan, *please*. Put yourself in her shoes. She's ready and able to work and no one will let her try. You'd be helping all of us, most especially yourself, because you'd have someone who actually *wants* to work instead of spending her days flirting with you."

He eyed the mess on the desk then thought about the reception area, her words pulling at his conscience. "It's not a good idea."

"Why not? How many *credible* applicants have responded to your ad? You know very well there would be more, but a lot of husbands don't want their wives working with you because of your reputation. Janice is an exception and if her husband didn't have the utmost faith in her and their marriage, *she* wouldn't be there. And do you really want to deal with Sierra's temps week after week? Bryan, you need help and Melissa is a viable solution."

True or not, he wasn't about to be sucked in by Ellen's argument.

"Think of it this way. You're not going to find the right woman when you're so busy shaking the wrong ones out of your bed and working overtime. *Hire Melissa,*" she ordered. "Do something good for her and for yourself."

"And you?" Silence met his words. He paced the room, swearing beneath his breath but knowing Ellen had him. If nothing else he owed Melissa for the hurt he'd caused her, and for the time they'd spent playing together as kids. He also owed Ellen for all the meals she'd provided as a neighbor. "Fine. I'll do it." A squeal erupted over the line and Bryan held the receiver away from his head, a rueful grin tugging at his lips.

When the squealing stopped, he hesitantly brought the phone back to his ear. "I'll give her an *interview*. We'll see how things go from there. She won't want to work for me, and when this doesn't work out, you're back to square one and I'm off the hook. Got it?"

"Oh, Bryan! You're the best! No wonder you've won so many of the awards in the *Tribune*."

He winced at the reminder. "Ellen, a piece of advice—don't ever bring up the newspaper's moronic contest."

Happy laughter came over the line. "You make it sound like being a small-town hunk isn't all it's cracked up to be."

"Ellen."

She laughed again. "I'll see you at the barbecue. Melissa will be there and you can talk to her then."

"Tonight? But—"

"Bye!"

Bryan rubbed his eye with the flat of his palm and replaced the receiver onto the base with a mutter.

Women. What had he gotten himself into now?

CHAPTER TWO

MELISSA PAUSED long enough for her eyes to adjust to the dim interior of the police station before making her way past the paper-cluttered desks and down the hall. Outside the small kitchenette, she skidded to an abrupt stop and clamped a hand over her mouth to stifle her choked gasp.

She flattened herself against the wall out of sight, her shell-shocked brain struggling to process what she'd seen. No matter how many times she blinked, it was still there. Her father and the social worker. Their passionate R-rated embrace. One of his hands on the woman's breast, the other on her rear and did he have his...*tongue down her throat?* Blood rushed past her ears in frantic gushes.

"Did I tell you how much I missed you last night?" Ellen asked huskily.

Melissa didn't mean to eavesdrop, but her legs wouldn't move. They were locked at the knees to keep her upright. Nathan Turner might be the station's official grill master and quite good at the job, but no way on God's green earth would she step foot into that kitchen to get the spatula he'd sent her after.

"I couldn't stay any longer. Melissa's having a hard time of it and I hate to leave her alone so much. Just today she said she didn't know what she'd do without me."

Her father discussed her with that woman? Closing her eyes, Melissa moaned softly. How could she not have realized what was going on? The late hours her dad had started working to catch up, the way he'd begun taking more care with his appearance. *And the lipstick stain she'd dismissed as an itch?* Is *that* why he'd stopped the swinging door? To keep her from seeing his…his *girlfriend* on the other side in some state of—

She blinked, unable to imagine her father messing around in the living room in broad daylight and yet able to imagine it all too well after what she'd just seen. Why hadn't he said anything?

The sounds of more kissing ensued, and she wrinkled her nose, distinctly nauseous. No matter their age, no child wanted to see her parent in an openly sexual embrace. It was too…*eww.*

"Oh, Hal, I want to tell people and show them the beautiful ring you've given me. Please, promise me you'll talk to Melissa soon."

She straightened. *What ring?*

"I should've made your proposal more romantic, but I couldn't wait any longer. I can't wait to wake up beside you every morning, Ellie. Kiss you every night. It won't always be like it is now."

"No, it's fine. It was *beautiful!*" The woman sniffled softly. "And I understand. Melissa's in such limbo you can't leave her yet, but maybe that'll change soon."

She *had* been upset lately over not being able to find a job, but she hadn't come across that pathetically…had she?

A gusty sigh left her dad. "I hope so. I don't want to wait, but we have to. Just a little while longer," he promised. "Then we can start the next part of our lives and figure out what we're going to do in our old age."

Melissa swallowed the lump in her throat and unclenched her hands, her short nails leaving crescent moons embedded in her palms. Without considering the consequences but knowing she had to do—*say*—something, she stepped into the doorway and cleared her throat.

Her father jerked away from Ellen and clasped his hands behind his back. "Mel?"

"Sorry to interrupt, but I had to come tell you my news."

"News?"

She didn't look at Ellen Morton. "I've got a lead on a job." She laughed, but instead of happy and joyous, the sound came out high-pitched and strained, her smile nearly impossible to maintain. "Isn't that great?"

"A job with whom?" her father demanded.

Floundering, Melissa opened her mouth, her brain scrambling for a response. "Uh…"

"Me," a deep masculine voice answered from behind her.

Melissa whirled around, inordinately grateful her back was to her father when she realized Bryan Booker had come to her rescue. She stared at him in shock, her reeling senses in a time-stilled blur.

"'Evening, Chief. Ellen." Bryan dipped his head in greeting. "Melissa," he murmured, his steady gaze meeting hers and holding for a long moment.

What are you doing? She mouthed the question while sending him a suspicious glare, but other than a discreet wink, the handsome physician didn't respond. Why would he say he'd offered her a job? Given their history, she couldn't help but think it was because Bryan felt sorry for her.

Her father cleared his throat, a sure indication that he was working up a lecture and fast losing patience, and even though she'd like nothing better than to pull Dr. Booker aside and demand to know what was going on, two seconds later she found herself nodding her agreement that she had agreed to interview for the position of Bryan's office manager.

"That's certainly news. Ellen, if you and the doc don't mind, I'd like to speak to Melissa alone. We have some things we need to discuss."

"Dad, that's not—"

"Of course, Hal."

So much for putting him off. Was her dad going to question her about the job offer or what she'd seen? Melissa gulped back a nervous laugh and worked up her nerve to step into the room. She had to get away from Bryan's cologne. The woodsy, citrus scent teased her nose and caused an instant spike of awareness.

She moved to the window and tried to gather her scattered wits, pulling a childhood memory of Bryan from her mind and concentrating hard to dissect the details. Shaggy blond hair, dirty, sweaty little boy. A cowlick and a purple mustache due to a seemingly endless supply of grape juice. Those things she could think of and smile about, but not the way he was now.

"Ellen, would you like to go get something to drink?" Bryan extended his hand toward the woman, palm up.

While the social worker gathered her things from the kitchen table, Bryan flashed Melissa a steady stare that made her think he'd support whatever story she told her father. Question was why? Maybe they'd played together as kids, but that was a long time ago. She didn't want his pity, either, and after the mortifying scene in her living room late last summer, he couldn't be backing her up for any other reason.

Bryan and Ellen left the kitchen and their footsteps faded down the hall. Lacking another distraction, Melissa shifted uncomfortably and tried for nonchalance. "What's up?"

"How long were you standing out there?"

"Out there? Oh, not—"

"How long, Mel?"

She shrugged her shoulders and sighed. "Long enough."

When her father's gaze narrowed on hers, she felt much the same as she had at sixteen when she'd had to tell him she was pregnant. And unwed. The police chief's daughter knocked up. Now there was a fun night.

"You saw it all, didn't you?"

"Take it easy, Dad. I'm scarred for life, but after everything I've been through, what else is new?"

His expression darkened even more. "That is not funny."

Neither was his marrying a stranger. "I stumbled upon you and was surprised so I...eavesdropped a little," she admitted, lifting her chin. "I didn't mean to, and I'm sorry. There, happy?"

He seated himself on the metal table. "No, honey, I'm not happy. *I'm* the one who's sorry." His hand gripped the edge tight, his knuckles turning white. "You shouldn't have seen what you did. Not only was it out of line considering our location, but I should've told you about me and Ellen sooner. Told you we're a couple."

"Yeah, you should've. So why didn't you?"

"I wanted to, Mel. It just never seemed like the right time."

She walked to the cabinet and pulled out a glass, ignoring the tremor in her hands. "Or maybe you didn't tell me because you think I'm so fragile I can't handle the thought of you being with anyone but Mom." She turned on the tap and filled the glass.

"Melissa Ann—"

"I can handle it." The words came out sharper than she'd intended, plaintive. She tried again. "I can, I just—" Water sloshed over the brim before she realized the glass was full, and she dumped the contents, the force sending the water splashing out of the sink onto the counter. She ignored the mess and set the glass in the sink with a clatter, not caring that it toppled over when she swung around to face him. "How long have you known her? You can't possibly be considering *marriage!*"

A smile touched his lips. "It seems sudden to you, but we've seen each other about every day since she set up her office."

Taken aback, she blinked at him, the pain of being kept in the dark slicing deeper with his words. "But…that was months ago."

He nodded his agreement. "Six, nearly seven."

Her knees weakened and she leaned against the sink for support. The water she hadn't cleaned up soaked into her clothes, but she didn't move, didn't care. Seven months and he couldn't find the right time to tell her?

"At first we met to discuss cases, ways the station could help the families in her care. Then it became more." He looked up from his study of his callused hands. "I should've told you sooner. I regret that, but…I wanted to be sure of my own feelings before bringing it up."

"It's too fast."

"I love her."

She sucked in a sharp breath.

"And it's not too fast. Ellen makes me happy. She's a good woman, beautiful and kind and compassionate. When we're together…well, we forget ourselves and it's nice, Mel."

A smile flashed across her father's face, one she hadn't seen the likes of in a long, long time. "I see… Well, now I know," she murmured uncomfortably, dazed from having to absorb the news all at once. "Still, y-you kept your relationship a secret and that makes me think you're not sure of your feelings."

"I'm sure."

"No. You can't be. Y-you're *lonely*. That's understandable, but, Dad, rushing into—"

"I'm not rushing."

"Of course you are! Joe and I had dated a long time before I got pregnant, and you were adamant that we couldn't get married!"

"Joe was barely out of high school and you weren't—there's a *big* difference."

Her father's expression revealed his vulnerability, his need for her to be okay with this relationship. But she wasn't okay and she wasn't sure why.

"I love her, Mel. And I'm tired of being alone."

Her dad was lonely. She knew loneliness, lived in that deep, unfaltering, empty void that overwhelmed her when she least expected it. God knows she felt it every day of her life, endured it. *Hated it.*

Sometimes in the middle of the night she couldn't sleep, and she'd lie awake staring at the ceiling because she ached to have someone beside her. Someone to hold her, to share her nightmares and be her shelter in a storm of uncertainty and fear because she knew she'd never—*never*—

"Melissa, sweetheart…please try to understand."

She blinked back tears, refusing to give in to them. Her father had found his companion. She should be happy for him. Shifting sideways along the sink until she stared down at the dirty dishes, Melissa found herself thankful for something to busy her hands. She grabbed the utensils and coffee mugs, putting them in the dishwasher, thoughts sliding in and out of her mind faster than she could identify them.

"I should've told you. It's come as a shock, huh?"

"Yeah, it has. I guess I never thought of you dating someone else. There was just you and Mom." She laughed softly. "That sounds really self-absorbed, doesn't it?"

"It sounds like you had your own problems to deal with."

Yeah, she'd had problems. And through it all, he'd taken care of her. But who had taken care of him? "I just never—"

"Because it didn't happen, Mel. Since your mama's been gone, I haven't dated anyone seriously."

She turned to stare at him in surprise. Her mom had been gone nearly *thirteen years*.

"You're thinking in terms of a relationship and that's something I haven't experienced since your mother. I've had a date or two, but nothing meaningful or long-term," he admitted, head down. "I couldn't because…I wasn't ready."

"But all these years…"

His eyes were bloodshot and filled with undeniable emotion. "All these years I've grieved, Melissa. I loved her and always will, but I'm done mourning now. I'm ready to move on and I want to do that with Ellen." A bittersweet smile touched his lips before a dark scowl closed in. "What I'm *not* sure about is why you'd even consider working for *Bang 'em Booker*. Honey, I know you need a job, but are you seriously going to work for that—for *Dr. Love?*"

She wrinkled her nose at the nicknames. When Bryan had first moved back to town, she'd been dating Nathan, going to college and working. Then she'd been diagnosed with breast cancer, and her focus changed to that of dealing with the anger and the fear and the fallout. She'd been drop-kicked into cancer hell and it had ruined everything. Life as she'd known it had ground to a halt. Cancer hadn't allowed her to finish college, had ended her relationship with Nathan and required she quit her job because she just didn't have the energy or ability to perform it. One after another the blocks of her life fell, tumbling beneath the weight of her illness.

"Mel?"

"Yeah," she heard herself say, "I am." She'd heard the gossip. It was impossible not to considering how much time she'd spent at the hospital undergoing consults and checkups. Treatments. The nurses, the doctors, the aids. Everyone had a story to tell about Bryan's sexual antics with legions of willing women who took one look at his model-beautiful appearance and melted at his feet. He was a player, a one-night-stand wonder. "He's not hiring me because he's interested in me, Dad."

"Are you sure about that?"

"Absolutely." She pulled herself from her thoughts with a self-deprecating grin. "Get real. Bryan Booker has his choice of women fawning all over him. He wouldn't want someone like me."

Moving faster than she'd ever seen him move, her father closed the distance between them, gripped her shoulders and slid one hand to her chin to tilt her face up to his. "*You* are a beautiful young woman. Nathan might not have been able to handle things, but your mother had the same surgery and we—"

"Stop!" Melissa closed her eyes in a grimace and raised both her hands in a pleading gesture. "*Stop,* Dad, please. I mean it, do *not* give me any more mental images to deal with today. Walking in on you groping the social worker was a sight I'll never be able to obliterate from my brain. Besides," she continued when her father released a gruff laugh chock-full of embarrassment, "*you* are a special man and what you and Mom had was special." Opening her eyes, she blinked up at him. "Don't you remember?"

His hands dropped to his sides. "Of course I remember." The scowl returned, making him look older. "The point is, there are men out there who'd understand what you've gone through if you'd only give them a chance."

She smiled drily. "We'll just have to agree to disagree there. I think Nathan is a more accurate example of the male species." She shrugged, looking away. "I understand why he backed off, and I don't blame him."

"Mel—"

"But it doesn't matter because I'm not ready for that, and if I *were*," she emphasized before he could interrupt her again, "we've *both* heard of Bang 'em Booker's reputation. He'd be the last person I'd choose and I'm quite sure Bryan feels the same way about me. For pity's sake, we used to dare each other to eat worms."

Her father studied her closely. "So long as you're aware of the talk."

"I am, and you have nothing to worry about," she stated firmly. "Who knows if I'll even get the job, or accept it if I do? Now, can we get back to what caused these sudden realizations?" She raised a brow, hugged her arms around her stomach and tried to release the tension in her neck and shoulders because she knew it was bad for her. "You're dating again… Are you using birth control?"

"Mel!" Eyes wide and horrified, her dad turned away, his strides carrying him swiftly to the other side of the room. "You can't talk to your old man that way."

She'd rattled him. Good. Maybe it would get his focus off her. "You're only forty-seven. Everyone knows men can produce—"

"I am *not* having this conversation with my daughter." He groaned long and low. "It was bad enough when I realized I hadn't had it with you. Now you're trying to give *me* the sex talk?"

She laughed softly, amazed at what time and distance could do to otherwise pain-filled memories. "Fair's fair."

"Hey, Chief!" Nathan's booming voice echoed through the building and bounced off the walls. "Mayor's here! Mel, where's that spatula? My burgers are burnin'!"

Her father's shoulders sagged with relief. "Thank you, God. Mel, we'll talk more later. Duty calls."

She shook her head while watching him rush from the room. "Saved by the bellow," she murmured, opening a drawer and retrieving the spatula Nathan needed. Gripping it tight, she smirked. Maybe she could hand it to him without slapping it upside his head. Then again—maybe not.

BRYAN WOULD'VE LIKED to talk with Melissa more about the interview and position, but found himself back in his practice within moments of stepping outside the police station. A child running across the pavement had tripped and fallen, colliding with another on the way down. Both kids needed stitches and he'd instructed the parents to bring them to his office.

He patched up the second child's head one stitch at a time to minimize scarring and wanted the long day to be over. His stomach growled, reminding him he hadn't had dinner…or lunch. "Almost done, buddy. You're doing great."

The little boy sniffled softly, big tears rolling out of the corners of his eyes. The kid's mom comforted the child, allowing Bryan to complete two more stitches before tying off the special thread. He added clear bandage cream to the top and straightened.

"Done," he said, winking. "And since you held still and allowed your friend to go first, I think you deserve a treat."

The boy looked to his mother and she smiled. "Don't forget to say thank you."

"Thank you," the kid repeated dutifully, knuckling his eyes.

Bryan smiled and pulled off his gloves, moving to the cabinet across the room where he kept stickers and candy stashed on the top shelf. "Think you'll ever forget to tie those shoelaces again?"

The boy's dark head jerked back and forth. "Stupid shoes."

A noise in the doorway drew his attention, and Bryan turned to see Melissa standing outside. An anxious expression crossed her face, her startling blue eyes solemn.

"Sorry. I didn't mean to intrude. The door was unlocked."

"You're not intruding. We're done, right, buddy?" Bryan handed the boy a handful of stickers and a sour candy before lifting him from the exam table. After giving the mom a few instructions, the woman and child hurried out of the room and then he and Melissa were alone.

She shifted nervously and shoved her hands into her back pockets, the move stretching the material of her loose T-shirt a little more snugly across her small chest. Bryan tried hard not to notice. What was her treatment? A lumpectomy? Maybe a mastectomy? It wasn't any of his business, but having spent his residency in one of the top cancer-treatment centers in the country, the doctor in him was curious.

"So…did you mean it?"

His eyebrows rose. No niceties, no small talk. Definitely not a flirtatious tone. Just straight to the point though a bit shy. He liked it. Her behavior was quite a change from the norm, a reminder of the girl he'd known. "The job is very real, and so is my offer of an interview." He began putting the medical supplies away. "How did the toy drive go? Does Santa have a big haul?"

"The bin was filled three times at last count." She moved over to where he stood and picked up the liquid numbing agent, handing the bottle to him. "But the, um, guys got called out on a domestic-violence run, and Ellen Morton left to take one of her elderly cases to the hospital."

He glanced her way. "Any names mentioned?"

Melissa lifted a shoulder in a shrug. "My dad said something about Crimshaw Road. I...didn't talk to Ms. Morton much."

After witnessing Melissa's earlier surprise firsthand, Bryan wasn't about to touch that subject. He finished putting the supplies away in a cabinet and yanked the paper sheeting from the table with a jerk. "Sounds like we're all having a busy night. Does this mean you're interested in the job?"

She stared at him as though measuring his words. "Actually...I came to say thank you."

"For what?"

A brief smile touched her lips. "Because you heard them," she stated bluntly, "saw my not-so-subtle reaction and guessed my pride had me lying about the lead I mentioned— which I was. But you backed me up anyway. Thanks."

Bryan smiled. "What are friends for? Anyone else would've done the same."

"Maybe. The problem is that I don't want a job offer because you feel sorry for me. So thanks, but I'm sure I'll find something else soon."

"Melissa, wait." Bryan caught her arm before she could leave the room. Maybe he did feel sorry for her, but he certainly wasn't about to confirm it, not when pity was obviously the last thing she wanted. Acutely aware of how delicate she felt beneath his palm, he released her. "I feel sorry for *me*, okay? I just spent the last two hours patching up a couple squirming kids, and both parents left without paying me even though I saved them a trip to the E.R. in Baxter."

She blinked. "Really? They just *left?*"

He put the last of the supplies away. "Yeah. Maybe they'll stop by Monday to settle up, but who knows? It doesn't matter because I don't know how to enter payments into the computer system, and I haven't had any luck with the temp agency."

"You sound desperate."

He felt the heat of her stare and noted how her eyes had narrowed and her arms were crossed over her front. Unease slid over him and he knew exactly what she was going to ask next.

"So this job offer has nothing to do with you feeling bad about being the one to tell me how…my baby really died?"

CHAPTER THREE

BRYAN LEVELED his gaze on hers and frowned. "No."

"No?" Her chin lifted. "What about my medical history, then? Does that bother you?"

He leaned against the exam table, his temper rising because of the challenge he heard in her voice. If she didn't want the job, fine. All the better for him. Being around her, knowing what she'd experienced, brought back too many memories. "You couldn't have prevented Josie's death," he murmured, focusing on her questions and shoving the past away. "Too many factors played into her reaction to the medication, none of which were in your control. Your health, her premature birth. I imagine you and Joe will always maintain a certain feeling of guilt as Josie's parents, but you couldn't have done anything differently. Guilt is like that. All-consuming," he stated knowledgeably. "And while I'm sorry your baby girl died, that's not why I offered you the interview. As to your other question, what kind of doctor would I be if your cancer diagnosis didn't bother me?"

"I meant—"

"But I wouldn't not hire you because of it," he stated firmly. "Melissa, I have a business to run and patients to care for and I can't help but think that your experiences will give you a little more patience and empathy in comparison to some of the others I've interviewed."

"I...thank you," she murmured dazedly, blinking. "I'd like to think it would."

"I take it the diagnosis has kept other potential employers from hiring you?"

She nodded, her teeth sinking into her lower lip, her blue eyes soft, untrusting, and yet hopeful. It was the hope that got to him. Ellen had no right to dump this—her—on him, but he only had himself to blame. For not saying no, for letting the battle-weary hope in Melissa's eyes remind him of someone else. He should send her on her way, ignore Ellen, but he couldn't and he knew it.

Bryan shoved himself off the exam table and kept going, conscious she followed him into the waiting area. Facing her, he indicated the front desk with a hand.

Her eyes widened at the sight of the mess.

"This isn't an easy job. My last full-time person updated the computer system before she quit, and I'm no help at all figuring it out. Janice Reynolds is my R.N., but she only handles patients, not the phones, the files or the insurance forms that have to be filed. You'd handle those administrative responsibilities *and* take charge of planning a major fund-raiser that'll require working extra hours. And you'd earn every penny I pay you and all the benefits provided. Are you interested?"

"Getting insurance for me won't be cheap."

"It never is."

"What's the fund-raiser for?"

"An urgent-care clinic. Too many people have suffered irreversible damage from their injuries during the drive to Baxter. With a clinic, they could be stabilized and then sent on to the hospital or better yet, not have to make the trip at all."

She nibbled her lower lip. "Any estimate of cost?"

"Half a million to start."

"You're serious."

"Very." Bryan waited, torn between wanting her to refuse and recognizing Melissa might well be his only hope of getting his office under control again. During their conversation, Melissa hadn't once sent him any coy glances, hadn't flirted or murmured come-ons. Nothing. And her cancer?

Once again Bryan blocked the memories trying to surface, the pain that demanded he take a step back and keep Melissa as far away from him as possible. *If* he hired her, she would be an employee, he reminded himself. Nothing else. "Are you still interested after seeing and hearing what you'd be getting yourself into?"

"Yes."

He wasn't expecting that as her answer. "Then how about a trial run? A few weeks from now if this is working out for both of us, fine. If not, we'll go our separate ways with no hard feelings and two weeks' severance?" He added the latter for his conscience's sake.

The muscles of Melissa's throat worked as she swallowed. Bryan waited and watched, aware of how her eyes projected her thoughts. Her eagerness to dive in and get started on the challenge he'd just tossed out.

"The, um, position—is it hourly or salary?"

He stated the specifics and waited again.

Another blink. Her eyebrows pulled together in a frown, but then she squared her shoulders and nodded. "I'll take it."

Bryan smiled despite the uncertainty pouring through him. "Then I guess I'll see you on Monday."

HAL BANGED on the door of Dr. Booker's practice with the frustration of a man who had better things to do. Like find the slimeball punk who considered the girl in his arms a punching bag. "Booker, open up!"

He heard the sound of running footsteps across the floor of the old house, the chirp of an alarm being disarmed and a lock sliding free. He was relieved the doc was home instead of out partying around town. The rumors had the number of women Booker was involved with in the double digits.

Finally the door swung open. "Is this the domestic-violence case?"

Hal didn't ask how Booker knew. He simply nodded and stepped inside carefully, trying not to jostle the young woman sagging against him. The girl's dark hair was caked with blood, her delicate features and stare stark with pain. "She refused to go to the hospital, but if she checks out okay, Ellen said she could spend the night at her place."

"I want to go home," the girl gasped, her voice reedy and high.

"What's your name?" Booker asked.

"Anna…Anna Pritchard."

Hal half carried the young woman into the first exam room and, together with the doc, helped her onto the table. "I'll wait in the hall." He left the small room, but positioned himself on the wall outside the open door so he could hear everything that took place inside.

"I changed my mind. I want to go home," she repeated, her clenched teeth making her words slur together. "M-my boyfriend will take care of me."

"Let me treat you first. It'll only take a little while." When she didn't protest, Booker got to work. "Anna, what happened to you?"

"Nothing. I—I tripped over something and fell."

The doc paused long enough to slide his patient a disbelieving glance before going back to what he'd been doing. "Must've been some fall. Anna, we know of a safe place for you to stay tonight. Or maybe you'd like us to call your parents? A friend?" Booker checked her eyes with a mini-light, his protective rubber gloves tinged with the girl's blood.

"No, I—no one."

"Not even your boyfriend?"

She set her jaw, but whether it was to fight against the pain or in deference to the doc's words, Hal couldn't judge.

"Then you can stay with Ellen. She won't mind at all." The doc glanced at Hal quickly, a slight smirk to his lips. "You'll be safe, and I'm sure the chief won't have a problem with hanging out nearby."

Hal glared at Booker. His relationship with Ellen was certainly healthier than anything the playboy doc could claim. Which made Hal wonder again: Would Booker really leave Mel alone?

"I can't stay there—I want to go home."

The doc's expression hardened. "Sweetheart, if you go back there, you're putting yourself at risk. You realize that, don't you? Abusive situations only get worse. Your boyfriend—"

"I fell."

"Anna, you need to get out. *Tonight*."

Anna shook her head but didn't say anything.

The doc listened to her breathing. "How old are you?"

The girl wet her lips, wincing because the lower one was split. "Eighteen."

"You look younger."

"I'll be nineteen soon. In a few months."

Straightening, the doc lifted his hands, gently inserting his fingers into her hair. "Will you let us take some pictures of the bruises?"

Eyes low, she shook her head. "Nothing happened. I just tripped over something, that's all. I bruise easily."

"The chief and I will back you up in court. You have nothing to be afraid of. You can end it now and the guy who did this will go to jail. You'll be free."

The young woman's face crumpled with tears momentarily before she pulled herself together. "I'm all right! Stop giving me such a hard time, okay? Nothing h-happened!"

"Shh…calm down." Booker braced his hands on either side of Anna's knees, hunkering down until his nose nearly touched hers.

Hal shifted, uncomfortable with the sight until he realized that with his change of position, he got an unfettered view of the doc's face and was able to see the other man's upset and anger—emotions the doc apparently tried to get across to a girl who thought it normal to be knocked around. Despite the man's reputation for using women and tossing them aside, his impression of Booker went up a notch.

"Take it easy. Honey, listen to me, okay? You are eighteen years old. It's Friday night. You should be out having fun with your friends, *not* getting beaten up by some jerk who doesn't appreciate you. Before you say you fell again, let me show you something. See those marks right there on your shoulder? That's where he smashed your skin between his fist and your bones. Those bruises right there?" He pointed. "That's where he grabbed you so tight he bruised you. I can tell the difference between someone falling and someone getting beaten, Anna. So can a lot of other people."

Hands clasped tightly in her lap, Anna looked away from the doctor's gaze and picked at a broken nail, tears trickling silently down her cheeks. "M-my head hurts…and my s-side. Can you… Do you have anything you c-can give me?"

Mouth tight, Booker hesitated a long moment before he shoved himself away from the table and walked the two steps it took to get to a cabinet. "I need to watch you for a little while to make sure you don't have a concussion before I can give you any meds," he informed her. "But I'll give you some later when you leave."

"Thank you."

"Taking the meds will ease the hurt now, but they won't do you any good next time, Anna." The doc turned back to the counter and ripped a bandage partially open in preparation for using it. "So tell me, how'd it feel?"

The doc's voice was quiet, soft, like he wasn't asking her hard questions, but was merely discussing the weather. Hal had to give him credit, he was getting the point across without raising his voice or yelling, something the girl probably wasn't used to.

"Were you scared he wouldn't stop?"

Anna sniffled and dropped her chin. A nod?

"Scared he'd do more?" Booker got to work on her scrapes and cuts, murmuring all the while. Little comments about how he thought women should be treated, how if her boyfriend loved her, he wouldn't hit her. Through it all Anna stayed quiet, fighting tears the entire time or else hissing in pain when the doc checked her sore ribs and declared them bruised but not broken. Her sprained wrist needed to be wrapped, her index finger splinted, but surprisingly, she didn't have a concussion, just a bloody cut and bump.

"I'll get you some samples for the pain."

Anna nodded gratefully, but when he was about to move away from her, she reached out and touched his arm. "Is it... Are you going to take pictures?"

Hal straightened at the question.

"Think you might give the chief a chance to use them?"

"I fell," she murmured stubbornly. "But if i-it happens again…"

"Knock, knock!" Ellen's greeting announced her arrival and she entered the practice through the unlocked door, hurrying toward him. "Sorry it took me so long. I had a couple more calls that had to be dealt with. Must be something in the air tonight."

"Ellen? Come on in," Booker called.

"How is she?" Ellen paused inside the exam room. "Oh, honey."

Hal listened with half an ear while Booker introduced Anna to Ellen. Before he had finished, the girl started to cry. Whatever Anna hadn't seen in the two men, she saw in Ellen because the young woman immediately reached for her with a sob. Ellen wrapped Anna in her arms and rocked her back and forth on the exam table, smoothing her hand over her hair and crooning softly.

In that second, he thought of Mel, of how she could've used a woman's touch during her illness. If she'd give Ellen a chance, he knew they could be friends. Would Mel be all right on her own?

Sometimes he wasn't too sure.

THE NEXT MORNING Melissa got out of her car and smoothed her hands over her hips to wipe away the moisture. The reception desk had been an awful mess last night. So much so she'd dreamed about stacks and stacks of paper towering above her head and weaving back and forth, ready to topple on her. No way could she face the mess, the patients, the gossip *and* Bryan all at the same time.

She raised her hand, paused when nerves balked, then

forced herself to knock on the door. A window above her opened, and Melissa shaded her eyes with her hand, stifling a gasp when she spied Bryan's sleep-tousled head. When that sight was followed by a naked chest and the top of a tightly honed six pack, she found herself wondering just how far out the window he'd lean.

"Melissa?"

Good grief, even his voice was sexy. She remembered when it cracked and squeaked. "Uh, h-hello, uh—" What should she call him if he was her boss? "—Dr. Booker."

He blinked at her, braced one hand on the windowsill and lifted the other to rub lazily over his chest. A slow grin tugged at his lips. "There's no need to be formal."

"Oh, um, okay. I'm sorry I woke you. G-go back to— I'll go." She dropped her hand and turned. Stupid, stupid, stupid! Why hadn't she called first?

"Don't move," he ordered. "I'm coming down."

"No, you don't—"

"Just stay put and give me a sec to get dressed."

Wondering who he had up there with him that would require him to not already *be* dressed at ten o'clock in the morning, she debated the merits of ignoring him and leaving. She could come back later. *Much* later. Or not at all? Was she nuts to consider this?

A woman laughed.

Melissa jerked her head up toward Bryan's still-open window, but when the sound came again, she traced it to the house positioned on the right of the medical practice. Was that…

Squinting, she focused on the fluttering lace curtains and sucked in a sharp breath. It *was!* Ellen Morton was talking on the phone, her voice carrying the short distance between the houses. The woman's laughter was low and teasing. Had she just said her father's name? *Her* name?

The door behind her opened, and Melissa spun around to face Bryan with a glare only to wind up gaping at him instead. Getting dressed apparently involved pulling on low-riding, body-molding jeans and a black T-shirt that defined his broad chest and muscles. Yesterday he'd worn casual slacks and a button-down dress shirt, but now Bryan looked like he'd stepped out of an ad for Abercrombie & Fitch or a rough-and-tumble Ralph Lauren spread.

Forcing her gaze to his and hating the fact she stood one step lower, which put her at ab level with him, Melissa ignored the crick in her neck and stared up into his hypnotic green eyes, trying in vain to gather her wits. Not an easy feat considering the sight of him made her nervous and…sick.

Because he was perfect. Completely, totally, absolutely *perfect* from his sandy-brown hair finger-combed off his face and left to curl on his neck, to his bare, big-man feet that balanced a six-foot-plus frame. Corded muscles, ripped abs that could be seen beneath the well-worn shirt, a muscular build any male model would envy. Bryan was the prime example of a man.

He leaned a shoulder against the doorjamb and crossed his arms over his chest with a lethal half grin that made her insides tingle and heat in an unfamiliar way. But that was absurd. Because as perfect as he appeared to be, that was how *imperfect* she was in comparison. If she were a normal woman she might have appreciated the welcoming, flirtatious smile, but she wasn't normal, never would be, and a man like Bryan Booker only made her more aware of all her shortcomings. Why couldn't he sport a purple mustache now or still think it funny to fart?

Bryan tilted his head to the side, his indecently long lashes adding to a sexy, sleepy expression few men could pull off without looking ridiculous.

"Melissa?"

He said her name patiently, as if he was accustomed to the chore because other women had done as she had and been rendered speechless at the sight of him. Coming out of her daze, she cleared her throat only to be sidetracked yet again by the sound of Ellen's laughter carrying from next door. She raised an eyebrow. "Ellen Morton is your neighbor?"

"Yeah."

Everything came together at once. "So you'd seen my dad hanging out over there, and when you saw my reaction yesterday at the station—" She groaned, closing her eyes briefly. "I must've looked like an idiot to you."

"You didn't look like an idiot at all. You looked like someone had pulled the rug out from under you," he admitted, his voice gently teasing, "but not an idiot."

She smiled wearily and lifted a hand toward the other house. "Do you know her well?"

"The way neighbors do these days. Why don't you come in?"

She hesitated, but when he moved back, she climbed the remaining step and entered the hallway leading to the reception area. Exam rooms lined both sides, four in all, with a public restroom and Bryan's office taking up the rest of the space. Diplomas, both his and his R.N.'s, lined the white walls, and a bulletin board full of pictures hung over a water cooler located toward the front of the old house.

"Why don't we talk in my office?"

She nodded, her thoughts focusing on Bryan's comment about Ellen. What exactly did being neighborly mean given

Bryan's reputation with women? Clearing her head with a shake, Melissa followed him into the paper-stacked room and tried to smile. What a mess. How on earth would she get everything straight?

"Have a seat and tell me what brings you here on a beautiful Saturday morning," he ordered, dropping into a worn but comfortable-looking leather chair. His grandfather's?

She glanced at the rolled arm. Yup, same one. There was a deep scratch where the buckle of her shoe had damaged it when she was six. It was amazing that it had lasted this long, and she found it sweet that Bryan had kept the old chair. "I'm sorry I woke you. I thought you'd be up."

His lips curled up slightly at the corners, and she felt a blush flood her face when she caught on to the double entendre. He didn't comment further, but propped his elbow on the cushioned armrest and tilted his head to the side, his hand rubbing over his chin as he regarded her with an intense stare. Bryan's gaze was probing and warm and way too slumberous for her liking, so she turned her back to him and studied yet more diplomas and awards. "I, uh, came to work."

"You're a couple days early. I'm not open on weekends."

"I know, but I wanted to get a head start," she informed him while discovering he'd graduated at the top of his class. She moved on to the next frame, this one closer to the door. "Things were such a mess, I didn't think you'd mind, but since you obviously do—"

"I didn't say that. I'm just curious as to why you want to spend a beautiful Saturday morning cooped up in here."

"Like I said, to make Monday easier."

Bryan rubbed his face again, the bristles on his jaw and chin rasping crisply against his fingers. "Hey, if you're willing, by all means, let's go for it."

She didn't like the surge of mixed-up emotions she felt in response to his words. Bryan was a flirt by nature, and she'd seen him in action on numerous occasions. At the book-club discussion meetings at the library, in town and the B and B. He smiled, he winked, he *spoke* in a way that made women sit up and pay attention. She knew better than to take it seriously, but at the same time it was distracting and she didn't want to be distracted. Not by him. Not ever. Maybe she should set that straight? Take the guesswork out of the equation?

"Look, let's go upstairs and—"

"Upstairs?" she repeated huskily.

"Yeah. We can grab something to eat and talk about today before I get started showing you what I need from you. Something wrong?" Bryan stopped in front of her, standing too close for comfort, his expression and bad-boy looks appealing far too much to a woman who had to think with her head.

"Yes—I mean, no. N-not technically, but—"

"Spit it out, Melissa."

"I think we need to talk." She followed that up with a nod just in case she wasn't clear.

"Aren't we talking now?"

His tone teased, bringing another blush to her cheeks. She felt silly, unsophisticated, but determined. "Before I consider taking on this job, I think we need to get some things straight. Important things."

"Important things," he repeated, drawing the words out. "Like what?"

CHAPTER FOUR

BRYAN STARED at Melissa, his gut twisted into a knot of unease. She had that look. The look women wore when they were determined to put a guy in his place. A look Melissa had worn often as a kid. He'd learned the hard way that he might have always been bigger and stronger, but Melissa was smarter.

The four-year age difference hadn't mattered much, even though she'd been five to his nine. Throwing rocks, climbing trees, riding bikes. They were kids being kids, a group of them who'd hung out and played during the day. But when the others went home, Melissa had stayed, her father's long hours matching his grandfather's.

"What kind of 'important things'?"

"Well…" She clasped her hands in front of her and squeezed until they were red. "Flirting, for one."

He stared at her, unsure where this was headed. "Flirting?"

"Are you going to repeat everything I say?"

"I'm giving myself time to process things," he said. "Give a guy a chance to wake up."

"Bryan, we used to be friends—"

"We're not friends?"

She waved a hand as though batting away the question. "Honestly? We're more like acquaintances, as you well know."

He conceded that point with a nod. The years had wrought a lot of changes in them both.

"We played together as kids, didn't see each other for a long time, and then you came back and you saw me—" she closed her eyes "—at one of my worst possible moments."

She was worried about—

"You stood in my living room and told me my baby died not because of the things I helped the prosecutor convict Joe of doing to her, but because I neglected—"

"I never said you neglected her!" He planted his hands on his hips and glared at her. "I've never once said that."

"But in that instant, I'd not only lost my daughter again, I'd lost my hair and my dignity and very nearly my sanity, and *you* saw it all. So just…ease up. I'm not going to be another Holly or Crystal or Lisa, or any of the others you've—not that you've asked me to—" she clarified quickly, holding up her hands so he wouldn't interrupt. "But I just want to set the record straight. I want a job, Bryan, nothing else, and the effort you're putting into being…nice and—and flirtatious isn't needed because it's wasted on me. You don't need to be that way with me."

"Is that right?" She was giving him hell because he was *nice?*

"Don't take it personally. It's not you, it's me," she said, echoing his words to Tricia the Temp, but making it so much worse by adding that last part. "I'm just asking you not to bother, that's all. You can relax. There's no pressure for you to be…you know, *Bang 'em Booker*. That's the last thing I want. Just be my friend again, my boss. If you can do that, we can work together." Melissa held out her hand. "Deal?"

He took her soft, trembling palm in his. She'd taken the lead and said everything he'd wanted to say to her. Well, not quite the same things, but close enough. The no-flirting rule, keeping things professional. It was all good. "Deal," he murmured, ignoring the slight punch in the gut he felt because she looked so relieved.

TWO AND A HALF HOURS later, Bryan quietly walked down the hall carrying yet more of the files that had accumulated in his office. While he'd unearthed his desk, Melissa had sorted through the collection of papers and files covering the reception area, moved into the waiting room and now had everything divided into neatly stacked, organized piles. In record time, too. She'd accomplished more in a couple of hours than the other temps had completed in weeks. And after her little speech about being friends, the tension and worry he'd felt about hiring her eased. "Looks like you've gotten a handle on things. You ready to stop for lunch yet?"

Distracted, she stuck a note on top of a chart and nodded, her eyebrows pulled down as she wrote on the yellow sticky. "Soon."

"How about now?" he urged with a low laugh when he heard the distinct sound of her stomach growling. "I'm hungry again and you've proved you're up to the task by being so engrossed you've backed yourself into a corner."

Melissa added the file to the top of a stack and looked up, her face coloring slightly when she noted the truth of his words. She stood and, with careful placement of her feet, crossed the small waiting room, trying not to cause any of the piles surrounding her to topple. Tall and graceful, she looked like a dancer with her short, trendy hair and lithe form.

Long gone were the carefully braided pigtails, buck teeth and the kid who'd tripped over her own feet nearly as often as he had. Melissa held her arms away from her body for balance but wobbled on the next-to-last step. She adjusted quickly and then hopped the last files without incident.

"Oh, I almost forgot." She knelt down and grabbed a pile of thick file folders. Rising and turning, her head low because she concentrated on what she was doing, she hadn't seen him step forward to help and he didn't have time to get out of her way. Melissa bumped into him, the files she held sliding to the right. Bryan scrambled to help her keep the foot-thick stack from falling, but ended up grasping her arms and smashing the files between them to do so.

Color spread up Melissa's neck into her face. "Sorry."

"No problem." Except it was.

He couldn't move, because if he did, everything would wind up on the floor. She shifted and tried to straighten the files again, her elbows digging into his stomach in the process. The mass of paper kept them from full contact, but desire raced through him regardless. Now? His body was responding *now?*

"I've got them. Oops, wait a sec. Now I do." She smiled up at him. "Thanks."

Up close, her hair smelled of raspberries and looked so soft his fingers twitched with the need to touch it. The sprinkling of freckles across her nose were undisguised by powder, but the sight of them made him want to—

"You can let go now."

Bryan released her and stepped back, more than a little surprised at himself for feeling like a hormonal teenager on a rampage. Melissa turned and walked away, seemingly unaffected by what had just happened. And him? Biting back a curse, he ran a hand over his mouth and rubbed hard to erase the temptation of kissing those freckles.

Melissa was the epitome of the girl next door—blond,

blue eyed, long legged and thin. But thanks to her speech earlier and because of his past, he couldn't ignore the fact she was *too* thin, her hair *too* short and her eyes shadowed by light circles born of prolonged illness—one he didn't want to ever have to acknowledge again. Not on an intimate level.

Melissa walked over to the desk to place the files on the corner and then began gathering up the dozen pens scattered across the top of the long counter. Within seconds, she'd put a fistful in the nearly empty container and went on to another task. Did she feel the tension, too? Somehow he doubted it. She seemed...oblivious. Simply trying to get as much work done as possible before she had to leave.

Curious, drawn by some invisible, unrecognizable force, Bryan moved to lean his elbows atop the high counter. His mind warned him to back off and not go where his thoughts led, but he couldn't help himself. It was too strange. He wasn't used to being dismissed by a woman.

Melissa glanced up at him. "Is something wrong?"

"No." He reined in his thoughts once more. "Just wondering if you like Italian?"

"Oh, right, lunch. Sure, Italian's goo—"

The phone rang and he glanced at the caller ID screen. "It's the station, probably the chief."

Melissa hesitated. It was obvious to him that she didn't want to pick up, but why?

Ellen's comment about husbands not wanting their wives under the same roof as him bounced through his head. Would the same apply to Melissa's police chief father? Hal hadn't liked the antics Bryan and Melissa had gotten into as kids: letting the air out of Melissa's piano teacher's tires at the grocery so the woman would have to cancel and Melissa wouldn't have to stop playing; climbing the old oak tree in the park with backpacks full of snacks so it couldn't be cut down. Fun times. Great memories. But big trouble for the chief.

The phone rang a third time. "Want me to get that?"

Groaning softly, she snatched the receiver from the base. "Dr. Booker's office. Hi, Dad. Yeah, things are okay. No, I'm—we're ordering lunch here." She glanced at Bryan before turning away. "No, we've only just taken a break for lunch... Dad, no. Yes, I appreciate the offer, but... No, I can't make it... Yes, I'm sure..." Her voice lowered. "Because we're working... I *know* it's right next door," she said cryptically, shooting him a wry look over her shoulder. "No, I don't have time right now... Yes, that's really why... I'm sure. Goodbye, Dad. *Goodbye*. I'm hanging up now," she stated firmly before she pressed the button.

Bryan raised a brow, impressed. "Did you just hang up on the chief of police?"

Amusement lit Melissa's features. "No, I just hung up on my dad." She released a weary huff and replaced the handset. "And I said goodbye, so that doesn't qualify as hanging up."

"Right. Well, don't say no on my account. Lunch with Ellen sounds like a good way to get to know each other better, and she's a great cook." That comment earned him a glare. "I take it you're not okay with him marrying her?"

He could see her struggling with an inner debate. "I never said that."

"But you don't want to go over for lunch?" He watched while she bustled around the desk grabbing more pencils and pens, Hi-Liters, staple removers and paper clips. "For what it's worth, she's a nice person. If you give Ellen a chance you might like her."

Melissa's teeth sank into her lower lip while she opened

various drawers and began tossing the items. "It's not—" She broke off with a groan. "I *know* I need to go. From the way it sounds it's practically a done deal."

"She does have a ring." That got him another glare.

"She's taking advantage of him, of his loneliness. Why can't he see that?"

"Maybe she's not," he suggested mildly. "Maybe she's in love with him. Either way, there's only one way to find out and that's by spending time with them together. See how they are around one another."

Her shoulders slumped and she was silent a long moment. "I suppose if I went now, it would mean a short visit. I'd have to finish up what I started here, right?" She paused, obviously considering her alternatives. "It *would* give me an excuse to leave, rather than getting stuck there indefinitely on another day when I have no schedule to keep."

He couldn't stop the smile that formed. "Melissa, she doesn't bite."

She looked up at him, staring at him as though she'd momentarily forgotten he was there—and then was suddenly glad he was. Unease had him straightening. "What?"

"Nothing… I'm just glad you feel that way. Remember when you ran into Mrs. Borwick's rose planter and broke it? When your grandfather caught us, you made me go with you to tell her you were sorry."

"So? That was a long time ago."

"Doesn't matter," she informed him, "because you didn't return the favor—until now. You're coming to lunch with me."

Bryan shook his head. He didn't want to be involved in the family squabble any more than he already was. "I wasn't invited."

She tossed aside a phone book. "You are now. I'll call Dad back and let him know."

THE FIRST THING Melissa noticed when she entered Ellen's house was the homey feel. Unlike Bryan's Edwardian-style home/medical practice, Ellen's home was a mixture of ranch, farmhouse and Victorian all rolled into one. They entered through the kitchen door after a cheery "Come in!" followed their knock, and Melissa listened to the other woman's hurried footsteps heading in their direction while taking in the sunflower wallpaper and bright decor. Reds and yellows brightened the oak cabinets and furniture, and the hardwood floors, dotted with rag-hooked rugs in a variety of shades and textures, were yet another welcoming touch.

"See? Not the dungeon you imagined your father trapped in, huh?" Bryan teased quietly. "And do you smell that? That's not gruel, but Ellen's sweet-potato casserole. Best I've ever eaten. I think I'm going to enjoy being your date."

Date? Melissa did her best to ignore the way her heart rate increased at his choice of words.

Yeah, like Bang 'em Booker would do someone like you.

Melissa stepped away from him to establish some much-needed distance. Her reaction was a physical one, nothing else, the result of being unable to remember the last time a man other than her father or a hospital orderly had touched her. She didn't want Bryan to *do* her, wasn't interested in him *at all*. It was just a thought, fleeting, one of those what-if's that came from out of nowhere when she least expected it.

She knew whoever consented to sex with her would wind up feeling a certain amount of pity. She supposed that was inevitable. But she couldn't tolerate pity from someone like Bryan, someone so perfect.

"Bryan! What a nice surprise. I'm glad you could join us."

"Do you mind?"

"Of course not," Ellen said with a smile. "You know you're always welcome. Anytime."

GRATEFUL FOR the distraction from her too-strange musings, Melissa watched Ellen's approach only to be even more upset when she noticed the way the woman's engagement ring sparkled in the sunlight.

She'd never been offered a ring.

The thought sliced through Melissa's overstressed brain. It might be mean, maybe even catty, but how fair was it that she'd never had a chance to walk down the aisle and probably never would?

"Melissa, I'm so glad you could join us. Please make yourself at home."

"Thank you." Her voice emerged raspy, earning a suspicious glance from Bryan that she ignored.

Ellen's hands fluttered at her waist. "Your father just arrived. He's in the bathroom washing up and will be in shortly."

Silence filled the air and they stood in the kitchen staring at each other. Seconds ticked by and still no one spoke.

Finally Bryan looked back and forth between the two of them and cleared his throat.

"Uh, why don't Melissa and I help you set the table or something? The sooner it's done, the sooner we eat." He rubbed his hands together as though he couldn't wait, and the act drew a soft, high-pitched laugh from Ellen along with a touch to his arm.

Melissa wondered at their familiarity and studied the woman more closely. Ellen's short hair framed a face gently lined but youthful. She wore a light dusting of makeup that enhanced her features, stylish glasses, a rust-colored shirt and a denim jumper with fall leaves and scarecrows stitched on the pockets. Men might not be scrambling to do a surgery-mutilated woman, but there was something homey about Ellen that put her in the do-able category.

"Thank you, Bryan, but everything is almost ready. Why don't you go sit down? Melissa, maybe you'd give me a hand?"

Bryan disappeared in a flash and Melissa glared at his back, wondering why she'd thought for a moment he'd stick around as a buffer. He was obviously on Ellen's side.

From somewhere in the interior of the house a door opened and familiar footfalls sounded across the old wood floors. She heard her father greet Bryan and the two of them began talking, the walls muting their deep voices.

"I guess we'd better get this on the table so you can all get back to work." Ellen set to work dishing the food into large bowls and platters, and Melissa watched for a moment to see where things were kept before stepping forward to help. They performed the chore in tense silence, but when everything was ready to carry into the dining room, Ellen stilled and Melissa knew the moment had come. Her heart picked up speed and sweat beaded her forehead. *Why had she let Bryan talk her into this?*

"Melissa, before we go in there I—I'd like to say something. I—I love your father very much. We never meant to hurt you by keeping our relationship private."

Private, not secret. Melissa's grip tightened around the lip of the bowl she held, and she faced the woman who would become her stepmother at this late date in her life. Unless she made her father see that dating was one thing, and perfectly okay, but *marriage*—

"Well that's all I wanted to say. I guess we'd better get this in there before it gets cold."

Melissa nodded readily at the excuse to escape and started toward the dining room where Bryan and her father waited.

"Melissa?"

She should've known she couldn't get away so easily. She paused in the doorway.

"I don't expect you to like me right away, but please try to understand that we just want to be together. Hal needs to be loved for the man he is, not because he's your father or the chief or anyone else, but as a man. Surely you understand that?"

Melissa ignored Ellen's question and forced herself to put one foot in front of the other. The best thing to do was get the luncheon over with as quickly as possible and get out of there.

And she intended to do just that.

THE NEXT HOUR CONFIRMED Melissa's fear that she had to work fast if anything she said or did was going to change her father's plans. The problem was exacerbated by the fact she still couldn't decide if Ellen's behavior was an act or not. Her dad was handsome, yes, but Ellen couldn't seem take her eyes off him. She touched her hair and smoothed it away from her cheek, listened with rapt attention to every word her dad spoke. She waited on him, refilled his iced-tea glass and smiled nonstop albeit shakily when she caught Melissa watching.

The woman displayed all the classic signs of being in love, but that didn't make it any easier to accept. Ellen was taking advantage of her father's loneliness. His pain. Why couldn't he see that? Melissa shoved her food around on her plate, not the least bit hungry.

"Anna was gone this morning when Ellen got up," her father informed Bryan. The statement brought Melissa out of her daze.

"I just hope the poor girl called someone to come get her and didn't walk all the way home. She was hurting pretty bad when she went upstairs to lie down last night," Ellen murmured.

Bryan sat with his head down, his gaze unfocused. He'd been devouring Ellen's cuisine seconds ago but now set his fork aside and shifted in his chair. "Sometimes no matter how much you want to help there's only so much you can do." Bryan lifted his glass of tea but paused when the mug neared his lips. "Accepting it isn't easy, but you can't let that stop you from helping others."

"I agree. And she'll be back," her dad said with a nod. "Once the abuse starts it only escalates. I have a feeling we'll be getting more calls about that girl."

The mood around the room darkened even more, but thankfully Bryan changed the topic by asking about the toy drive. From then on Bryan and her dad kept the conversation on lighter subjects and ignored her poor manners and silence. While they discussed town politics, gas prices and upcoming events, she felt the gap between her and her dad widening.

Finally an hour had gone by, and Melissa pushed herself to her feet. "Um, you know, lunch was great, but I've—we've got to get going." Her dad shot her a disappointed look she ignored. "Sorry, but we've got a lot of files to go through and put away before I leave to get ready for Ashley's baby shower. Right now they're covering the entire reception area."

"She's right," Bryan agreed, scooting his chair back to stand. "I'm Joe's entertainment while the ladies are partying, so if I don't show up to get him, Ashley'll have my head. Ellen, lunch was phenomenal as always. Thank you."

"You're welcome. I'll be sure to save some leftovers for you. Come get them this evening for dinner if you like."

Melissa watched the exchange, noting her dad didn't look particularly happy at the thought of Bryan dropping by. Why? Did he know something about the two of them? Had Bryan and Ellen had a thing? If the rumors of his conquests were true...

Bryan picked up his plate. "How about we help you carry in the dishes?"

Melissa glanced at her father and flushed when she read his expression. She should've been the one to offer, not Bryan. She should've thanked her hostess, should've been more friendly. Should've eaten her food and not been the first to jump to her feet to leave. "The least we can do is clear the table for you."

"No, no, don't worry about that." Ellen looked as relieved as she was that the gathering had come to an end. "I'll take care of them, you two go on. The last time I was in that office, it looked like a hurricane had blown through." Ellen shooed them again. "Leave those dishes alone, and go get your work done so you can have some fun later."

Melissa avoided her father and followed Bryan to the dining-room door, adding her goodbyes to his. They made their way through the kitchen and out into the afternoon sun before she could comfortably breathe a sigh. "Thank you so much for talking me into that."

Bryan winced. "The claws came out, huh? I thought we'd have to leave when you came into the dining room looking ready for battle. You barely spoke at all and didn't eat a thing."

"Trust me, I wasn't hungry after Ellen pulled me aside for a little talk in the kitchen."

"Are you that upset that Ellen called me to help you find a job?"

She nearly stumbled going up the steps. *Ellen had called him to—*

Bryan unlocked and opened the door. "She cares for your father, Melissa, no doubt about it. Like I said— What?"

"You *hired* me because of *her?*" Anger surged through her, propelled by hurt and embarrassment. "How could you— Let go!"

Bryan had grasped her upper arm and was looking over her shoulder toward Ellen's home before he maneuvered her inside.

"Let *go!*"

He did. But only after he'd shut the door and placed his broad palm against the metal panel by her head, trapping her. The hair on his forearm teased her cheek and all her senses reacted, leaving her no room to escape.

"What do you think you're doing?" Her breathing became gasping pants she tried to control, every inhalation bringing with it the tantalizing scent of his cologne. Bryan used to smell like boy and dog and peanut butter sandwiches.

"I'm setting the record straight before you embarrass all of us." His head lowered until he was at eye level with her. "You and Ellen didn't talk about that in the kitchen, did you?"

She almost smirked, would've if she'd found the situation the slightest bit funny. But Bryan admitting he'd only hired her because of Ellen... She couldn't laugh about that. "Nope."

He swore softly. "I'm sorry. I shouldn't have opened my big mouth and—"

"Don't be sorry. I'm glad I know. It makes things a lot easier."

He stilled. "What things?"

"I quit."

"Oh no, you don't. Melissa, it isn't what you think," he murmured huskily.

"How do you get that? Because what I *think* is that Ellen somehow convinced you to hire me, which gets you the help you need, me out of the way and Ellen the marriage she wants."

"I admit Ellen was the person who told me you were looking for work, but she didn't make me hire you and to insinuate she has that power implies a deeper relationship than friendship. Something I'm certain your father wouldn't appreciate."

Meaning they were more than friends—or had been—and her dad suspected? Was that why her dad hadn't liked the idea of Bryan returning for leftovers? "If not because of her then why *did* you hire me?"

Did it matter why? Melissa tried to sink into the unyielding door to escape, but it didn't work. And it did matter. She might be desperate to reestablish her independence, but she couldn't handle being thought of as a charity case by her childhood *friend*.

"Didn't we go over this last night? I hired you because I figured—" Bryan's voice lowered to a gravelly pitch "—you'd want to prove everyone who thinks you're too fragile or ill or unemployable wrong. I hired you because a long time ago, we were friends." His eyes glittered in the dimness, the Exit sign above their heads giving his sandy-golden hair and body an orangish cast. "We're both in a predicament here. I have an opening, you need a job. If you've changed your mind, tell me now and let's be done with this, but don't blame Ellen or me because you're not up to the challenge of working for me."

Not up to the— "It's not that simple and you know it." She shook her head, thankful the movement had him taking note of the lack of space separating them and drawing back. For once he appeared as uncomfortable as she felt, but she was too angry to appreciate the fact. "I don't like Ellen or you or anyone else thinking I can't find a job on my own."

"Then prove you're up to keeping it."

"Prove I'm up to— You think I can't do it?" Melissa shoved a finger hard into his chest. "Back off, Booger Boy," she said, using the nickname he'd earned long ago, "and watch me."

CHAPTER FIVE

MELISSA FITTED the floppy hat more firmly to her head and tried not to notice the surprised glances sent her way. She opened the back door of her car and retrieved Ashley's baby-shower gifts, resisting the urge to dive inside and hide.

How she had wound up here in the first place was still a mystery. At least to her. The party was being held by Mrs. H. and the garden club that Ashley belonged to, and while Melissa had always adored Mrs. H., she wasn't quite sure she was ready to face the townspeople at so public a function. Attending the B and B's opening-day celebration was one thing, but Ashley's *baby shower?*

But she couldn't decline. Not when the news would spread and cause more gossip. So she had to attend the baby shower with a smile on her face and pretend it didn't hurt to think of Joe becoming a parent again.

She wanted her ex to be happy. He deserved to be happy after all he'd been through because of her and the town that had judged him so unjustly—but wanting him happy and dealing with it while oohing and aahing over tiny diapers and baby outfits was just too much. Or maybe just punishment?

After coming to the house with Bryan to tell her the truth about Josie's death, Ashley had periodically called to check on her. Short conversations about nothing and everything. As

Melissa's recovery had progressed so had their relationship. Now she considered Ashley a friend, but still... Did Ashley realize what kind of attention and gossip Melissa's attendance would bring?

Melissa stepped onto the carefully laid stepping-stone path leading around the house and pulled at the neckline of her dress. Several women passed, touring the grounds, and Melissa managed a strained smile in response to their polite nods. Realizing she still tugged at her dress, she forced her hand to her side as she approached the bricked patio off the back porch of the B and B, noticing her reflection in a nearby window. She grimaced when she saw how her wide-brimmed hat covered her short hair and made her look bald. Compared to the tiny, ribboned concoctions the other women wore, her hat was close kin to a sombrero.

Panicked, Melissa yanked the hat from her head. Short hair did have some advantages after all—it didn't mess easily. Hat in hand, she discreetly checked her reflection again. Her loose, A-line dress looked more matronly and old-fashioned than anything the other guests wore. Filmy, halter-style sheaths with cleavage-baring Vs and split hems were the items of choice. Unease filled her and she struggled to maintain her composure. This was such a mistake. Maybe she could go in, leave her gift and sneak out the front?

"Melissa! Hello, dear! I just heard your wonderful news."

Mrs. Hilliard, known as Mrs. H. by most everyone under the age of forty due to the woman's many years of teaching high school English, held out both her hands in greeting. Smiling shakily, Melissa allowed the woman to draw her close for a hug.

"What news?" she asked, smiling at the older woman's cherry-red hat and fifties-style purple dress. On Mrs. H. the look was perfect.

"Your job, dear. Working for Dr. Booker will put you on the right track for earning some money to go back to college. You'll finish your teaching degree in no time."

Melissa blinked. "Oh, but I'm not going back to school."

Mrs. H.'s gaze narrowed shrewdly. "I see. And why not?"

Melissa faltered beneath the other woman's stare. "Um…"

"You had nearly completed your course work when you got sick, correct?"

"Yes, but—"

"Then you must return and get your degree." The older woman peered intensely through the wide black rims of her glasses. "My dear, you were a wonderful student and one of the brightest, most courageous young women I know."

"I'm no one special, Mrs. H."

She patted her hand. "Nonsense. You are a fighter, child. The fact you're standing here proves it, and that ability and insight is something children need. Now I insist you go to the college the very next chance you get and pick up a course listing."

Melissa stared at her, wondering why everyone seemed to have more faith in her and her recovery than she did. "Mrs. H., the cancer might come back."

"Of course it might," Mrs. H. confirmed, "but it might not, and then what will you have to show for yourself? You won't have lived up to your potential." Mrs. H. patted her hand again and nodded firmly before she walked away to greet another guest.

Melissa mulled over her former teacher's comments during the next hour as the party moved inside out of the heat. She'd always dreamed of following in Mrs. H.'s footsteps and becoming a teacher. So why not return and get her degree?

Investing in college, applying and fighting for a position

meant she planned to *have* a future. But the one thing she'd promised herself from the moment she'd been diagnosed with cancer was that she wouldn't lie to herself. Treatments had advanced so that the survival rate was excellent, but how could she be sure?

She studied the women occupying Ashley's large parlor room, hearing bits and pieces of their conversation. Nearly all talked of kids and grandkids and activities, husbands and weddings in the works. The only thing she could think about was Mrs. H.'s words.

"Melissa? You okay?" Ashley murmured, returning from the bathroom for the third time.

She blinked and focused on her friend, her smile weak. She was supposed to be writing down the gifts and who'd given them, not people watching or feeling sorry for herself. "I'm fine."

"You look really distracted." Ashley glanced around at her guests, a frown pulling at her lips. She leaned down and lowered her voice. "I've heard the talk, too, but you have to ignore it and let the old busybodies eat their words later when we don't wind up in a catfight over Joe."

Melissa laughed. Leave it to Ashley.

"That's more like it. See? If it doesn't bother me, it shouldn't bother you. Did someone say something insensitive to you? Because if they did—"

"I'm *fine*," she insisted with another small laugh, seeing Ashley's protectiveness surfacing and appreciating it because it was directed at her. Having grown up in a group home for children, Ashley was very protective of those she considered friends. "I'm just…thinking about something that's going on with my dad. I'll tell you about it later."

"Are you sure?"

"Sit down and open your presents," she ordered with a smile. "If you keep going to the bathroom every two minutes, you're never going to finish unwrapping all your gifts."

Ashley smiled, but for the first time since her friend had returned, Melissa noticed a difference in Ashley. A big difference. Her posture, her expression. "Ashley?" Her eyes widened. "Ashley, are you in—"

"Yes."

"Then shouldn't you—"

"No." Ashley gave her a *keep quiet* glare, inhaled deeply and locked her jaw. A moment passed and then Ashley smiled, but it was tense. "I want to stay home as long as possible. I went to the hospital way too early with Max and hated it, all the waiting and being stuck in bed. I want to be home and comfortable. Please, don't say anything. I have plenty of time. My contractions only just started."

"Ready for more gifts, Ashley?"

Ashley seated herself beside Melissa and turned to face Mrs. H. The older woman set a gift bag on Ashley's knees, but when Ashley gasped from the onset of another, obviously harder, contraction, Mrs. H. removed the bag, and then clapped her hands together in rapid succession much like she had in high school.

"Ladies! Congratulations *are* in order today. Ashley is in labor!"

Melissa smiled at her red-faced friend. "So much for keeping it quiet."

BRYAN WATCHED while Joe dribbled the basketball and prepared to make his move. Before he could, Bryan charged forward and stole the ball from Joe with a taunting grin.

"Think you're something, huh, pretty boy?"

Bryan pivoted, careful to keep the ball out of Joe's reach. His heart raced from exertion and he dripped with sweat, but since discovering sex with greedy, manipulative, superficial women had lost its appeal, this was the next best thing. "Voted Number-one Doctor by my patients," he drawled smugly, using the one title he didn't mind receiving from the *Tribune*'s contest.

Joe snickered. "That newspaper contest is rigged. Number-one Bozo is more like it." He made a grab for the ball.

Bryan spun away, feinted, took a shot and made it. "*Yeah!* We're tied!"

"I've been taking it easy on you."

"Bull." Bryan used the bottom of his shirt to wipe the sweat from his face and jogged over to retrieve the ball. "Since Ashley fell, you haven't made love to your wife and it shows. No wonder she asked me to get you out of the house for the baby shower. She didn't want you hanging around scaring away the guests."

Joe lifted both hands, fingers making a *bring it on* gesture. "At least my celibacy makes sense. Yours makes me wonder if you've decided you like guys. You and Holly broke up a long time ago—"

"We were never dating exclusively."

"—and Ashley didn't want me around because she felt ridiculous in the getup she had to wear. Who's ever heard of a tea party for a baby shower?"

Bryan shrugged and the game began again. He started with the ball, Joe took it, but Bryan blocked his shot.

"You won't hurt her, Joe. If her OB says she's fine, she is. Sex might actually help the process along. *And,*" he continued, waving his arms high, "if I want sex I can get it. Anywhere, anytime. That's not the problem. I've just…decided to be more selective. I like a challenge." Bryan didn't follow Joe's lunge to one side as expected and when Joe swung around to shoot again, Bryan was ready for him, the ball his.

Sweat dripped off Joe's nose and he positioned himself to guard Bryan. "So long as that challenge isn't a short-haired blonde who wouldn't give you the time of day *despite* the way you kept staring at her."

Bryan stumbled before quickly regaining his balance, but it gave Joe the advantage he needed to steal the ball and score.

"Twenty-nineteen," Joe crowed. "The pretty boy's goin' down!"

"I wasn't staring," Bryan groused. "And if I learned anything from getting involved with Holly, it's what a disaster it is to mix business with pleasure."

Joe gave him a befuddled look. "What's work got to do with Melissa?"

He grabbed a water bottle to rinse his dry mouth and spit. "If you haven't heard the gossip you're probably the only one. I hired her yesterday." Bryan regretted his words when Joe's eyes widened.

"Seriously?"

"Yeah," he murmured uneasily, aware that Joe wasn't thrilled by the idea. "What?"

"Nothing. Just keep it on the up-and-up. Mel's a sweet girl."

"She isn't a girl."

"As her boss you shouldn't be noticing that."

But how could he not notice? He'd arrived at the B and B to pick Joe up and found himself surrounded by women in floaty, ultrafeminine dresses and hats, Melissa included. The wide brim of her hat had drawn attention to her delicate face and wide, full mouth. The dark blue of her dress had high-lighted her eyes, deepening the color to cobalt, and the sight of her had stunned him because while the majority of the women's blatantly skimpy dresses were fashionable, Melissa's modest choice had affected him more.

Not notice? Despite unearthing that nightmare of a nickname she'd taunted him with as a child, seeing her had almost sent him over the edge with lust. He'd actually wanted to stay, to watch while Melissa smiled and chatted. She'd looked...fresh. Different from the other women and infinitely more appealing. Enough to make a man want to kiss the protest from her lips and slip his hands beneath the simple skirt and—

"She looked nice," he muttered, yanking himself away from his fantasy before it got too out of hand. Melissa was his *friend*. "Big deal. It doesn't change the fact that in a couple hours at the office she did more than all the others combined. Why would I do anything to screw that up?"

"Who said you were thinking about it?" Joe countered, bouncing the ball with irritating ease. "Wait—*you* just did. I'm warning you, B., back off. She doesn't need you messing with her the way you did the others."

Bryan tossed the water bottle aside and rejoined the game, closing the distance in three long, running strides and ignoring the arm Joe stretched out to hold him back. "She's an *employee*."

"But you were just thinking about her as more, weren't you?"

"Talk or play, Brody."

Joe lunged to one side, dribbling the ball with him. "She's a nice girl."

"I never said she wasn't," Bryan snapped, wanting Joe to drop the subject...and the ball.

"Too nice for you. But Ashley claims you're a decent guy—"

"Your wife talks about me, eh?"

Joe's already dark expression turned thunderous. "Not that way—and if you hadn't kept your hands to yourself when you two went out that night, you'd be choking on this ball, so get that look off your face."

Bryan grinned, the advantage his once more. "Uh-huh. Have to admit, Joe, she is a good kisser."

Instead of egging him on, Joe abruptly tossed his head back and laughed, the hand possessing the ball unwavering. "Nice try, pretty boy. Ashley ended your date by kissing you *on the cheek,* but I guess a loser who's gone so long without gettin' any would look back at that and consider it a kiss."

Bryan prepared to make his move. "Maybe I've just been hanging around you too much and become addle brained by your endless musings about how great marriage is."

"Marriage *is* great," Joe said with a snort.

"Even when you're sleeping separately?"

"She doesn't sleep well now and I thought it would help to give her more room."

"Whatever gets you through the night." Had they not become such good friends, Bryan would've been intimidated by the look he received from the solidly built ex-con.

"Don't know why you're so focused on *my* sleep habits when yours are the talk of the town. Now that I think about it…isn't the *Tribune*'s new contest going on right now?"

The mention of the newspaper's annual reader poll gave Joe just enough of an edge that Bryan struggled to keep up, huffing for breath while he fought to block Joe and get the ball. "I should sue that damned newspaper."

"Why?" Joe smirked over his shoulder. "Because you're

not *up* to satisfying the women who come out of the woodwork to chase you anymore? Ah, man, wait till I tell Wilson and Pop!" *Bounce, bounce*.

Bryan glared, his ego clamoring for defense. "I'm not up to *marrying* them, you mean. Every woman out there wants a ring on her finger. I can't just date anymore, and I got tired of the fights and tears when I turn them down and say I'm not the marrying kind."

Joe paused. "Ever?"

"Ever," he stated decisively.

The dribbling slowed, and the intensity disappeared from the game. "Are you serious?" Joe demanded. "You don't ever want to get married?"

"You gonna stand around all day talking like a woman or play?"

Joe ignored the question and stared at him like he'd lost his mind. Maybe he had. "You told me your parents have been married forty years."

"They have."

"Then what do you have against marriage?"

Bryan stole the ball and backed away. Joe lunged to get it back, but Bryan was ready for him. "Marriage is fine for other people—just not me."

"Then you'd better stay away from Melissa or you'll answer to Hal *and* me."

He didn't like being told what to do, or the tone Joe used to say it. Bryan feinted right, left, turned and jumped, making the shot. "Tied again."

Out of the corner of his eye Bryan noticed some of the local kids had come to play on the court, but now stood with their fingers looped in the chain-link fence.

"Watch your language when you lose," he taunted, drawing

on a comment he'd overheard when he'd picked Joe up at the B and B. "We have an audience. And I thought things were over between you and Melissa. Ashley doesn't strike me as the type to share. Mess around on her and I'd say you'd be treading water with lead weights around your ankles. I might even help her for old time's sake."

"They *are* over, and I don't cheat," he bit out, his voice low.

Bryan grinned. "But you have forgotten that I knew Melissa before you met her."

"Hanging out on the street corners for three summers doesn't count. What's that matter, anyway?"

He wasn't sure himself. All he knew was that he felt the need to establish a bond with her any way he could since Joe and Melissa had once shared a child. "Shut up and play—or tell me what Max repeated to put you in the doghouse."

"Nothing his mother wanted to hear." Joe growled the shamefaced admittance. "The swear jar got a big donation that day. Pick your prize," he ordered now that they were down to the winning point, "so I can rub it in your face when I win."

"You fix the leak in my shower. I'll supply the parts."

"Box seats at the next game."

"Which one?"

"Whichever."

Bryan laughed. "You want me to pay the way for you to avoid Ashley's wrath? Not a chance."

"Make it the next *two* games." Joe shot him a terse grin. "Labor's expensive. You had too many women in there at once and broke the thing, didn't you?"

"I don't kiss and tell, but you can dream about it since I doubt you'll be indulging in water sports with Ashley anytime soon."

Joe's expression became grim a split second before he took off. Bryan had a hard time keeping up with him as they scrambled across the court, both of them trying to get and keep the ball. They bumped into each other, shoved, fouled, but kept going, the rules, the rough play, all part of the game.

"Joe?" Melissa called sharply from somewhere behind them.

Joe immediately paused, and Bryan took advantage. He stole the ball and made his basket with ease, releasing a whoop of triumph. Joe hadn't budged.

Bryan followed Joe's fixed stare and saw Melissa's frantic wave, Ashley sitting silent in the car behind her.

"Joe, it's time!" she called excitedly. "Bryan! Ashley's water broke and she doesn't think she can make it to the hospital! The baby's coming! *Hurry!*"

Bryan's soft laugh echoed off the school building when he took in Joe's dazed expression. Bending, he grabbed the ball before he wrapped his arm around Joe's shoulders and prodded his fear-frozen friend toward the latched gate. "Come on, Daddy-o, let's go. Looks like you'll be in the doghouse at least six more weeks while I'll be getting a new shower."

CHAPTER SIX

"PERFECT, ASHLEY. Come on, *push!* This baby's in a rush."

Melissa held her breath along with Ashley while her friend bore down and pushed again. She'd driven Ashley to the schoolyard to pick up Joe hoping Joe could drive his wife to the hospital in Baxter, but along the way Ashley had said there wasn't time and she'd been right. Less than ten minutes after arriving at Bryan's office, the baby had crowned.

"She should be in a hospital," Joe muttered for the fiftieth time. "Ashley needs monitors and medical equipment."

She was thinking the same thing, remembering. Ashley was three weeks early, not necessarily dangerous but the risk was there.

"People had babies at home before," Ashley stated through her clenched teeth. "And at least…we're in…a medical practice." The contraction over, she collapsed into Joe's supportive embrace.

"Ashley's doing fine." Bryan smiled at them encouragingly, sweat beading on his forehead. "This little one is impatient like its daddy."

Melissa's heart raced, both from the adrenaline of being involved in something so unexpected and intense and Bryan's expression. Happy, obviously thrilled to be delivering a baby, he looked wonderful.

Ashley gasped sharply, the sound ending on a moan. "Here comes...another one—*oohh*."

"Wait for it. Breathe. Good, you're doing great, Ashley, breathe through it and let it build. Good! Now deep breath, come on. And push! That's it, push!" Once again Joe supported his wife, his arms around her, lifting her into position. But one glance at Joe's face revealed his bone-numbing fear. Melissa stood to the side, out of the way, stepping forward only when Bryan or Ashley needed something. A cool cloth, a soothing word, a strong hand to grip, or to slip the portable oxygen mask over Ashley's mouth and nose.

Through it all Melissa watched. Her mind replayed Josie's birth and how the nurses and doctors had exchanged silent, worried glances with one another when they couldn't stop the contractions and the monitors beeped crazily.

She'd been alone. No Joe, no friends. No mother or father. No one in the cold, sterile room to keep her company. Young and scared, unprepared for motherhood, much less the fear and pain of what was occurring. Memories assaulted her. None of them good. Images stole her breath until she had to resist the urge to put the oxygen mask over her own face.

Her baby. Oh, how she ached to hold her baby girl, just one more time. It had taken her a long time to feel comfortable around Ashley and Joe, the whole town, after learning her daughter had died of complications from a vaccination and not Shaken Baby Syndrome as they'd all believed. Sometimes she still wasn't comfortable. How could she be? She blamed herself and Joe had spent ten long years in prison, innocent. Convicted with the help of the things she'd said, the things she'd believed. All of them wrong.

"Head's out...shoulder. Slow and perfect. Come on, Ashley, one last push should do it. Good! Joe, looks like you and Ashley have a beautiful…" Bryan glanced up with a wide grin "—baby girl!"

Melissa inhaled sharply and strangled on a tear-choked gasp, praying no one noticed. The baby cried shrilly, upset at being shoved from its warm, comfortable home into a cold world.

Bryan suctioned her little mouth and nose, laughing softly. "That's not a weak cry. This kid's got a good set of lungs."

Ashley and Joe watched Bryan's every move, staring in wonderment at the precious miracle they'd created, their expressions a combination of awe and happiness and relief. They hugged and kissed, their laughter tempered with tears, their love for each other obvious.

Bryan laid the squalling baby on Ashley's gowned stomach while he showed Joe where to cut the cord. That done, Bryan waved Melissa closer to take the warmed blanket she'd prepared, and she stared at the red-faced little girl, the ache of her empty arms sharper than ever before.

Bryan awkwardly tried to swaddle the baby, but when he continued to fumble at the task, Melissa nudged him with her shoulder. "Let me do it."

He hesitated. "Melissa, are you—"

"Let me do it, Bryan." Her gaze met his and in that moment she didn't care that he saw everything she felt inside. "Let me…please?"

Hands shaking, her heart thumping, Melissa waited for Bryan to move out of the way before she carefully bundled up the baby girl. Her lungs burned from the effort it took to suppress her tears because she remembered swaddling Josie the same way, remembered her honey-sweet smell, the downy texture of her hair and how the baby would stare up at her and blink her beautiful blue eyes. But most of all, she remembered the way Josie had fit so perfectly in the cradle of her arms, her skin soft and perfect, her mouth a tiny little bow.

She tucked the edge of the blanket into a fold to hold it in place and lifted the precious baby, relishing the brief contact before she had to transfer the newborn into her mother's outstretched arms. Seeing Ashley's anxious face, Melissa forced a smile. "Ten fingers and toes," she murmured, but then she made the mistake of looking at Joe and found his eyes bloodshot and bright with tears.

Breathe. Just breathe.

Joe deserved another child, another chance. Deserved to be a father because she'd denied him that honor before. No doubt Joe struggled with the same loss, the same memories of their baby girl. This child wouldn't replace Josie, but she would certainly ease the pain for him. But Melissa would never have that. How could she ever risk bringing a child into this world considering the gene she carried?

"Sounds like the EMTs are getting restless," Bryan murmured. "Melissa, would you let them in?"

She nodded, grateful for the excuse to leave the room. She was happy for them, she was. But it *hurt*. Oh, Lord, how it hurt.

Why did Josie have to die? What did she do to deserve to lose so much?

Her legs trembled beneath her, but they carried her through the practice to the waiting room where the EMTs paced. Within moments, Ashley and her baby were fastened to a gurney, an anxious Joe at their side.

Once they were gone, the quiet of the medical practice deafened, broken only by the sounds of Bryan washing up in the exam room down the hall. Adrenaline-fueled strength dwindled to shaky weakness and sadness, and she swallowed repeatedly, leaning against the window and watching while the ambulance pulled away with proud-daddy Joe visible in the back.

The carpeted floorboards creaked before heavy hands settled on her shoulders. "You were wonderful in there. I couldn't have done it without your help, Melissa. Thank you."

Unable to speak, unable to breathe, she lowered her head and nodded. Then a tear escaped. A ragged sob followed and that was all it took to release an avalanche she couldn't stop. No matter how hard she tried to control herself, to clamp her mouth shut and hold in the cries, she couldn't. They kept coming, ragged, belly deep. All-consuming.

"Ah, honey, I'm sorry. I'm so sorry. Don't cry. Sweetheart, please—" Bryan turned her around and pulled her against his chest, his lips at her temple murmuring nonsense meant to soothe. The heat of him warmed her, the scent of him comforted.

While she and Joe had helped get Ashley settled in one of the examination rooms, Bryan had gone upstairs and hurriedly showered. Now he smelled of soap and man, and his soft shirt soaked up her tears while he rubbed her neck and shoulders in soothing strokes. Melissa relished the embrace, the tender touch. And while her brain railed at her to pull herself together, another part of her simply begged to curl against him and stay there.

She cried for Josie, for herself. For her own mother, and the grandmother she'd never gotten a chance to meet. Josie was better off where she was, wouldn't have to endure the suffering, the painful surgeries, the chemo treatments. Heaven was better. Josie was better. But *why* didn't it feel that way? Why did it hurt so much?

"Melissa...sweetheart, don't. Honey, you're killing me. Please...stop."

Head buried in his chest, she smiled weakly at his words, laughed, the sound raw and rough. Imagine that, the infamous Bang 'em Booker upset by a few tears. She'd have thought Bryan would be used to tears since he'd broken so many hearts.

Sniffling, she took a deep breath and, moments later, she wiped her face with shaking fingers and raised her head only to find her gaze caught and held by his. "I'm s-sorry."

"Don't be. Anytime you need to cry, Booger Boy is here."

The nickname caught her by surprise and she laughed, glad he didn't push her away, because she wasn't sure she could stand without his support. Time stilled. The large house was silent, dim where they stood leaning against each other in the unlit reception area. Blood pounded in her ears as she watched Bryan's mouth slowly lower. Moving closer and closer until...

Her lips parted the moment his lips brushed hers, his breath warm and musky, tantalizing to her overwrought system. Before she could draw a steadying breath, before her mind could register a protest or give it a voice, Bryan sealed their mouths together. His tongue entered and built a fire that spread through every inch of her body, making her forget all about protesting and professionalism, all about sadness and death.

For a moment, that moment, she forgot the past, the pain. Forgot everything but the feel of Bryan's arms. Who would've thought the boy she'd known could pull such a reaction from her?

The kiss went on, a bit rough, a little out of control, a lot hotter than her most private fantasies. Bryan's hands roamed her back, her waist. Her shoulders. His fingers slid into her short hair to better angle her head. He rubbed, nudged, the heat of him penetrating the material of her dress until she wasn't lonely and cold and sad.

Bryan's teasing fingers skimmed the base of her hips, slowly glided up. The sensation was seductive, dreamlike. A slow drag of fire wherever he stroked, teasing, overwhelming her every sense...until Bryan's fingertips settled over the fastener of her bra.

Cold reality smacked her. A hard, if-he-only-knew-the-truth slug to her stomach that stole her breath. She jerked away from him, and then staggered back two more steps when Bryan reached for her with an expression of pure eagerness.

Something about her hasty retreat made Bryan's eyes clear, and he dropped his hands to his sides with a curse, the sensual fog fading from his expression until it turned to one of slack-jawed horror.

Dear Lord, what had she done? Fingers pressed against her mouth, she tried to quell her trembling, torn between closing the distance between them because she wanted more of the heady pleasure, and running, *screaming,* until she was as far away from Bryan as she could possibly get.

"I'm sorry, Melissa. I didn't mean to do that."

She flinched. Of course he hadn't meant to kiss her. Swallowing tightly, she turned. "I've got to go."

Bryan caught her arm but let go when she rounded on him, angry at herself, at him. At the unfair world that had taken everything from her.

He held his hands up in a pleading gesture the total opposite of his normal devil-may-care attitude. "Melissa, hear me out. I did *not* mean for that to happen."

Could he stop saying that? Did he think she *hadn't* realized that already? A huff escaped her instead of the laugh she intended. Shaking her head, she headed toward the door once more.

"You have every reason to be upset with me, but I promise you, Melissa, it won't happen again!"

He had that right. She needed time to process things. To delve deep and figure out if she could handle working here when it was quite obvious Bryan was used to his advances being welcomed.

Her face burned with embarrassment. He didn't know she hadn't had the reconstructive surgery. He didn't know she was a breastless freak by her own choosing, but it didn't matter.

Melissa shoved the door open and ran outside, noting that, this time, Bryan didn't try to stop her.

HER DAD HAD JUST LEFT FOR WORK the next morning when the phone rang. Melissa had deliberately lazed in bed so she wouldn't have to talk to him about Ellen, or risk him taking one look at her and guessing Bryan had lived up to his reputation. Nor could she undergo his questioning her about helping to deliver Joe and Ashley's daughter.

By now everyone in town would be gossiping about her presence in the delivery room. What she'd done, what she'd thought, how she'd reacted to the news Joe had a second baby girl. The stories would grow with every telling, and one glimpse of her would send whispers flying.

Was it her father calling? Had he heard already? The caller ID box was in the other room and she was too tired to go check.

But as much as she wanted to stay in bed buried beneath the covers today, she knew she had to put in an appearance around town. Be seen out and about, a smile in place. It was the only way to stem the rumors. *Fake it till you make it.*

And if she saw Bryan? Why, why, *why* had she kissed him?

The phone stopped ringing, but after a slight pause it began again. As if whoever it was had hung up and called right back.

She rolled over onto her stomach and stretched to pick up the receiver. "Hello?"

"Give me a damage report," Bryan ordered huskily. "But whatever you do, please tell me you'll show up tomorrow morning."

The image of him leaning out the window, shirtless and drowsy, smiling down at her, entered her head with frightening clarity. Had that only been yesterday?

"Melissa?"

"I'll…" What choice did she have at this point? "I'll be there. So long as we agree that what happened yesterday will never, ever be repeated or talked about again. To *anyone*."

"Deal. I apolo—"

"We're not talking about it, remember?"

His warm chuckle filled her ear. "Understood. Now that the unmentionable has been taken care of, I'll be there in twenty minutes to pick you up."

"Pick me up?" She sat up in the bed. "For what?"

"Not what, whom. We've got a baby to see. I thought we could go together."

Together? She'd tossed and turned all night, dozing fitfully only to wake up with a jerk when their kiss played out in her head again and again. She'd fantasized about Bryan taking it further. In her dreams she hadn't had cancer, was the way she ought to be, a woman Bryan could be attracted to, until the dreams had changed to nightmares. In those, her breasts were gone, Bryan had been joined by Nathan, and both men had said they didn't want to be with her, couldn't be with her. They'd laughed at her attempts to kiss them, to attract them, disgust on their faces, contempt in their voices, because her body repulsed them.

"Hello…Melissa, are you there?"

She dropped back to her pillow and rolled to her side, rubbing her sleep-deprived eyes. "I'm here, but— Bryan, look, I'm sure you understand why I feel the need to reestablish employer-employee distance? Let's just forget the k— *yesterday* ever happened, and I'll see you tomorrow morning."

"Today. We need to move beyond what happened and we can't do it with the phones ringing and patients watching. And it's a perfect day for a drive. Forty-five minutes to the hospital, forty-five minutes back, a half-hour stay at most so we don't tire the new mother and lunch. How's that sound?"

Melissa pressed the heel of her hand to her forehead. It sounded like a date. She pulled the sheet up to her chin, undecided, her instincts screaming. He'd agreed the kiss was a mistake, but if she spent the afternoon with Bryan, how could she *not* think of the kiss? Not remember her dreams? Her imagination had been quite detailed, painfully so.

To even consider Bryan a possibility as a companion to her loneliness was a joke...on her.

"Come on, it's a gorgeous beginning to September and the last of the really pretty weather. I'll put the top down so we can enjoy the day. How about it? I'd hoped to discuss the fund-raiser since we didn't get a chance yesterday. Maybe toss around a few ideas and get things rolling? Layer on the sunscreen and let's go."

Melissa reminded herself that Bryan—men—viewed things differently than women. A date to her was a business lunch to him. Go figure. Then again, if Bryan's reputation was anything to go by, the last thing his dates entailed was a drive to visit a friend in the hospital. It was something he'd do with...a sister. Or a friend. She did need to see the baby, make sure Ashley knew she'd simply been a little overwhelmed and that she didn't resent her or Joe's happiness.

"Do you have other plans?"

"No, but—"

"Great. So how long do you need?"

"Need?"

"To get ready. Longer than a half hour?" He chuckled softly, the sound friendly. "Are you sure you're awake?"

The teasing in Bryan's voice made her smile, as well, before she squelched it and shook off her hesitation. Bryan might be a player when it came to women, but he was also her boss. One who'd readily agreed to her demand of not repeating the same mistake because he'd regretted it himself. Instantly.

She was the only one making a big deal out of things. What happened in Bryan's office was nothing to someone like him, a man who dated multiple women. No, he'd gotten caught up in the moment, forgotten her history and—

It wouldn't happen again. "Thirty minutes."

"I'll see you then. Don't forget the sunscreen."

BRYAN HELD Ashley and Joe's daughter in his arms, amazed how something so tiny could hold everyone around her so enthralled. The infant scrunched up her face, yawned, then blinked her eyes open to stare at him, and he knew in an instant the girl would grow up and break some hearts. "Beautiful. It's a good thing she takes after her mother, though," he murmured, never taking his eyes off her little face.

Wilson Woodrow, the man who'd unofficially adopted Ashley when she'd bought his large Victorian home to open a bed and breakfast, laughed gruffly. "Wouldn't Joe's ugly mug have been a sight?"

Joe took the ribbing in stride. "Hush up, old man, or you'll be getting diaper duty."

"Serve him right. He never does his share of the dishes," Joe's father added. Ted Brody shook a finger at Wilson, but the grin on his face belied his gruff tone. "Always out playing bingo with those widows from Baxter. I told him if he ain't careful, one of these days he's going to find himself in front of a preacher again."

Wilson looked so horrified at the thought they all laughed. Bryan continued to chuckle, noting belatedly that the group had quieted down and was now focused on something behind him. He turned. Melissa stood outside the door holding a bouquet of flowers that shook slightly. "There you are. I wondered where you'd disappeared to."

Her face flushed. "Sorry. I ran into someone and then…I didn't want to visit empty-handed."

"Oh, Melissa, you didn't have to buy flowers! Come in," Ashley greeted warmly. "I'm so glad you're here!"

Melissa stepped forward, her eyes down, her cheeks bright pink, which caused the sprinkling of freckles across her nose to stand out against her pale skin. "How are you feeling?"

"Actually much better this time than after Max was born."

"That's wonderful."

Ashley waved Melissa deeper into the room, looking nothing like a woman who'd just given birth hours before. "Come on, don't be shy. Isabella and I need another female in here to help even up the numbers," she said with grin. "And I want to thank you for helping us yesterday."

Melissa handed Ashley the bouquet, giving her a hug and murmuring something Bryan couldn't hear. Ashley's face softened and she shared a look with her husband before discreetly shooing Joe away. Joe placed his hand on Melissa's shoulder and squeezed gently before leaving the bed and moving to Bryan's side.

"Quit staring."

"Shut up," Bryan muttered, unable to take his eyes off Melissa's heart-shaped rear when she bent over the side of the bed rail to hug Ashley again. Dressed in snug jeans and a loose, button-down shirt, Melissa looked great. Healthy. But he'd noticed the exhaustion around her eyes when he'd picked her up this morning, and knew without a doubt she hadn't slept, either. But why? The baby's birth? The kiss? She'd suggested never speaking of it again. Because it hadn't mattered to her? Didn't affect her the way it had him?

He heard Melissa softly say Joe's name and jealousy made itself known. How healthy was it that Melissa was friends with her ex-lover's wife? Was it a way to be close to Joe?

The two women stopped whispering, and Ashley smiled as she patted Melissa's hand. "The flowers are beautiful," she said, her tone a little louder and now including the rest of them in the room, "and they smell wonderful. Thank you again, Melissa. For everything."

"Mommy, Mommy!"

Before Melissa could respond, Ashley's son barreled into the room pulling a young hospital volunteer behind him. He let go of the girl's hand once he spotted Bryan.

"Unc' B.!" Max torpedoed himself against Bryan's legs and wrapped his arms tight, grinning. "Me, me! Up!"

Bryan chuckled at Max's antics and saw Melissa watching them, a smile on her face. The first true smile he'd seen all day.

"Would you like a turn?" Carefully, keeping his movements steady and sure, given the munchkin pulling on his legs, Bryan shifted the baby in his arms while Melissa eagerly stepped close. During the transfer to Melissa, a minuscule hand escaped the hospital blanket.

Melissa's laughter filled the air, her face instantly softening with love. "Well, hello to you, too. Oh, Ashley, she's *beautiful*."

"See? Everybody knows who's got the looks in the family," Wilson teased from the corner of the room.

Bryan picked up Max, distracted by the expression on Melissa's face. She stared at the baby, transfixed, her lips curled up at the corners, her eyes sparkling.

Beautiful was right.

Everyone went back to chatting, but Bryan couldn't take his eyes off Melissa even though he knew he'd get some ribbing later from Joe.

Wilson made a joke, and they all laughed. But still he watched her. That's why he saw the instant she started and stiffened like she'd been stabbed. The color left her cheeks and then returned in a blazing rush. A split second later, his heart slammed into his chest when a tear trickled down her cheek and Melissa hurried to wipe it away. "Melissa?"

At the sound of Bryan's voice, Ashley turned her head and gasped. "Melissa, what's wrong? Why are you upset?"

"I'm fine. *Really*." She sniffled and released a strained laugh, but no more tears escaped. "I think I'm having sympathy mood swings for you," she joked huskily, trying to add a smile and failing miserably. "She's beautiful, Ashley. Just so…so *perfect*. I'd forgotten how—I'd forgotten. That's all."

Unable to go on, Melissa carried the baby the three steps it took to pass her to her mother and then fled the room with a hastily murmured goodbye. Bryan turned and found Joe waiting for his stepson, arms outstretched. Two seconds later Bryan rushed into the hall, barely catching sight of Melissa's blue blouse as she went around the corner. He jogged after her and followed her into an otherwise empty elevator. "Melissa—"

"Don't." She wouldn't look at him. "I'm fine. I feel like a fool, but I'm fine. Go back to them."

"Not a chance." The elevator doors closed and, assured of their privacy, Bryan stepped forward to take her into his arms.

CHAPTER SEVEN

THE MOMENT Melissa noticed his approach, she stalked to the opposite side of the elevator. Bryan fought his frustration and settled his butt against the metal bar, arms over his chest. "What happened?"

Using both trembling hands, she wiped her face and rolled her eyes. "What an idiot. I feel like an absolute *idiot!*" She slumped against the elevator wall, her face pale. "This was such a mistake. I shouldn't have come. Why did you have to insist I come with you?"

He stepped forward, but she distanced herself again, sliding along the wall to the back of the elevator. *"Melissa."*

"Leave it alone, Bryan. Leave *me* alone or I'll quit before I ever start work tomorrow morning. I mean it."

"Why can't I hold you? As a *friend?*"

"Because I'm fine!"

"Lie to yourself if you can, but don't lie to me."

It dawned on her they weren't moving, and Melissa slammed her hand against the elevator button. A second later they began the descent to the lobby. "I can't believe it. What must they *think?*"

"I'd say they think you're upset over holding a baby girl not much smaller than the one you lost. Melissa, they understand that you're happy for them and yet sad for yourself."

His gaze narrowed when he felt a surprising stab of jealousy once again. "Unless there's more? Does this have something to do with Joe?"

Her eyes widened. "What? No!" She shook her head firmly. *"No,"* she repeated, a glare and her tone lending truth to her words. She groaned again, palms pressed to her forehead. "Joe and I were never really more than friends. We were just too young to realize it at the time."

Relief flooded through him. He had no business feeling relief or jealousy or any other emotion where Melissa was concerned, and yet he did. But only because he didn't want Joe and Ashley's marriage to be endangered.

The elevator chimed and the doors began to slide open. Bryan watched Melissa raise her chin and square her shoulders, the tears gone or at least under control. He supposed that's how she'd managed to survive the cancer, by standing her ground, pride intact, head high and fighting. But in that instant he wanted to fight for her. With her. But how could he do that when, having moved back to town and discovering she battled cancer, he'd neglected to visit her? He'd told himself he was too busy taking over his grandfather's practice, convinced himself that there had been too many years between visits to still be friends, but he knew none of those were the truth.

Shaking his head at his own actions, Bryan smothered a groan and followed her out into the lobby. Melissa hadn't even worked her first official day and already he was in over his head. He could already hear Joe laughing at his dilemma. And threatening to kill him if he stepped out of bounds and hurt Melissa in any way.

Minutes later Bryan unlocked his car with a bleep of the key-ring control, and they climbed inside. Neither of them spoke until halfway between Taylorsville and Baxter when he turned onto a narrow driveway and slowed the powerful sports car. Trees lined the road and created a sun-dappled haven of cooler air. With the wind no longer a factor, he decided to appease his curious mind even though he told himself to leave well enough alone.

"Enough already. Melissa, what happened back there? The truth this time, please."

She tensed, glaring at him briefly before averting her head once more. "I don't know what you mean."

A grim smile lifted one side of his mouth. "You'd rather I guessed? Let's see…you came in with flowers, hugged Ashley and were fine. You smiled. Chatted. Smiled some more."

"Bryan—"

"Then you took the baby and wound up white as a sheet. Muscle spasm? No, I don't think so. Maybe a—"

"*Bryan.*"

He slid her a glance. "Something happened, Melissa, and since I *do* care what happens to my employees—my *friends*—I'd like you to feel you could talk to me. Surely whatever it is, it isn't so bad that you can't tell me?"

She stared out at the slowly passing scenery, her profile revealing her turbulent thoughts. "It just felt…strange. Holding her, like you said."

Uh-huh. That might be part of it, but it wasn't all. He wished he'd kept his mouth shut and not given her a ready excuse. "It's been—" he quickly tabulated "—nearly twelve years since Josie's death? Surely you've held babies since then?" Thinking fast, he latched on to a memory. "Yeah, I know you have. I've seen you with Max several times, and little Katie Morgan."

"Drop it. Please," she begged huskily. "You have no right to ask these questions."

"I do when Ashley and her family are my patients. Are you going to disappear or get upset every time they come in for a visit?"

Her head whipped toward him. "Of course not!"

"Then tell me what happened today instead of giving me lame excuses. Let me be the friend you say you want," he challenged. "Come on, Melissa. A long time ago you told me everything. Now it's truth time again—*what happened?*"

Bryan split his attention between the road and Melissa. She appeared to be trying to look through him instead of at him. Slowing even more, the car crawled along at a snail's pace.

"I suppose if I don't tell you we'll go five miles an hour until we get there?"

"If that's what it takes."

"I guess it's no big deal. Everybody knows, anyway." She sent him a dubious glance. "As a doctor, you must know what's involved with the type of cancer I had, right?"

"Breast cancer can be treated numerous ways." What did her cancer have to do with the baby? "A lumpectomy or mastectomy, radiation and chemo are standard."

"Yeah." She inhaled and blew the breath out quickly, her cheeks turning pink. "Okay, well…I had a double mastectomy."

His grip tightened on the wheel. "Why a double?" he asked hoarsely, knowing he had to give her some kind of level, doctorish response. Curiosity, medical expertise, something other than the bone-crushing fear tumbling through him. She'd lost *both* breasts?

"I carry the breast-cancer gene and they thought it would be best with my family history."

Her words brought another face to mind. Rachel's image had blurred over the years since med school, but he still remembered her smile, her laughter. The way she'd maintained her sense of humor despite the trauma her body had endured.

"I never thought I'd see you speechless."

Bryan glanced over to where Melissa sat and caught himself before he murmured the thoughtless *I'm sorry*. He'd learned working in the cancer unit that a lot of families didn't want to hear placating words because they didn't fix the problem—and they wouldn't fix Melissa. The last thing she needed or wanted was his pity. "What did the baby do?"

"The baby..." She laughed softly. "Let's just say she did what all newborn babies do."

Given the poor condition his brain was in, it took him a second or two to catch on. "You mean she...*rooted* you?"

Melissa nodded, but avoided his gaze. "And even though I have held babies since Josie, that hasn't happened. Let's just say it brought home a whole lot of truths in the space of a second, and even though I was already aware of them, I—I guess I hadn't completely, I don't know, accepted them."

"I understand." And he did. Looking at her one would never have known what she'd suffered, but Melissa was very aware of her body's altered state and changes since the surgery. "And I appreciate your telling me."

"I know it's silly. I mean, it's been nearly two years since I was diagnosed and the surgery was immediately after that. I should be used to it."

"It's not silly at all, Melissa. Your reaction was perfectly understandable. You're certainly not the only woman who would've reacted that way."

"Maybe." She looked out at the goldenrod they passed, a

twist to her pink lips. "But now I'll have to call Ashley and apologize for running out like that. She'll be— Bryan, where *are* we?"

Thankful for the change in mood, he grinned at her awe-struck expression. "My granddad's," he said, trying to see the large house through her eyes. "I hope you don't mind, but I thought we'd have lunch here and spend a little time with him?"

Melissa shook her head quickly, her expression softening to one of concern. "Here I've been going on and on, and I never once asked. How's he doing? I heard about the stroke. You found him?"

"Not me. The housekeeper, Meg. She's also the cook and all-around wonder woman. She's worked for my granddad for years. A home-care nurse comes by every day, but Meg fills in the gaps." Tearing his eyes away from hers wasn't easy. "The first hour after a stroke is critical because sometimes the damage can be reversed if care is given quickly enough, but Granddad had the stroke during the night and didn't get help until hours later."

"The damage is permanent?"

Bryan nodded and stopped the car. No amount of money or ability could change his grandfather's health now, but he'd do his best to see to it his grandfather's sacrifices wouldn't go unacknowledged.

"He's the reason the clinic is so important to you."

Leave it to Melissa to understand. "It might have started off as his dream, but it's become mine."

Melissa flashed him an understanding smile. "Then we'll make sure it happens. Your grandfather was a wonderful doctor, well respected and loved." Her expression turned thoughtful, speculative. "Maybe with his permission, we could play up that angle? Use him to remind the people of Taylorsville what they lost or could lose in not having the clinic we all need?"

"I like the sound of that. It gives the clinic a more personal feel. I'm still considered the newcomer to town, but if Granddad shows his support—"

"We'll have the majority of the town," she stated confidently. "He doctored so many people, their children. *Grandchildren*. Bryan, that's it! That's the key to making this fund-raiser a success."

He stared at her, taking in her conquer-the-world expression and the smile that pulled her lips up at the corners. In a matter of moments Melissa had gone from being sad and teary eyed to determined to see the job done.

Yeah, he liked it. He liked it a lot.

INSIDE THE six-thousand-square-foot house, Melissa looked around, unable to keep her mouth from hanging slightly agape while Bryan closed the massive double entry doors. The house was absolutely beautiful from the outside, but inside it was a designer's dream. A mixture of old and new, antiques and modern furnishings.

A complicated block pattern in what appeared to be cherry inlay dominated the floor. Darker stained wood encircled the entry, giving the floor the look of a cherry-bound wooden rug. Leaded-glass doors stood open off the elegant foyer, and a peek inside showed it to be a salon or parlor, the furnishings proudly holding time-worn knickknacks and antiques. "It's beautiful."

"Like stepping back in time," Bryan agreed. "I'll give you a tour before we leave."

She followed him dazedly. Along the hall were black-and-white photos of the original Dr. Booker, shiny silver tags with descriptions and dates at the bottom. One picture was of Dr. Booker standing outside his practice with an early-model Ford parked alongside a horse tied to a porch post, another of him and the first baby he'd delivered, another in a hospital surrounded by children. "Bryan, is that…?"

Bryan chuckled. "Yeah. Granddad was on vacation in Rome when he heard about some kids getting sick at a local orphanage. He went to see if he could help and had been there three days when he heard a commotion. A group of nuns came into the room with a man in long white robes. Granddad said he was so exhausted it took him a minute to realize who it was." He smiled. "Come on, I'm hungry. Granddad is usually in the sunroom this time of day. You can ask him about the photos and hear the stories firsthand."

Eager, she allowed Bryan to pull her deeper into the interior. What looked like Tiffany lamps lit the way and wind-up clocks were everywhere, some with pendulums swinging, some with suns and moons.

"When he moved back to this area and began practicing medicine, a lot of the people didn't have money to pay him, but they had their pride so they brought him other things. Family heirlooms, farm stock." He lifted a hand. "Clocks and quilts. He refused the majority of it, but over the years he still managed to accumulate quite a collection."

They turned a corner. Ahead of them, Melissa heard a woman's voice followed by a sharp, inhuman cry.

"That's Charlie. He's a cockatiel and one of Granddad's many payments."

Bryan rounded another corner and hesitated, slipping his hand from her arm to the small of her back where it rested lightly. He appeared unaffected by the contact, but Melissa felt a surge of warmth shoot through her when he guided her into the room, his chest brushing her shoulder.

"You two up for a visit?" Bryan called, smiling.

"Dr. Booker!" A smock-clad nurse turned away from her patient in surprise. "Aren't you a sight for sore eyes! Come in, come in! I was just about to go ask Meg about Randall's lunch. Would you like me to tell her you'll be joining your grandfather?"

"That'd be great."

Melissa recognized the nurse immediately, but before she could form a greeting, she saw Randall Booker. He watched them from his wheelchair, his head lowering once in a nod of welcome when he saw her looking at him. She smiled. "Hello, Dr. Booker. You have a beautiful home," she murmured, trying hard not to let the old man see her dismay at his appearance. The once robust man she'd known was no more. Dr. Booker looked his age and then some. Forcing the sting of tears away at how fragile the old man appeared compared to when she'd seen him last, she turned her attention to his nurse. "Hello, Tilly, it's nice to see you."

The woman's mouth dropped open in surprise. *"Melissa?* Oh, honey, don't you look wonderful! I didn't even recognize you!"

Bryan glanced from Tilly to her. "You two know each other?"

The nurse crossed the room and pulled her into a hug. "I should say we do!"

"Tilly was my home-care nurse for a while," she told Bryan, "and she took wonderful care of me."

"Because you made it so easy," the older woman said, patting her like a proud parent.

At Bryan's gentle prodding, the three of them moved closer

to Randall. "How's your son?" Melissa asked along the way. "Has he settled down any since we spoke last?" She hated that the sweet woman worried herself sick over a child who didn't appreciate his mother's love.

Tilly shook her head. "I don't think that boy will ever settle down. He's living with his girlfriend, but I see him about every day or so. He comes over quite a bit in the evening and just sits around the house, but I don't mind. I like having him there. It gets too quiet otherwise. Oh, listen to me prattle on. And look at the time!" She bent and picked up the book and chart from the couch. "I'm going to have to run, but first I'll let Meg know you two will be staying for lunch."

"She won't mind?" Melissa asked, sending a hesitant glance Bryan's way.

"Ha! Meg loves showing off her cooking skills anytime she gets a chance. Right, Randall?"

The old man nodded.

Tilly winked and patted Melissa's arm again. "While I'm in there, I'll see about getting you some lemonade or iced tea, too. Sound good?"

"Sounds wonderful," Bryan said, rubbing his hands together. "I could use a drink. Thanks, Tilly, we appreciate it. The drive in the sun made me thirsty, and Meg's lemonade is the best."

The nurse hugged Melissa one last time, told the elder Dr. Booker to behave himself, and then excused herself with a murmur.

Bryan took her elbow in hand. "Granddad, do you remember Melissa York? Starting tomorrow she's my office manager. Brave of her to take it on, huh?"

Only the right side of the old man's mouth curled up. "Good see you 'gain."

"You, too. You're looking well, Dr. Booker."

He shook his head. "Too many Doc Bookers-s. I—I'm juss Randall n-now."

"Randall it is then."

A large bank of windows dominated one side of the room, the sunlight warming the space. On his perch in front of the windows, Charlie shifted and squawked, apparently tired of being ignored. A sharp whistle split the air, followed by, "Pretty girl, pretty girl."

"Charlie, h-hush," Randall ordered firmly.

Melissa laughed. "No, please, don't hush him. That's the best compliment I've gotten all day."

Randall's eyebrows rose in response before he glanced at Bryan.

"You know me better than that," Bryan countered, grinning rakishly. He stepped forward and gave the old man a hug, then shook his hand, holding it in both of his. "Melissa and I went to visit a friend in the hospital, and thought we'd drop by to see you."

"I hope you don't mind, but Bryan has promised me a tour of your house later and I plan to hold him to it. The pictures along the hall are amazing."

Randall nodded, smiling his lopsided smile. "Good years-s."

Melissa took the seat Bryan indicated and stared at the men, noting that Bryan looked very much like his grandfather. They shared the same angular features, the same intense green eyes. Randall's once-blond hair had long ago turned white, and the stroke had marred the man's physical appearance, but he cut quite a striking figure all the same. He sat in a wheelchair dressed in green patterned pajamas, a throw over his legs, his bifocal glasses perched on his nose.

"Has Meg treated you to any of her desserts this week?" Bryan asked.

Randall shook his head. "Mean w-woman—won't share."

"In other words, your sugar must be acting up and Tilly's watching her like a hawk. Don't be too hard on them. You know it's for your own good."

"Man's-s got to die...s-sometime. M-Meg's desserts good...way."

Melissa laughed softly, earning Randall's appreciative glance. He gave her his lopsided smile again, the sight causing her heart to constrict painfully. What would Bryan do when he lost the grandfather he loved so much?

"Melissa has agreed to help me come up with some fund-raisers for the clinic, and she had a great idea as we pulled up outside. Melissa?" Bryan's expression urged her to tell the story.

"Oh, um, well, I thought—hoped—we might put a more personal spin on things and remind people of all the years you cared for us." She tilted her head, trying to judge Randall's response. "And how you could've used the clinic's help yourself. We've all probably needed it at some time and will need it more in the future as Taylorsville grows."

The old man appeared to give it some thought before he nodded. "M-might work."

Bryan leaned forward until his elbows rested on his knees, his hands clasped as he tried to contain his excitement. "Then maybe you wouldn't mind if we used some of the framed pictures of you for the flyers and promotion? I'm still the new kid in town, but if we focus on the fact this started as *your* dream—"

"Don't m-make old m-man look foolish."

"Never," they said in unison.

"Absolutely not," Bryan added. "We wouldn't do that."

Melissa stared, struck by the tender, loving expression on Bryan's face, easily seeing how women could fall for him if they were on the receiving end of it. It was a good thing she knew better, otherwise after yesterday she very well could find herself thinking of Bryan as a man instead of a boss. What a disaster that would be.

"Y-you can u-use them."

"Great! You'll make this clinic a reality yet, Granddad."

Randall indicated Melissa by lifting his hand. "L-look like your m-mother."

Melissa had smiled at Bryan's boyish excitement, but just as quickly caught her breath at Randall's words. "Thank you, that's another wonderful compliment."

"P-pretty woman. B-beautif-ful."

"Yes, she was," she confirmed. "I— Bryan told me a bit about the pictures in the hall. I saw the one of you and your infamous candy jar. I'll never forget the horror I felt when the dentist said I had a cavity. I begged my mother not to tell him about your jar so he wouldn't be mad at you and make you stop giving the kids treats when we came to see you."

A gruff sound left Randall's chest, and it took her a moment to realize it was laughter. Smiling, she glanced at Bryan and found him staring at her, obviously pleased but seemingly aware of how his grandfather's compliment had made her feel.

Once, maybe, she could've been considered pretty. Beautiful was a long shot on a good day, but she hadn't appreciated her appearance then, hadn't thought about how it could alter. Now with her short hair, radiation-tattooed body and no breasts, well, beautiful wasn't even in the realm of possibility.

"You wore p-pigtails."

She made a show of grimacing and clamping a hand loosely over her face and peeking through her fingers. "Oh, no! Please don't remind me! My mother used to insist every little girl looked cute in pigtails, but I *hated* them."

Both men laughed as she'd intended.

"S-sad when your m-mama passed. Good w-woman."

Once again Melissa fought to keep her smile in place. *Couldn't they talk about something else?* She didn't need the constant reminders of what she'd lost. She felt those on a daily basis. "You gave her a lot of comfort in those last days."

"She made…best apple p-pie in town."

At least now Randall touched on a happy subject. "Did you know she won first place at the county fair every year she entered? Got to where she had to guard her recipes anytime someone came to the house." Melissa smiled. "I keep her recipe box hidden in my room because I'm determined to guard her secret ingredient."

All three of them laughed at the statement, but her laughter and Bryan's seemed strained. Her imagination? A moment passed, the room silent.

Bryan stood. "Tilly's awfully quiet in the kitchen. Makes me think Meg took a rolling pin to her. I'm going to check on her and give her a hand with those drinks."

Melissa watched Bryan leave, feeling awkward at his sudden abandonment.

"P-poor boy." Randall lifted his left, stroke-curled hand toward the doorway where Bryan had disappeared. "He still mourns that g-girl."

What girl? "I'm sure he's just checking on drinks for us."

"More'n that. Can't b-bear to talk 'bout it. Reminds-s him of h-her. She d-died, too. Canc-cer." He shook his head roughly, his gaze meeting hers, the slackness on the left side of his face not diminishing the intense look in his eyes, one that seemed to beg for her understanding. "He was g-going to m-marry her."

"Bryan was engaged?"

Randall shook his head, his green eyes bright. "They broke up before it h-happened. He w-watched her pass though. Such pain. Now he s-sleeps 'round…t-to forget." His eyes narrowed, his frustration with his inability to form the words fast enough obvious. "R-right woman make'm better though." He lifted his hand and pointed a trembling finger at her. "M-make'm love 'gain."

Melissa tried to calm her panicked thoughts. She scooted to the edge of her seat and fought the urge to get out of there as quickly as possible. "Um…I think you might have gotten the wrong idea about me and your grandson. We're not— I'm just an employee. I mean, we're friends, but we're not a couple or anything."

"Never b-brought w-woman here."

He hadn't? "It's not like that," she insisted, fighting the images in her head. Images of Bryan holding her, kissing her. Making love to her? But he'd never be able to do that. Even knowing what he knew about her illness, now that she knew he'd loved someone and lost her, it was unthinkable.

"You must not remember what happened to me." She shook her head and slipped her hands between her thighs and the couch to control their shaking. "I had cancer, too. The same as that girl and my mother, and Bryan's my *boss*."

"S-so? Many a d-doc married his h-help. My Penny w-was my nurse at f-first."

That might be so, but there were a million and ten reasons why she couldn't. Why Bryan *couldn't*. "But if Bryan's playboy reputation is based on seeking…*comfort* from all those women, the *last* person he needs o-or would *want* is someone like me."

The old man stared at her with Bryan's eyes, measuring, assessing. "Forgive me. Old man's-s wishful thinking. Was j-just glad my grands-son had f-finally brought a g-good girl home."

An incredulous laugh got caught in her throat. A good girl? Somehow, she didn't quite see herself as the catch Randall imagined. She'd been a pregnant teenager, a college dropout, a cancer patient. Yeah, quite a catch. "I'm not, Randall."

"He s-sees you that way. Always h-has."

Really?

"Here's the lemonade," Bryan called, walking into the room carrying a loaded tray. His attention fastened on her face and his smile faded. "Something wrong?"

"Wrong?" She felt Randall's knowing gaze on her and fought for composure. "No, why do you ask?"

"You're blushing." Bryan winked at his grandfather and set the tray on the table between them. "I haven't seen a woman blush in ages, have you?"

Randall laughed, his frail body shaking in the wheelchair, his eyes hinting at things Melissa didn't dare consider because if she did—

"S-see what I mean?"

—it would ruin everything.

Five hours later Melissa smiled weakly and waved at Bryan to drive away while he waited in his Mercedes for her to walk to the front door of her house and go in. She needed a moment to recoup from the day. Not only from the slam of emotions after the visit to the hospital, but from Randall's comment and all the weird thoughts that ran through her head as a result.

She'd spent the afternoon second-guessing everything Bryan said and did until she'd been ready to scream from frustration.

Footsteps dragging, she approached the front door and had just made it to the threshold when it was yanked open, startling her.

"Where the blazes have you been?"

CHAPTER EIGHT

HER FATHER'S large frame was in shadow, looming over her. Heart thumping, she blinked in the harsh brightness of the overhead light. "What's wrong?"

"I've been calling everywhere looking for you!"

She glanced at her watch and winced. "I'm sorry. I should've called but didn't think about it." His words sank in and she frowned. "Why were you trying to find me? Did something happen? I went to visit Ashley earlier and— Is she all right? The *baby?*"

"They're both fine."

"Oh, thank God. You scared me."

"I scared you? You left the hospital hours ago. Where have you *been?*"

She frowned at his tone. "Can I come in or do you want to discuss this while we get eaten alive by mosquitoes?"

Her father took several steps back, holding the door open wide enough for her to step through. When she did, she noticed two things at once: her father was so angry and upset he shook, and Ellen had been there. The whole house smelled of the woman's perfume. "Where's your—Ellen?"

"Home. Now answer the question."

"Bryan drove me to the hosp—"

"You've been with Booker the entire time?"

"Yes! After the hospital we went to visit his grandfather." Melissa dropped her keys inside her purse. "Why am I getting the third degree?"

Her father ran one of his hands over his uniform's tie and rubbed. "Ashley called this afternoon and said you'd left the hospital upset. When you didn't come home…"

Her eyes widened when her father's face began to heat with a ruddy flush. "You mean you thought Bryan and I were— Dad!"

"They don't call him *Bang 'em Booker* for nothing, Mel."

"I don't believe you! I suppose one glance might make some women happy to take whatever he's willing to give, but I'm not. *How* could you think spending one afternoon with Bryan would make me forget about everything I've been through and fall into bed with him?"

"Because it happened before!"

Her mouth dropped open in shock. He actually thought—

"Don't look at me like that. What on God's green earth were you *thinking* helping to deliver Joe's baby? You shouldn't have been there, Mel. Not only because of the gossip, but why would you put yourself through that?"

She stalked across the living room, resisting the urge to run to her room and slam the door the way she had as a child. Those days were gone. That innocence, gone. "One, I didn't have much choice since it was an emergency delivery and Bryan needed help! Two, for whatever reason, Ashley wants to be my friend— *is* my friend—and so is Joe even though I can't believe he's forgiven me. And three, I can't believe you just compared me to the sixteen-year-old child I used to be! I didn't handle Mom's death well, but when will you forgive me one little mistake?"

"It wasn't little."

"Nor was it bad! If I hadn't slept with Joe I wouldn't have

had Josie and despite her…her *dying,* I'm not sorry I had my baby the brief time she lived!"

"Neither am I!" Her father caught her arm. "Mel, I have every right to be worried. Any decent father *would* be worried if his daughter was out with that reprobate."

"We were with Bryan's *grandfather* and his cook discussing the fund-raiser. How many chaperones do you think a mutilated woman needs?"

"You're not—" He closed his eyes and ran his hands over his face, into his hair. "Mel…sweetheart, I'm sorry. I guess I overreacted."

Her anger dissolved, but without it she felt deflated, the hurt of his words cutting deep. "No kidding. But why?"

Jaw locked, her dad put his hands on his hips and stared down at her. "Ellen and I…we had a fight and I guess I—"

"Ah," she drawled, "that answers a lot." She shook her head and headed toward her bedroom, too tired to handle any Ellen stories now. How dare he accuse her? "I should've known. Sorry, Dad, you're on your own there."

"Mel, wait."

Something in his voice made her pause. When she looked at him she saw that he stood with one hand braced on the mantel lining the fireplace, his broad shoulders slumped.

"Maybe we could have lunch again? The three of us?"

"Dad, no. You can't expect me to sit through another meal without making it clear I don't think you should be getting married. Do us both a favor and don't put either of us through it." She was careful to keep her voice soft, steady. Hoping to coax him to reason. "Why not give this more time? Date her, have *fun,* but take your time before you—"

"I *love* her—I love *you!* Don't put me in the middle and make me choose!"

Would there be a choice? "You want me to care for her, right? Well, caring takes time. Give me a year," she begged. "Give me *six months!* At least then when you marry, it won't make me feel like you're rushing or trying to prove something!"

He shook his head, adamant. "I've made up my mind. And I've waited long enough. Too long."

"Says who? Is Ellen pushing you? If you love her now, you'll love her—"

His pager going off interrupted her, and Melissa wanted to scream. Couldn't they have a conversation without interruptions? "Let me guess—Ellen?"

"It's work," he said after a single glance down. "I've got to go, but we'll finish our conversation in the morning."

"I can't, remember? Tomorrow's the day I start my new job."

Her dad had crossed to the door, but stopped in his tracks when her words registered. "Don't do it."

"Why don't you like Bryan? Because he's all grown-up and friends with Ellen?" She couldn't help her snide tone.

"It's not that I don't like him."

She crossed her arms over her front. "Could've fooled me."

"I don't approve of his shenanigans," her dad said as if that excused his anger. "Call him, Mel. Tell him you've changed your mind."

"I will if you will," she countered, desperate, regretting the words as soon as they left her mouth. She wanted the job with Bryan. Not because she found him attractive, but because she needed to get out of this house. Needed distance. A life. *But if quitting would end or postpone things with her dad and Ellen?*

Then she'd do it. All he had to do was say the word.

Looking over his shoulder, her dad gave her a piercing look. Okay, so maybe she did sound like a child, tossing out ultimatums, but she was desperate to keep him from making a mistake.

He yanked the door open. "I've warned you against Booker, Mel. You might think no one would want a woman like you, but you're wrong. He'll break your heart and move on to the next conquest. It's what men like him do."

"Dad, of the two of us, I'm not the one going to get my heart broken. I know exactly who Bryan is. It's Ellen I don't trust." She stepped closer. "You're a widower, in good health but with a dangerous job. You've got a house—"

"She's not after my pension! Mel, the house is yours and she knows that. If anything, Ellen's taking me in."

"You don't have to go anywhere!"

"And you're getting off track. Booker will break you—"

"Ellen will break *you!*"

He shook his head. "She's made me whole again. You just can't see it. Mel, I'm marrying Ellen. You're going to have to deal with it, and the sooner you do, the better. Love doesn't break you, it heals. You'd know that if you'd ever experienced it."

IGNORING ELLEN'S DARKENED windows and car parked crookedly in her short driveway as if she hadn't been paying attention when she'd pulled in, Hal glared at the lights shining in the second-floor living area above Booker's practice.

Lights flashing, he sped past the homes on the edge of town and kept going, down Route 5 until it crossed Miller's Run. Turning left, he drove into one of the more isolated areas and slowed, squinting to see a road sign that might or might not be standing, depending on the teenagers' latest scavenger hunt. He found it, and three minutes later spotted the flash of his officers' lights through the trees. He pulled in behind them, and a shadow detached itself from the trailer's doorway.

"Hey, Chief, sorry to bother you, but she insisted she only wanted to talk to you."

"How is the old bird?"

Nathan shook his head. "Scared to death. Who wouldn't be after some punk breaks in and terrorizes her?"

Hal jogged up the uneven path to the wheelchair ramp and stepped inside the open doorway. The gray-haired old woman sat on the couch with her face buried in the bag of frozen peas in her hand. A female EMT smoothed the old woman's hair back to check the cut on her temple.

Hal crouched down in front of her. "Miss Molly, you okay?"

The sound of his voice brought the eighty-eight-year-old woman's head up, and he grimaced at the extent of the damage. One side of her face was already blue, her eye swollen shut, her mouth and nose bloodied. Hal silently cursed and vowed to find whomever had done this to a defenseless old woman.

Fresh tears appeared in her eyes, but Miss Molly nodded. "I'm fine." Her shaking hand caught the EMT's and gently patted. "This young darling is taking good care of me." The EMT smiled and kept working.

Hal shifted onto one knee, leaning his elbow on the other for balance. "Did you see who did it? Did you know him?"

Miss Molly winced when a cloth was pressed and held on her cut, but nodded. "He knocked on the door pretty as you please. The bulb had burned out on the porch so I couldn't see him too good, but he said he'd run out of gas and needed to use the phone."

"You let him in?"

The woman gave him a sour look. "I'm old, but I'm not a fool."

Grinning, Hal nodded his agreement. "I'd say not. So what happened then?"

"I told him to tell me the number and I'd call someone to come bring him gas."

"Smart girl. Then what?"

"He left. Least I thought he did. I watched him till I couldn't see him no more. Must've dozed off, but a little while later I woke up when I heard a crash. Next thing I knew he was in the house with me."

"Was he tall? Short? Dark hair or light?"

Now the woman frowned. "He broke my lamp first thing, but he had dark hair, short, but straggly. He was skinny, taller than me but I don't know how much."

Considering the woman was barely five feet, that could mean anything. "What then?"

"After he broke my lamp—my sister made that lamp," she said, growing agitated. "Sent it all the way from Washington because she knew it was my favorite color."

"Maybe she'll make you another one," Hal soothed. "Tell me what happened after he broke your lamp."

"He kept shoutin' something, but—" she ducked her head "—I couldn't make it out 'cause I was cryin' and scared."

"Don't feel bad about that, Miss Molly. Anyone would've done the same in your shoes."

"Maybe so." She nodded weakly. "But when I didn't answer, he slapped me and knocked me down. I hit the coffee table and that's all I remember until I woke up and called for help."

Hal transferred his attention to the EMT. "Any other signs of abuse?"

"Just her face and head that I can see. She'll need X-rays to check for fractures."

"Take good care of her and once you get her to the hospital, call dispatch and give me an update."

The EMT nodded. "No problem. Miss Molly, are you ready for that ride?"

Hal got out of the way of the gurney and looked around at the home's interior. Someone had turned on the kitchen light and from the looks of things, the place had been trashed.

One of his deputies stood in the impossibly tiny hall outside the bathroom and Hal made his way there, keeping a careful eye on where he stepped. Tubes and bottles littered the ripped linoleum floor.

"Our friend wasn't only after her cash and jewelry," the deputy said. "She said she had some Vicodin and Darvocet, but they're gone."

"Like the others," he muttered. "Any prints?"

Nathan left the bedroom farther down and joined them. "None so far."

"Keep checking. Make sure you do it all by the book, too. I want everything we can get to put this punk away."

An hour later Hal tiredly made his way back through town. When he approached Ellen's house he slowed, wondering if he should pull in and continue the conversation he and Ellen had begun earlier. The road was deserted, the houses dark when he turned left and drove down the street bordering Ellen's. Booker's sports car was parked in back. Alone.

He rolled to a stop and stared up at the house a long moment before his attention was drawn to movement taking place at Ellen's. A light switched on in the kitchen; the curtain moved. She'd heard him. Hal pulled in beside Booker's car and shoved the cruiser into Park. Moments later Ellen's arms welcomed him and he was well aware of the tension and stress draining from him the moment he inhaled her familiar scent.

"Are you okay? I saw Bryan when he came home a while ago, and he told me where they were today."

A heavy sigh left his chest. "She said they were working on some fund-raiser."

Ellen's head nodded against his chest. "The clinic. It's very important to Bryan because it's his grandfather's dream."

He tensed. "You know an awful lot about Booker's dreams."

"Hal, *stop*. We cleared that up a while ago and don't you go down that road again," she said, raising her head from his chest. Ellen stared up at him, and without her glasses on she squinted to see clearly. "Understood?"

"Yes, ma'am," he drawled with a teasing grin, tired of arguments and tension. All he wanted was peace. "I should go. I'm not in the best of moods. We had another break-in tonight, and on top of Mel's behavior—"

"She's afraid of losing her father, Hal. We were wrong to keep our relationship from her. This is too sudden to her."

"She's twenty-eight years old."

"But she's never been alone. She's dealt with one blow after another from the time she was a child and the only constant in her life has been you." Her arms tightened. "I'd hold on and fight back, too, if I were her."

"Maybe, but she'll be in worse shape if Booker does a number on her."

"Bryan is a nice guy. I wish you'd look beyond—"

"The man has slept with every woman in town. Almost," he added hastily when her face clouded with anger. "I've had a half-dozen drunken ex-boyfriends in my jail over the past three years because some girl thought she had a chance at being a doctor's wife and screwed her fella over for Booker, even though *he* didn't care about any of them."

"You'd better keep adding that 'almost' in there. As to the rest, Bryan's a flirt and sometimes a player, but he sets the women straight from the get-go. Hal, *they* are the ones wanting more, and you can't blame him for those girls' poor decisions."

He ran a hand over his hair. "You're defending him again."

"Someone has to."

"It doesn't have to be you."

Ellen tilted her head to the side, a strange expression crossing her face. She blinked, winced.

"What's wrong?"

She pasted a weak smile to her lips and pressed a hand to her stomach. "Nothing. I ate too late, that's all. Now I have some indigestion and our fighting isn't helping it."

"You sure that's all?"

She nodded. "Too much sugar. I had a huge piece of chocolate. Now I'm paying for it." She lifted her hand from her belly and indicated the kitchen table where a bottle sat. "I came down and took some Tums and then heard your car outside."

"I should've kept going."

"I'm glad you didn't."

He tugged her back into his arms, resting his chin on her head when she snuggled against him with a sigh. "Things will ease up soon, and Mel will come around. You're worrying about it so much you're making yourself sick."

"I'm worried about *you*. I don't want you and Melissa fighting because of me. You've both been through enough."

Hal tucked his hand under her chin and nudged it up. She

tasted minty and sweet. "Ellen, you're my wife in every way. God sees what's in my heart. The piece of paper is coming, but I don't want you to ever doubt what I feel for you no matter what Mel or anyone else says."

Ellen lifted her hand to his cheek, the engagement ring sparkling on her finger. "Can you stay? Just for a little while?"

"I'd love to."

She smiled at his words, but then her expression clouded again. In a split second she went from looking a bit green to being white as a sheet. She clamped a hand over her mouth before running for the bathroom.

Hal followed her, held her head while she tossed up the cake, and he pressed a cool, wet cloth to her face when she was through. "Better now?"

She nodded weakly, eyes closed.

"Sure?"

Another nod. He wasn't buying it, though. She'd been sick several times recently. Said her stomach was upset. "Ellie?"

"Mmm?"

"When are you going to tell me you're pregnant?"

Ellen's eyes snapped open and what little color she'd regained left her cheeks again. Fresh tears trickled down her cheeks, but these had nothing to do with hurling, and everything to do with the panicked, horrified expression she wore. "I can't be... I—"

He could almost see her brain counting up the days. "It's all right."

"No, it's not!" she cried with a moan. "You think Melissa is upset now? If I'm— Oh, *Hal!*"

Hal pulled her into his arms and held her close. Shock rolled through him, but then...then a grin started. One he couldn't stop.

"What are we going to do? Oh, Hal, I'm so sorry. I didn't— We didn't— We never talked about this."

He kissed her forehead and adjusted his hold until they both sat on the bathroom floor with Ellen cradled in his arms and looking up at him in embarrassed panic. He chuckled softly. "Maybe not, but don't be sorry. I'm not. As to what we'll do, we're going to get you one of those home tests. And then…" His grin widened even more. He didn't need a test to tell him the truth. The moodiness and fatigue, the changes he'd noticed in Ellen's body over the past few weeks. "Then we'll see if I'm going to be a daddy again."

MELISSA DIDN'T HAVE time to be nervous the next morning. She waited until she heard her father stirring and then locked herself in the shower to avoid him. After last night's fight she didn't think there was much left to say, and when she emerged he was gone. She figured it was for the best. No way did she want to risk another argument before work.

Bryan was waiting for her when she arrived, and he quickly ran over the procedure for handling patients, the phones, and taught her what little he knew of the new computer system. She wasn't afraid of technology and Bryan's setup was pretty self-explanatory. Within moments she had a general idea of how to use it, where to enter payments and schedule appointments. And then it was time for the real test of her abilities.

Bryan unlocked the door and the first fifteen minutes set the course for the day. People came in for their appointments and she became the talk of the waiting room, no doubt the talk of the town. Behind the chest-high wall surrounding most of the reception desk, Melissa tried hard to ignore them while keeping up with everything that needed to be done.

"That's Hal's girl, isn't it?" Mrs. McCleary's voice carried despite her attempt to whisper. "She sick again?"

"I was friends with her mother," another voice informed them. "God rest her soul."

A chair squeaked. "Who's sick again?"

"Hal's girl," said the second voice. "The one who said Joe Brody shook her baby to death."

"They say stress is bad for a body." Mrs. McCleary tsked. "Wonder if the news Joe was innocent made her feel so guilty it came back?"

"My Amy said Melissa was in the room when Joe's new baby was born," yet another female voice told them all. "That couldn't have been healthy for her, either."

"My niece has breast cancer. Only got a few months they said. Just got diagnosed a month ago, but it's everywhere."

"Betcha she'll die young, just like her mother."

Melissa gasped softly, wondering if they spoke of her or the poor woman recently diagnosed. Either way, it was a cruel thing to say. Thoughtless, mean-spirited. Why didn't people think before they spoke?

"Nice of Dr. Bryan to let her work while she's able, don't you think?"

"She must just be filling in. I mean—" the voice lowered "—everybody knows he likes his help to be…*friendly,* if you know what I mean. Do you think her and the doc are—"

"Mrs. McCleary?" Melissa called, standing. She studied the older women in the corner seats, hoping to shame them and their gossiping ways. Mrs. McCleary wasn't embarrassed, though. She simply lifted her chin higher, one of those people who thought age gave her the right to say anything she pleased. "Follow me."

The file shook in her trembling hand and Melissa clutched

it to her chest to still the telltale movement. Walking down the hall, Mrs. McCleary behind her, Melissa said a quick prayer for the unknown woman fighting the battle against cancer and held her head high when she settled the older woman inside an exam room.

"You filling in for Holly?" Mrs. McCleary asked, her earrings bobbing along with her chins.

"No, ma'am. I'm the new office manager."

"Is that right?"

Mrs. McCleary instilled enough doubt in her question that Melissa fought the urge to double-check her employment status.

"Guess I'm just surprised to see you here."

"Why's that?"

"Well…you know. You and Dr. Booker…you're seeing him now?"

She managed a tense smile. "No, ma'am. Like I said, I'm the new office manager. The doctor will be right in." That said, Melissa bit off the rest of the response she wanted to make and went back to her desk.

The talk continued. With every new arrival and departure word spread, the knowledge that she was, incredibly, *Bang 'em Booker*'s newest hire. The gossip began with rehashing her cancer diagnosis and ended with speculation as to whether she was sleeping with Bryan. If her father got wind of this, he'd be furious.

Didn't people have better things to discuss? World politics, famine, a cure for cancer? Spying a small radio on the far side of the desk, she leaned over and turned it on, tuning it to a local station. The chatter stopped for a moment and Melissa smiled. Maybe if they had to shout over the noise, it would keep Bryan's patients from talking about her?

Seconds passed, then the whispers began again.

CHAPTER NINE

THAT AFTERNOON Bryan stared at the back of Melissa's head. He told himself he needed to make sure she had things under control, but anyone could see she was fine. Melissa handled the job as if she was born to it, able to make order from the chaos of phones and people. Not just any people, either, but grumpy, impatient, nosy ones who didn't know when to mind their own business, and who had to inform him, repeatedly, that *Melissa had had cancer.*

The reminders didn't help, and they certainly didn't keep him from pausing in the hallway between exam rooms to watch her bend over her desk, phone jammed to her ear, scribbling on a pad of paper, her long legs showcased in gray slacks that hugged her rear with palm-itching appeal.

Melissa laughed at something a patient said. The sound set fire to his blood. Is that what she'd sound like in bed?

He ran a hand over his face and smothered a groan. He couldn't wait for Janice to get back to work so there would be someone else in the office. A chaperone of sorts. The only saving grace was that Melissa was blessedly unaware of his distraction.

Shaking his head, Bryan banked his thoughts and entered Room 1. "How are we doing today?" he asked automatically, belatedly realizing the patient was Amanda Warner, the mayor's latest wife.

"I'm better now that you're here. I was beginning to think you were ignoring me."

"I'm running behind."

"Well, you're here now." She smiled. "I've missed you, Bryan."

He flipped through a page or two in Amanda's chart and noted that Melissa's handwriting had started out neat on the page, but had gotten a bit shaky at the end. Had Amanda said something to her? Made some comment like all the others? "What's the problem today?" He decided to leave the door open a large crack behind him when he saw her expression.

He sincerely doubted she was here for anything medical. Maybe an open door would curb her typical brazenness. "Says here you hurt you knee playing tennis?"

She laughed softly. "I had to tell her something. Especially with all those old biddies out there listening to every word. But for the record, the pain radiates up to…here." Amanda stroked her inner thigh. "Close the door, Bryan. I need to discuss something private with you."

"Something medical?" he asked pointedly.

"A horrible ache I've been having." She patted the table where she sat. "Come on, get over here. I'll just slip off my skirt and you can take care of it for me."

"Amanda."

"My marrying George does not have to change what we shared," she insisted. "I remember how much you used to appreciate a little love in the afternoon."

"It was fun while it lasted, Amanda, but your marriage does change things and you know it. We've been over this. Why don't you go home to your husband and make him the same offer? I'm sure he'll appreciate it," he murmured. "I've got patients waiting."

Amanda's gaze narrowed, and she hopped onto her feet with the agility of a gymnast. "You don't do high-and-mighty well, Bryan."

He paused, his hand on the doorknob. "I'm not trying to. Have a good afternoon, Amanda."

"Does she do it for you?"

Don't ask. "Who?"

"The medical case study at your front desk. Does she get you off the way I did?"

"For the love of—"

"Everyone's talking about it, wondering. So tell me, are you desperate or just giving the poor girl a good time because you feel sorry for her?"

He closed the distance between them, lowering his head until he stood nearly nose-to-nose with her. "You're mad at me, not her. Leave Melissa out of this."

"Oh, touchy. I wonder why?" Amanda put her hand on his cheek, slid it down his neck to his chest and stroked. "Come on, Bryan, you can't seriously be saying no. You know as well as I do that you need a real woman to satisfy you."

"Melissa is a real woman."

Amanda drew back, her mouth curling up in a surprised smirk. "So you *are* sleeping with her? Get off on the boy look, do you? I wouldn't have taken you for a back-door kind of guy."

He swore softly. "*Goodbye,* Amanda."

Her nails dug into his arm. "You can't blame me for getting upset, Bryan. Are you seriously sleeping with Hal York's daughter?"

How had they gotten so far off course? "Who I'm sleeping with—or not—is none of your business."

Anger clouded her heavily made-up eyes. "Well, well. You

do realize, of course, the darling chief will have your—" her hand dropped to his groin "—head on a platter the moment she sheds a tear?"

He shoved her hand away.

"Bryan, play nice," she said in a cajoling tone. "You know I'm right. You and I are two of a kind. You have nothing in common with the little Goody Two-shoes out there. We understand each other and there's no reason we can't have our fun—"

"Trust me, Amanda, there are a lot of reasons." She sucked in an insulted breath he ignored. "The bottom line is we aren't happening. Ever. Now I've got to go. I have patients waiting who actually do need medical care."

Her cool gray eyes narrowed into catlike slits. "Your little receptionist isn't woman enough to keep a man like you satisfied for long."

Bryan didn't comment because it would do him no good to defend Melissa to Amanda or anyone else. They'd think what they liked. Shaking his head in disgust, he grasped the door handle and pulled, but got a kick in the gut when he spotted Melissa in the hall. Hoping against hope she hadn't heard, he glanced back at Amanda and saw her smiling widely and doing a piss-poor imitation of surprise.

"Oh, dear. Caught in the act," Amanda murmured.

Bryan stepped forward. "Melissa—"

"You've patients waiting, Dr. Booker."

Melissa raced past him. He wanted to grab her, stop her, but didn't. She'd heard him and Amanda talking, knew what had occurred between them, but maybe that was best for them both. Safer. But from the look on her face, the revulsion she felt that he'd been with Amanda, not for the first time he wished he could go back and change the past.

"Poor little thing." Amanda slid her fingers over his chest. "You really shouldn't tease her so. I don't think you're sleeping with her, but now that she's seen how you treat your lady friends, well…I don't see it happening at all, do you? I mean, she certainly can't afford to have dear old daddy disappointed in her *again*. Her little oops with Joe Brody was enough to tighten her chastity belt." She wrinkled her nose and shivered delicately. "Although there's something to be said for big, brawny men. Rumor has it she and Joe are still quite close."

"Get out, Amanda, and find a new doctor. Whatever you do, don't step foot in here again."

MELISSA LOCKED the front door to the practice that evening and forced herself not to drop her head to the surface with a groan.

"It wasn't what you thought."

Tensing, she squared her shoulders. Smiling was more difficult, but she managed a weak attempt. "Your sex life is none of my business."

"I didn't have sex with her in the exam room."

"Sneak her into your office instead?" *Shut up, shut up, shut up!* "Sorry. It's been a long day." She didn't look at him as she stalked over to the desk.

"For the record, I didn't invite her into my office or anywhere else in the practice for a quickie. I don't sleep with married women."

Relief poured through her at his words. "Good for you. Especially if you're serious about this fund-raiser. A big no-no is sleeping with the mayor's wife. People have a tendency to frown on such things, and he won by a landslide."

"Amanda was a mistake I made when I first moved here. I ended it right afterward, but she hasn't taken the hint and comes back periodically to try again."

"I'm sure the mayor appreciates that." Melissa yanked open the drawer that held her purse. She was going home. Then maybe to the B and B. Some time spent baby snuggling would surely lower her BP, and right now it had to be sky-high. *Not woman enough?*

It didn't take a *woman* to sleep around or cheat on a husband. In her opinion, it took one not to.

"Melissa." Bryan turned her to face him. "I'm sorry she took her anger with me out on you."

"Forget it." She pulled away. "I know exactly what I am, and she's right."

"Right in what way?"

"Oh, please, isn't it obvious? You practically made a puddle right there on the floor when she flashed her cleavage at you! And that remark about being woman enough? It takes more than playing the sex kitten to be 'woman enough.'"

"Then we agree, but how is she right?"

"Because it's also normal to think a female with big boobs and a decent set of features is attractive, married or not, and *that's* how she's right—because men have brainwashed women to measure their worth through the size of their breasts, and regardless of my history and what people know about me, *I'm* woman enough to realize that isn't true."

"What if I told you it's not just women who can make the distinction?" he argued. "What if I said guys like more than breasts in a woman?"

She raised her brows high and crossed her arms over her front—her *flat* front. "I'd say you're wrong. There's no need to lie or sugarcoat the obvious. Guys like *breasts*. Her comment didn't hurt me, what *hurts* is the fact that the general population thinks the same way she does."

"Why do you think that?"

Swallowing, she rolled her eyes, her anger surging up with tidal-wave strength and gushing out of her. "The first *thing* guys notice is a woman's breasts, the bounce, the jiggle, whether or not their shirt is *see-through*. But if a woman doesn't have the necessary body parts or, let's say she does and they're not to the guy's satisfaction, then lo and behold, he suggests augmentation. It comes down to this—guys can be less than impressive, but heaven *forbid* a woman doesn't have a body like a model, the breasts of a porn star or the sex drive of a teenaged boy because *that* upsets them! *Men* have no idea what *real* women are like—and neither does Amanda Warner."

His mouth turned down at the corners. "You can't lump men into a single category. Not all of us are obsessed with breasts."

She snorted. What did he know about not being perfect? "Yeah, well, argue all you want, but when faced with some-one like me in bed I'd bet you'd be all talk and no action."

Silence.

Melissa stared up into Bryan's face, her heart pounding so rapidly she actually saw spots in front of her eyes. Had she really just gone off on Bryan like a bitter, *breastless* shrew? He was her boss! Her words had come out like a challenge. Like she begged him to—

Whirling, breathless, Melissa grabbed her purse and ran for the door, well aware Bryan's eyes bored a hole into her back. What had she done? What had she said?

She'd never be able to face Bryan again.

MELISSA HELD the baby close and smiled. "I can't get over how much she's changed already." She looked up at the tired mother. "Or that they released you so soon."

PLAY THE Lucky Key Game

and you can get

FREE BOOKS
and FREE GIFTS!

YES!
I have scratched off the gold areas. Please send me the 2 FREE BOOKS and 2 FREE GIFTS for which I qualify. I understand I am under no obligation to purchase any books, as explained on the back of this card.

334 HDL EL4G   134 HDL ELT5

FIRST NAME	LAST NAME

ADDRESS

APT.#   CITY

STATE/PROV.   ZIP/POSTAL CODE

www.eHarlequin.com

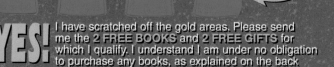

2 free books plus 2 free gifts   1 free book

2 free books   Try Again!

DETACH AND MAIL CARD TODAY!

(H-SR-06/07)

© 2002 HARLEQUIN ENTERPRISES LTD. ® and ™ are trademarks owned and used by the trademark owner and/or its licensee.

If offer card is missing write to: The Harlequin Reader Service, 3010 Walden Ave., P.O. Box 1867, Buffalo, NY 14240-1867

BUSINESS REPLY MAIL
FIRST-CLASS MAIL   PERMIT NO. 717-003   BUFFALO, NY

POSTAGE WILL BE PAID BY ADDRESSEE

HARLEQUIN READER SERVICE
3010 WALDEN AVE
PO BOX 1867
BUFFALO NY 14240-9952

NO POSTAGE
NECESSARY
IF MAILED
IN THE
UNITED STATES

"Insurance companies have a tendency to do that nowadays." Ashley leaned back against the couch with a sigh. "I'm just glad you're here. With Dara hustling to get dinner for the guests and keeping an eye on Max until Joe gets home from work, I was afraid to fall asleep. It's almost Issy's dinnertime, and I would no sooner shut my eyes than she'd be telling me that."

"Well," Melissa murmured, careful to keep her tone soft, "I'm more than happy to take care of Miss Issy's dinner. Miss Issy, would you like a pink bottle or a purple one?"

Ashley laughed softly. "Designer bottles. Who'd ever have thought I'd actually own *designer* bottles?"

"Hey, when Dad said to go for it, I did. It was so much fun shopping for stuff like that, and the least we could do for little Issy here after…everything."

"And the rest of the stuff you bought her?"

"Pure indulgence," she said with a grin. "Now go to sleep. You need to rest."

"The mood has passed," Ashley said even as she smothered a yawn. "I'd rather have company. And find out how your first day at work went."

Melissa wrinkled her nose. "It was okay."

"Uh-huh. Who said what?"

"Where do I begin?" She smoothed a fingertip over the baby's soft, chubby cheek and raised her head to meet Ashley's gaze. Had it only been yesterday? "I'm sorry for running out on you at the hospital. It was unbelievably rude."

"Don't think anything of it. I know it's got to be hard holding Issy when Josie wasn't much bigger when she died."

As it always did, her heart constricted at the mention of her daughter. "It is…but that wasn't why." Melissa bit her lower lip and shifted the baby slightly. "Yesterday when— Issy rooted me."

"Oh, Melissa."

"It's okay," she stressed. "I just wasn't expecting it and it came on top of everything going on with my dad and his sudden declaration he's getting married. Did I tell you he left a message for me to meet him downstairs for dinner at seven? To talk," she said, mimicking her father's stern tone. "If we were dating I'd think he wanted to break up with me and was trying to avoid a scene. I mean, no offense, but we could just as easily eat at home alone, you know? I can't help but think he wants to spring another surprise on me, and I wonder what I'll do if he does?"

"Run screaming from the room?"

She winced. "I already did that once today."

Ashley's eyes widened. "You *did?*"

"Practically, yeah. It's nothing, just that Bryan and I got into the stupidest argument. I was in a horrible mood after listening to the gossips describe my life from birth to what will be my death and then…"

"Then?"

"Then I overheard a married woman hitting on Bryan while insulting me in the same breath, and—"

"*Who?*" Ashley sat up abruptly. "Who did that?"

"It doesn't matter who."

"But he turned her down, right? *He did turn her down?*"

"Yeah."

Ashley fell back against the cushions in obvious relief. "So what did this woman say? How did she insult you?" She made a face. "And why don't I shut up now so you can get the story out and then ask my questions?"

"Good idea," Melissa said, smiling because she knew Ashley wouldn't take the teasing to heart. "I'm still not telling you who, but her cleavage was out to here," she said, lifting her hand in front of her chest in an exaggerated description, "and she rubbed herself against him and said I wasn't 'woman enough' for him, and he'd soon grow bored."

"That *witch!*" Ashley was up again, her hands fisted on her lap. "*Who* was it? Did Bryan put her in her place? He better have set her straight or I'll go talk to him my—"

"I didn't stick around to find out."

"*Melissa!* You can't pay any attention to people like that. Is that what you and Bryan fought over?"

"It's what led to the fight," she admitted sheepishly. "Bryan accused me of lumping him into the male-jerk category when I said all men are obsessed with breasts and he'd practically dissolved into a puddle due to the cleavage she presented him, and then before I knew it I practically whined, because he— oh, I can't repeat it again." She buried her nose in Issy's soft pink blanket. "It's too humiliating. One day and I blew it. I'll never be able to face him."

"That bad, huh?"

"Yes." Raising her head, she found her friend looking at her with a curious expression. "What?"

"Nothing. Just wondering why you're worrying so much about what Bryan thinks. Over the last year you've outright avoided him." Her eyes widened then narrowed, a suspicious grin forming on her full lips.

"Don't look at me like that. Ashley—no."

"Yes."

"*No!*"

"I wouldn't have thought so, either, but if you could see the expression on your face right now," Ashley drawled, her grin widening rapidly. "Melissa, you and Bryan would make—"

"Nothing. We would make *nothing!*"

"—a gorgeous couple. You're both tall, blond and—well, gorgeous."

She snorted. "Oh, please. Since when is a woman who looks like Peter Pan considered hot?"

"I don't know, the cut is very Halle Berry."

"Having a baby has affected your vision. That or the sleep deprivation is getting to you."

Ashley sighed. "If your hesitation is about the past—"

"How can it not be? Bryan might be gorgeous, but the man has boinked practically every woman in town."

"Did you just say *boinked?*"

"Even if—and there's *no way*—but even if we were to, how could I ever measure up to all those women? Ashley, after the mastectomy I didn't...I didn't have reconstructive surgery."

"What? Why not?" Ashley's face darkened with color. "If you don't mind my asking?" She waved a hand to where Issy lay cradled against her. "You mean that's not...?"

"Real? Nope." She inhaled and sighed. "It's a special bra. And I didn't have the surgery because I was never that big anyway and I guess I thought there'd never be a need for it because at the time all I could think about was my mom and grandmother and..."

"You thought you were going to die." Ashley's eyes filled with tears. "Oh, Melissa, do you mean to tell me you *never* believed you had a chance?"

"Would you?" she whispered softly. "It runs in the family, remember? And neither my mom nor my grandmother made it."

"But you did."

"Still, the odds are stacked against me. And implants would only make it harder to detect—and I should not be telling you this." She closed her eyes, ashamed, the sweet baby scent of Issy reminding her that there was such a thing as sharing too much. "You just had a baby, and here I am going on and on, laying this on you."

"I'm your friend, Melissa. You can tell me anything."

The baby began squirming in her arms, her little face scrunching up and turning red until Isabella opened her mouth and began to cry like a pro. *Saved by the bellow again.*

"Here, give her to me. Would you mind going down to the kitchen to get a bottle while I change her? Dara will show you."

Melissa shook her head, more than ready to escape. "Not at all." She handed Isabella over to her mother and had made it to the door when Ashley stopped her by saying her name. "Need something else?" Melissa asked.

"Yeah," she said, nodding. "Melissa, Bryan might be drop-dead gorgeous, but he's not like other guys."

"If you say so."

"I say so. Bryan's a lot of things, but he'd never make a woman feel inferior. Take the married woman, for example. You said he turned her down, but did Bryan ever come out and say anything horrible to her?"

She replayed the afternoon in her head. "No. Not really."

"I thought not. And he wouldn't, because that's not him. But anyway, what I referred to earlier when I mentioned the past was what happened with Josie and how Bryan was the one to find out the truth."

"Oh." Now she felt foolish. Why hadn't she kept her mouth shut? "What about it?"

"You've avoided Bryan since then."

"I have not."

"You don't come to any of our cookouts or dinners if he's going to be here."

"I've been busy. It's just coincidence." *But was it?* Her cheeks heated, and she hoped Ashley didn't notice. After that day at her house when Bryan had seen her breakdown—

"You might like to know that whenever the subject has come up, Bryan has repeatedly told everyone who'll listen that you weren't to blame, that Josie's reaction to the medicine could've happened to any parent under the circumstances."

He had? She gripped the painted doorjamb, her fingers hurting because she squeezed so tight. "Thank you for telling me." The whisper came out hoarse, choked. She'd always wondered what Bryan really thought. Wondered if he'd ever hinted to anyone that she should've done more. Should've been more aware or been the person sentenced to prison instead of Joe.

"Melissa?"

She blinked, shoving her pain-filled thoughts away. "Yeah?"

"Issy and I would like one of the hot-pink bottles," Ashley said with a perfectly straight face. "To match her outfit."

Melissa laughed softly. "Got it. One hot-pink bottle coming up!"

"ARE YOU ALMOST ready for the big day?" Hal watched Ellen closely, noting how she bit her lower lip in anxiety.

"Are you sure we're doing the right thing?"

He tried to remember when Maggie had been pregnant with Melissa. The mood swings, the tears. "I'm positive."

"Has Melissa said if she's coming?"

His arm tightened around Ellen's shoulders and he pulled her closer, his lips brushing her forehead. "Not yet. We've been busy and haven't talked much these past couple days."

A sniffle sounded a moment before he felt the hot warmth of a tear hit his chest. "I hate that it's going to be this way."

"She'll come around, just give her time."

"But you're not talking!"

"We've both been working a lot." It sounded like a lame excuse and he knew it. He didn't like it, either, but his daughter wasn't going to ruin the best thing that had happened to him in a long time.

"I…I invited Bryan to the wedding. I hope you don't mind."

"If you want him to come, that's fine."

"He's a decent guy, and I think deep down you know it."

He scowled. "At least I can keep an eye on her since she's right next door."

"See? You're focusing on the positive," she drawled, her tone revealing only a slight trace of sarcasm.

Hal rubbed her back and shoulders, feeling the tension slowly subside. They sat side by side on her couch, snuggled close. "You go to the doctor today?"

She nodded and her chin bumped his chest. "They did an ultrasound. I couldn't make anything of it, but the doctor said the baby looks fine."

Thank God. "Any worries about its mama?" His voice emerged husky and anxious, not what he wanted. Ellen squeezed him in response and Hal relished her strength, the lush feel of her pressed against him.

"I'm fine. Stop worrying."

His chuckle lacked humor. "I'll stop if you stop," he murmured, wincing when he realized how similar it sounded to the challenge Melissa had issued to him.

"I love you, Hal. I'm sorry for upsetting Melissa, but…I love you. Too much to let you go."

He smoothed his knuckles over her cheek. "Good thing. You'd have a hard time getting me to go anywhere. Better remember that if you ever decide you want a younger man."

"Who'd want a younger man when an older one has only gotten better with age?" Her eyes were sparkling, her grin seductive.

Chuckling, he kissed her, determined he'd show her just how much better an older man could be.

AN HOUR LATER Melissa stared across the table at her father, on the verge of jumping up to run from the room screaming as Ashley had suggested. He looked…calm. And considering he'd just come from Ellen's house—

Eww, eww, eww! When would the day *end?*

"I'll put your orders in and be out with your drinks." Dara, the woman Ashley had hired about a year after opening, gave them a quick smile and walked away.

Melissa fiddled with her napkin, unwrapped her utensils and arranged them, and then smoothed the napkin over her lap, well aware of her father's scrutiny the entire time.

"You've been avoiding me."

"I was at work and it was my first day on the job. I couldn't exactly talk to my father about his personal life every time he chose to call."

"Mel, can we drop the attitude and just talk? I need that right now."

"Ellen putting pressure on you again?"

"No, she's not. You are." He leaned across the table. "Why can't you be happy for me? Accept that I want to be with her?"

"You *know* why." The muscles in her shoulders tensed painfully. "You don't have to marry the first woman who comes along. Ellen might be nice, she might be great, but—"

"She's pregnant."

CHAPTER TEN

MELISSA BLINKED, unable to comprehend what he'd just said because of the blood rushing to leave her head. "That's *not* funny." Her dad stared at her, his gaze, his expression, dead serious. Remembering her comment to Ashley about her dad meeting her in public to drop yet another bomb, she laughed, the sound high-pitched. "I don't believe this— I don't believe *her!*"

"Stop right there and lower your voice." His cheeks took on a ruddy hue.

She was too shocked to care that her outburst had gained the other diners' attention. She sat back in her chair and crossed her arms over her stomach, unable to stop the near-hysterical laughter bubbling up and out of her chest. No doubt she sounded manic.

"Melissa."

"Oh, the irony!" She snickered, earning an even deeper scowl from her father. "This is just too good. I mean, she arranged for Bryan to hire me so she could get me out of the way and marry you sooner, but as a *backup plan,* she got herself knocked *up!*" Her father's face was awash with angry color, his eyes glittering dangerously, but it didn't keep her from saying what had to be said. "What, she didn't tell you about coercing Bryan into hiring me? Why am I not surprised? I wouldn't have found out myself if Bryan hadn't slipped. For the record, he defended her, too."

"You didn't have an interview set up with Booker that day at the station?"

Guilt stirred, but she clamped it down. She would not feel guilty. "No, I didn't. I was stunned when I heard you talking about your *old age* and how I was holding you back so I...fibbed and hoped for the best. Then Bryan appeared behind me, courtesy of Ellen, and the rest is history."

"I can't believe you thought lying would solve anything."

Leave it to her father to focus on that. "Yeah, well, despite everything, I guess I have some pride left, and being discussed like a *child* left me a little wobbly. Besides, you can't honestly blame me, can you? I mean, you can thank Ellen for all the time I'm spending with—" she leaned toward him and lowered her voice "—*Bang 'em Booker,* right?"

Her father shifted in his seat, unable to sit still. She heard his teeth grind together, felt the frustration rolling off him in waves and identified with it.

A baby? The air left her lungs. Growing up, she'd always wanted a little brother or sister, but not *now*. And certainly not like this when it meant her dad would have a new life with a new wife and a new kid to replace the old one, the sick one who'd caused so many problems over the years. How could she possibly fit into a situation like that?

Her father released his breath in a rush, a slow nod turning into two, three. "You needed a job," he murmured finally, "and Ellen thinks of Booker as a friend. She was trying to help you. That's why she did it. That's why he hired you, too. You played together way back when, were friends even though he got you into more trouble than not."

"Are you trying to convince me or yourself? Because personally, after what you just said about her being—"

"I've been around thieves and crooks too long to not be able to tell when I'm being played. Booker gets my back up because of the way he treats women, but I'm not his judge or jury, and the man does have a way with patients. He treated that girl Anna with respect, gave her the help she needed and he helped Ellen quite a bit before I came into the picture, too. Just like he helped you by giving you a job." He ran a hand over his face. "I don't care for his antics, but I see the good in him, too. Just like you need to see the good in Ellen."

"Seeing the good doesn't explain how Ellen got *pregnant*."

"Mel, Ellen isn't old by any means, but a baby at thirty-eight isn't something she'd do lightly. It just happened."

Could it really be an accident? *Like she could judge?* "You'll be fifty in three years. Do you want to be a dad now?"

"I planned on marrying Ellen months ago. This is just—"

"Rushing things even *more*," she declared, her throat closing up at the thought of the inevitable days ahead. "I didn't care for the idea before, but now I really don't like it. Dad, you can't marry her, pregnant or not."

His expression closed in an instant. "Your blessing would be nice, but I'm *not* asking for your permission. I wanted to sit down and talk to you, to tell you myself with the hope that we could settle things between us before word got out. It's important for a family to stick together, and like it or not, Ellen is your family now. I expect you to stand by her in this."

Melissa realized in that moment that she'd said the one thing she shouldn't have said. No one gave Hal York orders, and if they did, it was in preparation of being proved wrong. But she wasn't fighting against him, she was fighting *for* him, for her place in his life. And that angered her even more. "This is crazy. You know it is."

"Why?" His gaze was searching, hard. "Because I want a life with a woman I love? Because I refuse to live with one foot in your mother's grave the way you do? You look so much like your mama, Mel, but she wasn't a coward."

Shocked silence filled the void between them and Melissa stared at him, her body, her mind, reeling, her sharp gasp the only indication of her pain. The father who'd always supported her, stood by her and held her during the worst moments of her life, had broken her heart. He thought her a *coward?*

Her dad leaned over the table, hands clasped together atop the pristine tablecloth, his knuckles white. She focused on them, remembering when they'd felt like the strongest hands in the world. Now they were letting go. No, they'd *let* go.

"You're not living, Melissa Ann, you're existing. You don't want me to marry Ellen. Don't want me to have another child, but the truth is you don't want to live because you're afraid to. You're afraid to move on, *afraid* to be happy. Too damned afraid despite the second chance you've been given. I want you to have what your mother and I had. What Ellen and I *have*. I don't want to bury another person I love because *you're too afraid* to take life by the horns and live while you can for as long as you can."

Pain engulfed her. Her muscles ached and her stomach rolled, physical pain caused by overwhelming anguish that took her breath and left her gasping. She stared at him, lips parted, too angry to release the tears burning her eyes, too angry to do much more than hurt. "I'm not afraid. When the cancer comes back—"

"Not when, if!" His fist slammed down on the table. *"If!"*

She swallowed tightly then tried to wet her dry lips. Her chest hurt, and it took every ounce of pride she had to remain in the chair whispering over the table as if the topic of conversation held no more importance than the weather for the upcoming Little Miss Fall Parade.

"If you feel s-so strongly that you have to marry her, fine. Do it. But don't attack me or tell me how I should feel when you know *nothing* about losing a part of yourself. You don't *know* what it's like to have something in your body that's *killing* you and there's nothing you can do about it. I have every right to be afraid!"

His lashes lowered over his eyes, fuming yet full of tears. "Don't you sit there and tell me I don't know fear. I lost part of myself the day I lost your mother and don't you ever forget it or insinuate otherwise. Do not throw our marriage and the love we felt for each other in my face just so you can play the martyr."

"I'm just trying to get you to *understand!*"

"I do. Better than you think. But unlike you, I'm not done with my life. Almost fifty or not, I'm marrying Ellen, I'm going to be a father again—and I'm going to enjoy every minute God allows me. Mel, I want the same for you, but you're not ever going to find happiness when you don't choose to try."

"Things are different for me, and you know it. What guy wants to tie himself to a woman who's already got the scars to prove things aren't going to end happily? You can't compare my situation to yours and Mom's, and you certainly can't blame me for not wanting you to marry a woman who got herself pregnant to *trap* you!"

"Dammit, Mel, she isn't trapping me! And don't talk like that. We don't know how things will end."

"Some of us do."

"None of us do. *Some of us* just have to be in control, but it doesn't work that way. You live like you're already in a coffin. Have you ever considered that the man upstairs might have a plan that requires you to live to be a hundred and ten? Are you going to spend the next eighty years alone and feeling sorry for yourself?"

"How do you expect me to move on when everyone tosses me back into that coffin every time I try to claw my way out of it?"

He opened his mouth to comment when his pager went off. Her dad swore, glanced at the number and swore again. Quite a day for a man who tried hard to keep his language in check and set a moral example both for his officers and his town.

"I've got to go." He shoved himself up from the chair. "Mel, I'll pay the utilities until you draw a few checks and get on your feet. I talked to the judge today and to Joe before I came in. Ellen and I are getting married here in three weeks. If you want to come, do it with a smile on your face and acceptance in your heart, but if you can't—"

"Mind if I join you?"

Melissa turned to see Bryan standing nearby. She hadn't heard him approach. The few diners who'd been finishing up their dinners had mostly disappeared or chosen to take their desserts and coffee out on the patio. The rest openly gawked at them and she fought the urge to hide under the table. Had Bryan heard them?

"Yeah, Doc, you can."

Her eyes widened at her father's response, then widened even more when he closed the distance between him and Bryan, not stopping until he stood nose-to-nose with him.

"Dad... *Dad?*" She was afraid her father's boiling temper and dislike of Bryan might get the best of him under the circumstances.

"I don't think it's possible you're anything other than what the gossips say, but the other night you helped that girl and I saw the side of you Ellen keeps insisting is there. I'm going to give you the benefit of the doubt for the time being, but I want that man—the *doctor*—right here, right now."

Bryan's gaze slid to her, then back to her father. "You've got me."

"Good. In exchange for the meal I'm going to buy you, *Doc,* I want you to talk to Mel about living rather than dying."

"Dad!"

Her father stalked off without another word, without looking back. He paused only long enough to hand money to Dara with muttered instructions and continue on his way. Melissa gaped after him, uncomfortably aware of Bryan watching her, of the *room* watching her.

"That must have been some father-daughter chat." Bryan seated himself at the table.

She angled her head away from the other diners and fought back tears. It had been a long, mortifying day. Her emotions were threadbare and unraveling, and the last thing she wanted to do was talk to Bryan about her inability to—

"Melissa?"

"Enjoy dinner. I'll see you tomorrow morning—if you still want me to work for you after what I said to you today."

"We were both out of line, and of course I want you working for me. Melissa—"

"No." She shook her head firmly. "Please, Bryan, not now. I can't do this. Not after—" she waved a hand to where her dad had disappeared "—that."

His jaw firmed. "Fine, I'll see you tomorrow, then. But we will talk about this."

"No, we won't. I don't want to discuss this with you."

"Too bad." His gaze caught hers and held. "I can't disappoint the chief of police, can I?"

Melissa grabbed her purse and headed for the door. Maybe Bryan couldn't, but she obviously did.

HAL ENTERED the dim interior of the eight-hundred-square-foot house, his gaze sharp and on the lookout for anything his officers might have missed. Like Miss Molly's, the place had been ransacked. Tables were overturned, glass shattered and broken, the bent head of the white-haired victim gaining his attention the moment Hal spotted him.

"Same as last time," Nathan muttered, disgust heavy in his voice. "Right down to the running-out-of-gas excuse. The old man opened the door to help him out."

"Prints?"

His officer shook his head. "Nothing yet. The perp makes such a mess we don't know what's what, and our victims aren't the best of housekeepers so when he fingers something, he's pulling away dust and leaving nothing behind."

"What'd he get this time?"

"A VCR, a couple guns and a lot of pain pills and patches, things that'll give him an instant high."

"Just what we need, some idiot out there high as a kite and packing. Did the old man get a description?"

"Single Caucasian male, young, probably early twenties, average build, average height, dark hair. Describes half the guys in town."

Which left them nothing to go on. "Get the word out to the newspapers and churches. Make sure they warn people we've got a burglary scam going on, but have leads."

Nathan raised a brow at the last statement.

"You heard me. We don't want to start a panic. Let's just warn the community and go from there."

WEDNESDAY EVENING Melissa pulled on her shoes to go for a run, a poor attempt to take her mind off her problems and the humiliation of having to face Bryan after everything that had happened. What was she going to do?

She and Bryan spent their time at the practice avoiding each other and the awkwardness between them was growing. What she wasn't sure of was why Bryan felt he owed it to her father to talk to her. Employers weren't supposed to get that involved with their employees' personal lives. Doctors should care for others and Bryan used to be a playmate, but that was no reason to team up with her dad against her.

She groaned in frustration, locked up the house and walked down the street, her pace increasing as she went in a vain attempt to burn off some excess anxiety. The humid air had her clothes sticking to her skin before she made it to the end of the block, but the saunalike mugginess felt good after being in the air-conditioning all day.

She continued on past the high school where the football team practiced and used her worry over what to do to propel her faster. Who had time to take things slow? She certainly didn't.

"You have another run-in with Mrs. McCleary?" Bryan asked from behind her.

She stumbled and had to alter her stride to keep from falling on her face. Turning, she glanced behind her to make sure her hearing wasn't playing tricks on her, and sure enough, there he was. Bryan's thickly muscled arms pumped in sync with hers, his broad chest bare and glistening with sweat.

After their argument on Monday evening, they'd fallen into a routine, that of Bryan working the back of the practice, her working the front. When their paths did cross, it was always about a patient, always brief and to the point, and always layered with courtesy that had nothing to do with breasts or making love or even coffins.

"What are you doing here?" She huffed slightly, breathless, which angered her even more. Bryan wasn't winded at all.

"Same as you—running off some demons."

They jogged side by side for several blocks, Bryan thankfully silent, and rounded the corner where the courthouse park came into view.

"First to the center fountain?"

She hesitated for a long moment, then remembered all the challenges issued during those long summer days growing up. Why not? Running hard meant no talking. She shrugged. *"Go!"*

Bryan watched as Melissa took off with a burst of speed. She had a power behind her stride that any runner would envy. All the more impressive given her illness and whatever residual effects she suffered.

He increased his pace, realized he had to go even faster to catch her and pushed hard to edge her out at the last moment. They both slowed, gasping, and he bent with his hands on his knees, staring at Melissa in amazement because she grinned from ear to ear. Quite a change from the office.

"Oh, wow. I haven't done that in ages. That felt good!"

That it had. Almost as good as—he shut his mind off to where it was headed in relation to *her* and smiled back. "Too bad you didn't stand a chance of winning."

Her laughter filled the air and a couple old men playing chess under a shade tree looked their way, then went back to their game.

"Ha! You barely beat me. And, well, after all, you *are* my boss."

He straightened, enjoying her change of mood, wanting to try again to talk about that evening at the B and B, but unable to figure out a way to bring it into the conversation without sounding forced or—worse—ruin her good mood since it was the first he'd seen in days. "You did not let me win."

"If you say so."

Bryan took a couple of threatening steps in her direction only to stop when she began jogging in place. "Ready to go again?"

He was ready to go, all right.

BY FRIDAY things were looking up. The last patient had just left, and this time when she locked the door it wasn't out of exhausted desperation, but with the knowledge that her first week was over and—she could handle this.

After their run she and Bryan had gone their separate ways, and at work the next day she'd found herself shaking her head more than once at the antics of some of Bryan's female patients. And at him. Bryan enjoyed the attention the women gave him whether they were ninety or nine. The flirting, the smiles—everyone enjoyed playing with Taylorsville's Most Eligible Bachelor.

She shook her head at the drama, glad she was able to view it as the comedic forum it was, desperate to ignore the twinges inside her that resembled jealousy. She was not jealous.

"I'm going to the new Chinese place to get some dinner. You hungry? My treat. You can go with me and eat there, or I'll get it to go and bring it here before we work on the fund-raiser. What do you say?" Bryan asked from the other side of the reception's half wall. "Either way I'd like to celebrate."

Did she want to be seen in public with Bryan after what had happened at the B and B? "Celebrate what?"

"You. It's been a long, hard week full of problems and trials, but you're still here and the desk is visible. Come on, you in?" He grinned his wicked grin. "You need to replace some of the carbs you lost running this week and build up for next time."

Next time? Running with him had unintentionally become a habit in the evenings. If doing so two evenings in a row counted as a "habit." Neither of them had said a word about joining up Thursday evening at a specific time, but sure enough, as she'd rounded the corner of Tiger Drive leading to the high school, Bryan had been crossing the street behind her, their strides easily matching.

"Well?"

Considering the alternative was an empty house and walls that had a tendency to close in on her, Chinese sounded wonderful. "I'm in. Since you're buying," she clarified.

His grin widened. "Any special requests?"

"Surprise me."

"Ah, an adventurous woman. I like it."

She laughed softly and shook her head, determined the extra little *thump* her heart made at his response was normal. The man had flirting down to an art form, and she had to remind herself—often—that it was Bryan's nature, nothing to be taken seriously. At least not when it came to her.

"Wait. You mentioned dropping off the old printer to be repaired earlier. Any chance you might pick up a large pad of art paper? I'd like to sketch out a spreadsheet before attempting to use Excel."

"You got it. Be right back." He turned, then paused. "Lock up behind me okay? I don't want you here with the doors unlocked."

"Yessir," she countered, saluting. "You know, you're as bad

as my dad. Nothing major ever happens here, but I know to always keep the doors locked and do. Quit worrying."

"Even if it doesn't happen here, you never know what crazies are out there."

Melissa followed him down the hall while he gathered up the broken printer and left the office via the back door. Once she'd dutifully locked it, she retraced her steps and finished the filing on her desk, finalized the payments and made sure they coincided with the insurance forms and had just printed the list of patient files she needed to pull for Monday when someone began banging on the front door.

CHAPTER ELEVEN

MELISSA GASPED, startled by the loud noise. The blinds were pulled, but she knew it wasn't Bryan. He'd use his key or at least identify himself. Especially after their conversation.

The pounding had started off strong but grew weaker. Lower?

She ran for the door, hearing broken sobs on the other side. Regardless of the heart-wrenching noise, though, her dad's warnings sounded in her head and she peeked through the blind. Sure enough, a woman stood outside, her car sitting sideways in front of the glass door. No one else looked to be around, and Melissa fumbled with the lock.

"Help me. Please…"

"Shh, it's okay." She knelt beside her in the doorway. "You're okay. Let's get you in here and I'll call the doctor."

Melissa helped the woman to her feet and supported her long enough to get her to the closest chair. She got her seated, took in her swollen face and the bruises on her arm in the shape of fingers, and the sight had her running to relock the door before she called Bryan.

Voice mail. She swallowed a groan. "Bryan, it's me—uh, Melissa. You need to come back to the office right away. You have an emergency patient and I—" she turned her back and lowered her voice "—think she might have been beaten." She hung up and hurried over to the woman. "What's your name? Can you tell me what happened?"

The young woman shook her head, tears rolling down her cheeks. "Wh-where's the doctor?"

"He'll be here soon. I'm going to go call the hospital and get—"

"No. No hospital. The doctor can f-fix me. He's...he's done it before."

Her heart stilled. "Is your name Anna?" A sobbing nod was her answer. "Anna, please, I need to call the squad. I called Dr. Booker, but he might not get my message right away, and I don't know how to help you. I'm not a nurse."

"No. I just n-need the doctor."

Melissa brushed the girl's hair away from her face, careful to stay clear of the blood. She looked so familiar. "Anna..." Realization dawned, a flash of memory, that of big eyes and a ponytail, a bright smile. "Anna Pritchard? Macy Morgan's daughter?"

"Y-yeah. Who are you?"

"I'm Melissa York. When I was in college I used to work at the school as a teacher's aid for Mrs. Evans. You were in her class."

The teenager sniffled, her bleary gaze sharpening for a moment before pain dulled it again. "Yeah...I remember you."

Melissa heard a noise at the end of the hall, the sound of the back door being unlocked and opened. *Bryan.*

"We're up front!"

Bryan ran into the waiting area. "Who's the—Anna."

The girl wouldn't look at him. Bryan knelt beside her and Melissa caught her breath when she saw his expression. Bryan might be a player, but in that instant she saw how kind, how compassionate, how caring he really was.

"Come on, sweetheart. Let's get you to the exam room."

Her heart in her throat, Melissa followed them slowly.

"I h-had another accident," Anna said as Bryan settled her on the table.

"Save it, Anna. This was no accident."

The girl sniffled. "He's just…it's been so hard. He lost his job."

"That's no excuse to hit you."

"He—he was angry and yelling, and I backed up and tripped."

"Don't make excuses." Bryan's eyebrows pulled low. "That only makes it worse."

"But I did!"

"After he shoved you?"

Her face flushed. "He got mad because I broke something his mom g-gave him." She lifted her hand and gingerly touched the bruise on her cheek, wincing. "Do you… Could you give me some samples again? I—I only work part-time and I don't have any insurance." She lowered her head. "I'm sorry. I'm sorry to be such a bother when I can't… If you don't want me to come here anymore—"

"I want you to come anytime you need help, Anna. Regardless of whether you can pay."

Bryan continued to talk to the girl while Melissa retrieved supplies and bandages and helped where she could. Once he'd checked Anna over thoroughly, Bryan took a step back and smiled grimly. "I'll go get the meds from the closet. Hang tight, I'll be right back." Walking toward Melissa, his gaze met and held hers meaningfully. By her side, he paused. "See if you can talk to her?"

Melissa nodded, intimidated by the enormity of the request. How could she get through to Anna when Bryan and her dad couldn't? She moved over and sat beside the girl. "Bryan's right, you know. You deserve better, Anna." Melissa lifted her hand and smoothed the girl's hair back from her face, remembering her as she used to be. Now her eyes were filled with tears, the smile gone. Amazing how time had changed them both.

"It was an—"

"Don't. I'm not buying it, either. He hit you. He *hurt* you, and you're letting him get away with it by defending him. This isn't the girl I remember, Anna. *Why?*"

"Because…because I love him."

"What about you?" She waited until the teenager looked up, confusion on her features. "What about you?" she repeated more sternly. "Do you love yourself enough to protect yourself?"

She wiped her nose. "He…he always says he's sorry."

"Saying you're sorry afterward doesn't change—"

"He hasn't always been like this! And I'm *not* leaving him, no matter what you say, and if you and the doctor keep on at me, then…I won't come back."

She looked like she meant it, too. And the next time Anna's boyfriend beat her she might have broken bones, internal injuries. She could die from lack of treatment. Anna's life was at stake, just as Bryan had said.

"I won't say anything else except this." She nudged Anna until the girl reluctantly met her gaze. "Anna, love is meant to be patient and kind. It shouldn't hurt. Crying from a broken heart because you've fallen for someone unsuitable is one thing, crying because he *breaks you* another. If nothing else, try to remember that, okay? And when you're ready, know that you can come see me or Bryan and we'll do what we can to help you help yourself."

NEITHER OF THEM were in the mood to work after Anna left. Bryan hadn't stopped for food, hadn't had time to purchase the art paper, so instead they agreed to call it a day and regroup the following morning instead.

Fifteen minutes later they met up on Oak Street. By silent agreement they continued to jog, their strides matching, their rhythm synchronizing perfectly. No words, no glares. Just a good kind of companionship with no expectations.

Bryan found himself looking at Melissa instead of where he was going. At her worried expression, the way she held her head high, her shoulders back but tight. They jogged a mile or so in companionable silence. The act slowly eased the stress and tension of the day and bit by bit, her shoulders lowered as she relaxed.

"You hungry?"

A nod of her head was his answer. Veering off what had become their typical path, they continued on until he could sense her tiring, her body protesting its lack of food.

"Hot dog or hamburger?" The dairy bar was up ahead. Not exactly healthy, but it was better than nothing. "I said I'd buy you dinner, remember?"

That brought a smile to her lips. "The nitrates aren't good for—oh, what the heck. A hot dog. With *lots* of mustard."

A hundred feet or so away from the building, they slowed to a walk and took their time cooling down. The picnic tables nearby were crowded with families and teens, but while he stood in line to place his order, Melissa snagged them a bench in a prime location overlooking the Ohio River.

For the longest time they sat there and watched the boats, listened to the teens discuss their drama with overly expressive gestures. A breeze blew, carrying with it the heady scent of late-blooming roses, the musty smell of damp earth and old wood. The sun sank lower and lower into the multihued sky and still they sat there, unmoving. Not talking.

Melissa shivered. He knew he ought to get her up and back home to change out of her sweat-dampened clothes, but instead he positioned his arm along the back of the bench and scooted closer to share his heat. "Much as I hate to say it, we'd probably better head home. It's getting late."

"It's peaceful here, don't you think?"

"Beautiful," he murmured, not taking his eyes off her.

"I remember coming here for picnics with my mom," she continued softly, focused on the water, but unseeing. "She'd bring a blanket and let me pick a spot, and I'd walk the levy stairs all the way to the top because I didn't want to spread the blanket at the bottom." Her lips curled up at the corners and she laughed, the sound husky and warm and full of love. "Sometimes we had to sit with our legs spread out to keep our food from rolling down the hill."

He smiled at the image, fighting the urge to find a blanket and picnic basket and re-create the memory for her. Instead he sat beside her, silent, willing to watch over her while the sky turned dark and the moon rose. She told him bits and pieces of her time with her mom, growing up in Taylorsville, going to the county fair he'd always missed because he had to go home to Boston to begin school.

Bryan ignored the curious glances shot their way by the workers when the dairy bar closed for the night and turned out the lights. The raised eyebrows of the parents who packed up their families and left in their minivans. The teens walked in groups, crowding the sidewalks and roughhousing on the grass. Another hour passed and then all was quiet, more peaceful than ever. Every blink of her eyelashes more beautiful.

Warning bells rang in his head, but he ignored them and

tried to figure out what it was about her that drew him. Melissa was different. Unlike the women in town chasing after him because of the stupid titles or the prestige of marrying a doctor. Different, because she didn't look at him and see money or looks or any of those shallow things. But what did she see? He wasn't so sure he wanted to know. What if all he ever was to her was Booger Boy or Bang 'em Booker?

Melissa shivered again and Bryan found himself touching her, his hand on her shoulder and upper arm, rubbing. Warming. Her soft skin drew him like moths to a light that couldn't be dimmed. She was that light. Melissa had that inner essence some people had, indistinguishable, an aura of grace.

He'd spent many an evening with beautiful women. Dinner, dancing, partying. Lounging around in bed or else performing sexual romps that would leave the most adventurous women gasping. This was a first for him. A run, a hot dog and the river. Companionship and friendship that meant much more than satisfying his baser desires. Definitely a first and infinitely more attractive.

"Bryan, I—" She broke off the moment she turned her head and saw him watching her. He saw her expression change from memory-filled pleasure to panic-stricken fear.

Melissa sucked in a breathy gasp and something—a whimper?—escaped next. The sound burned through him. One moment he thought of how well they'd do if he'd just leave well enough alone, and the next his head lowered toward hers until she jumped up and scrambled away from him.

"Th-thanks for dinner."

He watched her hurry away, the streetlights over her head highlighting that golden glow even more. A police cruiser approached, and once the driver spotted Melissa, it slowed.

Bryan's eyes narrowed when he heard Nathan Taylor call out to her, asking if she needed a ride. Melissa glanced at Bryan, then crossed in front of the cruiser and got in. Bryan remained where he was, watching, and fearing the jealousy ripping his gut to shreds.

"YOU LOOK LIKE something Nam chewed up and spit out."

Bryan glared at Joe's mocking reference to his stray-turned-pet and kept dribbling. "You ever going to own up to your loss and fix my shower? I did deliver your daughter free of charge."

"Quite a baby gift." Joe's grin widened. "Thanks."

He made his move and growled again when Joe managed to snag the ball from beneath his hand. Bryan ran after him, jumping a split second too late to keep the ball out of the hoop.

"Crap!"

"Rumor has it Nathan drove Melissa home last night after she was seen in the park with you. That have anything to do with your less-than-stellar mood?"

"Lay off, Joe."

"Change your mind yet?"

"About what?"

"Mel."

Bryan shook his head with a glare. "She's not for me."

"What, she's not pretty enough?"

"Play ball."

"Nice enough? One of those women you can trust when you aren't around to keep an eye on her?"

"Leave the matchmaking to the old biddies and start the play already."

Joe tossed the basketball at him so fast and hard he

wasn't prepared. It hit his stomach like a fist, taking the air out of his lungs.

"Guess Hal could be a problem. He sure doesn't seem to like you none."

"That wouldn't stop me."

"Then what?"

He began to dribble, the steady *thump-thump-thump* doing nothing to soothe his frustration. No way would he tell Joe his fears of her cancer returning, so he settled on a different fact. "She's afraid of me. She pulls away anytime I get close."

Joe was in a defensive position, but he straightened at the words. "Seriously?"

Bryan scowled at him but nodded. "There's a lot of baggage there, and some of it I don't understand." He watched his friend turn thoughtful and hoped Joe might comment. He didn't. "What, no advice?"

"Thought you wanted to play ball?"

And with that the game began again.

SATURDAY AFTERNOON Melissa arrived at Bryan's practice bleary-eyed and dragging from her sleepless night. Nathan had driven her home, clearly not liking that she'd been alone in the darkened park even though she'd been with Bryan. The protectiveness Nathan displayed might've been nice under the right circumstances, but she knew it had more to do with Nathan following her father's example where Bryan was concerned.

Around midnight she'd given up all pretense of resting and before long, she'd scribbled two pages of potential projects for the fund-raiser. Now to set to work putting them into a semblance of order, get Bryan's okay and start to work. But how could she concentrate after the near-miss last night?

Bryan had almost kissed her—again—and while she knew she'd done the right thing and gotten out of there fast, the thought of Bryan kissing her sent heat blazing through her body to areas still tingling with unfulfilled need from the first time. She'd had a long, lonely night and a lot of unanswered questions, the first of which was what to make of Bryan's behavior?

He wasn't coming off the excited high of delivering a baby, which meant what? *Why* would he want to kiss her knowing what he knew about her? She honestly didn't get it. Maybe she was thinking about it *too* much? Sex was sex, after all. To a guy, anyway. And he'd turned down Amanda Warner's offer so maybe…Bryan was simply in the mood? Thought she was so desperate she'd accept any crumb of affection he might toss her way?

But would he be interested in making love to her? That was definitely something she had no business thinking about.

"I'm glad you're here."

She looked up and quickly smoothed her expression. Bryan stood before her in wash-worn jeans and a green T-shirt, his feet bare, his hair damp and fingered back over his head. It curled slightly at the ends, and she wondered once again what it would be like to touch before she mentally stomped the thought. Professionalism, *friendship,* was key.

"We said we'd work on the fund-raiser today. If you made other plans, that's fine, I just need your okay on a few things to get started."

"Melissa, about last night—"

She pushed by him and into the hallway. "I put together a list I want you to see."

Keeping things all business must've worked because Bryan's eyes lost some of their intensity. She couldn't read his thoughts, but he followed her down the long hall to the reception area. Along the way she turned on all the lights so there weren't any shadows, waited until he chose a seat and then sat across from him rather than beside him.

It was best to keep things professional. There was no reason to believe for a second she could compete with the women in Bryan's life. She couldn't. Nor could she ever match Bryan's perfection and feel adequate.

What woman could live with feeling second-rate?

THE NEXT WEEK PASSED in a blur of paperwork, gossip and fund-raising chaos. Neither of them spoke of the near-kiss in the park, and an hour after they closed on Friday, Bryan bent over the art paper Melissa had squared off and stared at the two-inch portion she wrote inside of. "What am I looking at again?"

"Eat and let me finish," she said with a grin. "The noise from your stomach is driving me nuts."

Happy to comply, Bryan watched as she continued to work, the pen in her right hand flying over the page, pausing every now and again so she could take a bite of the food she'd insisted he heat up on the stove rather than microwave.

Finally she set the pen aside. "Phase one complete," she drawled contentedly. "For as long as I can remember the EMTs in Baxter have had a running competition with my dad and his men. That competitiveness is going to be our first moneymaker."

"How so?"

"Basketball. For a price, they can play against one another tournament style until we have a champion."

"What's that?" he asked, pointing to another square where she'd organized the groups across the page horizontally, the events vertically. "Cook-offs? You've got to be kidding me."

"Hey, don't knock it until you see the results. You think guys are competitive? You haven't seen anything until you put Mrs. McCleary's Irish Stew against Maddie Harper's Vegetable Medley. Toss in the rest of the First Christian Church's Disaster Aid Team members because they feel ignored over the fuss made over Mrs. Harper and Mrs. McCleary, and you've got a huge cook-off on your hands."

"So where does all of this food go then? What if there isn't an emergency?"

Melissa gave him a tolerant smile. "You've never done anything like this before, have you? Hopefully there won't *be* an emergency. That way we can sell the food per plate and make even more than the entry fees charged."

Almost afraid to ask what she'd come up with that involved the high school boys' soccer league and the varsity cheerleaders, he pointed to the next square and received another explanation. And another. And another. The basketball tournament coincided with the cook-off, the bake sale went along with a kid's festival featuring games and inflatables the kids could pay to play in.

"I ran into Mrs. H. this morning. She said she'd get her friends at the retirement center in on the bake sale and recommended an online company the school uses for the game prizes. I spoke with the mayor, too, and we can use the park. He's waiving the permits and fees. Oh, and the riverboat captain said he'd furnish the boat and the crew, and that so long as we covered the fuel and insurance, we could charge whatever admission we wanted free and clear of him."

Bryan stared down at the grid covered in Melissa's neat handwriting and tried to suppress his excitement. If she could pull this off and get everyone involved… Was that number the—

"Yup. Enough for the estimated groundbreaking and construction start," she told him with a proud smile. "And that's without digging into the money you've got saved. I'm sure we'll need it later to finish things up, but this will get us started, and I've gotten confirmed commitments from almost everyone." Her grin widened. "I perfected a spiel about E.R. trips saved, the safety of the sports players getting care sooner and, um, told them about how important it is that stroke victims get care right away. If that didn't work, I hit them with your grandfather's name and how it's his life's dream. They caved every time. Next I'll put together a list of local businesses, other civic groups and the like and offer them advertising in the flyers in exchange for donations while, of course, urging their individual participation for the good of Taylorsville. Work for you?"

He stared into her beautiful, silvery-blue eyes and smiled. "Yeah, it does. Melissa, you did it."

"Pretty cool now that you can see it all spread out, huh?"

"This is way more than cool, this is *incredible*."

"Don't thank me yet. We still have to finish organizing it all."

"You think a big gala is the way to end things?"

"Absolutely. People around here never get a chance to dress up and show off. I say we do all the normal stuff first and play up the grand finale, let the excitement build, and then bring out the best for last. Taylorsville might be small, but it's cliquish, and if we make it a who's who special event, we'll be turning people away for lack of space. You going to eat the last of the noodles?"

Bryan laughed, happier than he'd been in ages. Granddad would get his dream after all. Thanks to Melissa. "No, have at it."

He watched her dig in and shook his head, smiling, his

thoughts drifting. She ate with delicate relish, not the picky I-can't-gain-a-pound mantra so many women held and certainly not the poor appetite of a chemo patient.

That thought sobered him quickly. He was attracted to her, no doubt about it, but it couldn't lead to more. He needed to back off, let Nathan patch things up between them if he could.

She paused, swallowing. "Something wrong?"

"No. No, not at all," he murmured, standing. "I think I'll get another drink though. How about you? Another water?"

"No. I'm good."

Bryan headed for the kitchen, but along the way, he paused. "If it's not too much, I'd like to set up a timetable for all this. It's the end of August now. Think we can schedule these events over the next month as a kickoff to fall and plan the gala for early December? Pull the heartstrings and use the season to give incentive?"

She froze in the act of eating. "Oh, um… I don't know. I hadn't thought about it."

He frowned at her expression. "You must have a date in mind?"

"No. Not—not really."

Forgetting the need to escape and get a drink, he retraced his steps and stared down at her. "What am I missing here?"

"Nothing," she said with a nervous laugh. "I'm just not— I don't usually plan that far in advance. I hadn't thought of that when I put this together."

"We have to set a date to tell people when they need to sign up, get the orders in. None of this will ever happen unless we have a target date to get it done."

"I know that." Her mouth twisted and she looked down at her carefully drawn plan, pushing the box of Chinese away.

Sensing more to her hesitation and remembering he'd never had that talk he'd promised the chief that he'd have with her, Bryan squatted down beside her, intent on getting an answer. "Why don't you plan ahead?"

CHAPTER TWELVE

"BECAUSE I DON'T have a crystal ball?"

Bryan scowled at her, not liking her cynical expression. "Knock off the comedy act and tell me."

Melissa lifted her shoulder in a shrug. "I'd made plans once and then... Now I just don't. That's it, no big, dark secret."

"*Why?*"

"*Because.* I don't like to make plans I might not be able to keep, so I only ever schedule a week or so in advance."

The reason tore through him and ripped out his heart. "Because of your cancer," he murmured bluntly. "You won't make plans because of a cancer diagnosis that happened over *two years ago?*"

She shoved herself to her feet and moved away from him, but he followed her, glaring down at her with all the anger and frustration he felt because he didn't know whether to shake her or kiss her. Each held equal appeal.

"Don't," she warned, eyes blazing, one finger raised up in warning. "Don't stand there and tell me how I should or shouldn't live my life. I don't make plans in advance. Big deal!"

"It is a big deal. That's what your dad meant that day in the B and B isn't it? About living with one foot in the grave?

I thought he meant because you don't date, but it's way more than that. Melissa— Dammit."

"Don't swear at me!"

He rubbed a hand over his mouth. She had to fight. It was too important and if she gave up... "Attitude is *everything* with that da—with that disease and if you don't make plans, you're giving it free rein to come back! You're letting it win!"

"I'm doing no such thing!"

"Liar."

Her chest rose and fell rapidly, her hands fisted at her sides. In that moment she'd never been more beautiful, but now, Melissa seemed to be more vulnerable than ever because she'd experienced the worst a hard-core illness had to offer and come through the other side living half a life.

"How can I *not* think about dying? I nearly did. My mother and grandmother *did*—and who knows how many women in my family lost the battle before cancer was officially diagnosed? I *can't* plan anything beyond my next test because I don't know what'll happen when I step foot into my oncologist's office. I don't *know* if I'll be able to keep the plans I've made, or what shape I'll be in when some future date comes around so why—" She shook her head, tears slipping from the corners of her eyes before she wiped them away. "*Why* put myself through that? I'd think you of all people would understand."

"I understand how frightening—"

"*Frightening?* Oh, please. You and my father are too alike in a lot of ways. Good grief, how scary is that? You're a doctor, Bryan. You know exactly what it's like to watch someone die, but you still think I should have some Pollyanna outlook on life? It's way more than 'frightening.' How can you stand there and blame me for being cautious?"

He stared at Melissa and thought of the way she'd told him about her mastectomy that day in the car, how brave she'd been. Now it was his turn. His heart thundered in his chest, but he had to get through to her, knew Rachel would want him to. "Melissa, I don't blame you. You're right, I do know what it's like, because I performed my residency in a hospital specializing in cancer treatments and I saw…I saw a lot, okay? And I saw more when my ex-girlfriend showed up one day and I realized she was there for an appointment and not to see me."

Melissa swallowed tightly. "She died."

He nodded. "She died," Bryan whispered huskily. "I worked with some of the best doctors in the country, but we couldn't save her, couldn't heal her. And after a particularly rough day, I couldn't take it anymore. The moment she opened her eyes, I told her I was quitting medicine, giving up my career because I didn't have what it took to be a doctor." A smile crossed his lips. "She looked me straight in the eyes and called me a loser. She did," he confirmed when Melissa glanced at him in surprise. "She said I couldn't quit, because nothing would be gained if I did, and I owed it to her to be the doctor I'd always wanted to be. We'd broken things off because of the schedules we kept with jobs and school. She refused to let me make that sacrifice worthless."

"She sounds like a strong, wonderful person."

"She was. And so are you," he told her firmly, holding her gaze for as long as she was able. When she looked away, he continued, determined. "The point I'm trying to make is that you can't stop living, Melissa. If you do, nothing is gained even though you've sacrificed everything in the process."

She blinked away tears but didn't speak.

"When Rachel was gone, I left that facility and got a job

at another hospital. I couldn't handle seeing those patients I treated on a daily basis because we got the worst of the disease, were their last hope. But even though I couldn't handle not being able to help them, I could help others and be a damn good doctor while I was at it. Colds, broken bones, *quality of life*. To some people it might not be as important as what I did back East, but to me, it was. It is." Bryan shook his head. "I didn't give up even though I wanted to, Melissa, and neither can you. I can argue with you about planning future events because *you* are still here. Taking precautions is one thing, but considering yourself cancer-*postponed* instead of cancer-*free* is no way to live. You're healthy. You fought a horrendous battle, but *you won*. And you deserve to live life no matter how the future plays out. Why shortchange yourself by living in fear?"

"You ask me why after *losing* her?"

"You got a second chance!"

"Maybe I did, but would *you* put someone through that if you could help it? I *can't!* Planning ahead or being with someone would only make dying that much more painful because I'd know I was hurting them, too!"

He stalked away from her, blinking rapidly to combat the burning in his eyes. He couldn't picture Melissa like that. Wouldn't. "You shouldn't think that way. Shouldn't be that way when you have—"

"Oh, please." She followed the comment up with a laugh, the sound full of unshed tears. "Don't stand there and tell me how I should be. Not when you just told me a heartbreaking story that has me thinking your grandfather is right."

He swung around to face her. "Right about what?"

Melissa lifted her chin, her posture defensive. "He has a theory about why you sleep around."

Bryan ran a hand through his hair. "For the love of— I've made some mistakes, but I've always taken precautions and everyone knew the score. There's no theory behind that."

Her cheeks took on a pretty blush. "Really? Some people might look at those 'mistakes' and think they were made because you're still mourning the woman you loved."

"That was a long time ago. We'd been broken up for a long time, too. I...I cared for her once, thought I was in love, but it was little more than a college crush."

"That makes it worse, Bryan, don't you see? You only cared for this girl and yet you were ready to give up your life, your livelihood, because of what happened." Melissa narrowed her eyes. "It *scared* you, and I understand that."

No doubt she did, but— "Why would Granddad say something like that to you?"

Melissa ducked her head and turned away. "That's not important. What is important is that before you examine my life, you need to look at yours. You sleep around, keep things casual. Why, Bryan? Do you really not know? Your grandfather thinks you want to forget her, but I think it's because you don't want to get hurt again."

"We weren't a couple," he argued. "We weren't even in love."

"I understand that. You didn't love her, but her death affected you more than you realized it would. What would happen if the woman you *loved* got sick? How would you feel then? I think that's why you keep everyone at arm's length."

"We're not discussing me."

"What's amazing is that you're still a wonderful doctor with a great bedside manner, but I've noticed something," she drawled. "You don't make eye contact with your patients. You study their charts, you listen to their symptoms. But you don't look at them."

"I look at them." He winced at his excusatory tone.

"You don't, not really. Oh, a cursory glance and a smile, sure, lots of teasing if they're fairly healthy, which most of your patients are, but the others—" she shook her head "—you don't. You see them, but you don't connect." She fingered a book on a shelf, the latest bestseller he hadn't had time to read. "Bryan, I'm not *judging* you. I—I understand that need to disappear, to forget and yet be able to feel again. I—I even envy your ability to keep things casual and pull away before things get serious." She closed her eyes briefly. "Sometimes I think if I were normal…"

That brought him out of his stupor. "What do you mean, if you were normal?"

CHAPTER THIRTEEN

"WHAT DO YOU mean by 'normal'?" he asked again when she didn't answer.

Melissa turned to look at him, her expression battle-weary and proud, vulnerable but determined. "Nothing. It's just that the normal part of me who planned ahead died like your friend. With every needle and cut of the scalpel, with every single hair that fell out of my head, I stopped believing in tomorrow. Bryan, don't you see? All I could handle was the day, *that* day, and sometimes I couldn't handle those! I had to live moment by moment because it was all I could manage, and if I refuse to put someone else through that, that's my right. You and my father need to respect that."

Bryan braced his hands on the edge of the sofa table, gripping it tight to keep from grabbing her and shaking her. She was running away from her inability to see herself as healthy by shifting the subject to him.

Melissa picked up her purse and he bit back an order to stay. They had a lot more to say to each other. He wanted her to fight. To live. But moments later he heard the soft *snick* of the door being closed, and her rapid descent on the stairs. Her car started and pulled away and still he stood there, his hands locked onto the table.

Finally he got his anger under control and lifted his head

to survey the remains of what had been another wonderful evening with Melissa until it had degenerated into a fight.

He prowled the room, went downstairs to lock up and set the security alarm, then headed upstairs again where he sat down and stared at the papers Melissa had left behind in her rush to get away from him.

In that instant he wanted her back, wanted to redo the night and erase the argument. Sit down beside her and make her laugh so he could see the way her eyes crinkled at the corners, the cute way her nose wrinkled up when she made a face. Watch the soft fullness of her lips when they curled into a smile or, better yet, feel them beneath his.

Dear God above, he wanted her to fight for her life. He wanted her to live and love, and he wanted her— He *wanted* her.

He wanted her not to be so right.

ASHLEY OPENED the door, her smile revealing her confusion. "Bryan? It's late. Is something wrong?"

"Is Joe up?"

"No, he's asleep, but I can go get—"

"No, that's okay." Ashley looked as muddled as Bryan felt, and he shook his head at himself. "Actually you might be the person I need to talk to."

"Okay." She bounced the fussy baby in her arms. "Come on in."

Bryan entered the remodeled kitchen and paced across the floor. "I'm sorry for coming so late. I was out driving around and I thought I'd take a walk around the pond, but then I saw the light come on—"

"It's fine. As you can see Issy is hungry. Would you like something to drink? Some coffee? Water?"

"No, thanks."

"Bryan? *Bryan?* What did Melissa do?"

He looked up and found Ashley watching him, curiosity clear on her pretty features. "Why do you think this is about Melissa?"

Ashley shot him an amused look before she grabbed the bottle she'd already prepared. She settled herself in a chair and gently inserted the nipple into Issy's searching mouth. "Because I've seen you watching her. You don't look at her like a boss, Bryan. You never have. Not from the moment I met you and saw the two of you together."

He shook his head. "You're wrong. When I moved here she had already been diagnosed with cancer and was undergoing treatment."

"I know."

"How do you— What do you *think* you know?"

She smiled at him, one of those tolerant, humoring smiles he used to see his grandmother give his granddad. "Do you remember when you invited me to the book-club discussion at the library?"

He nodded.

"Well, I was getting Max out of the car seat and had just turned around when Melissa walked by. You two were aware of each other even then. She blushed after receiving a single look from you, and you…you told me she was sick and you could barely get the words out. You couldn't stand the thought of her being ill and left the room after I asked about her."

"That was rude."

Ashley's rich laughter warmed the room. "I'm not telling you this to give you a hard time about your manners. You had a connection to Melissa back then, and I imagine it's become stronger since you started working with her."

"It's there," he admitted reluctantly. "A long time ago I spent a few summers here as a kid and Melissa and I played together a lot." He smiled, remembering. "The Popsicle Gang," he said with a laugh. "That was our club. Stupid name, huh?"

"I think it's sweet."

"But that's not— Ashley, I know more than I care to know about the ravages of cancer. I have a connection to her because I know what's been done to her. I know what might— I *understand* what she's been through, that's all."

"Not quite. Empathy is one thing, but it doesn't explain why you're out wandering around at midnight."

No, it didn't. "We were working on the fund-raiser tonight and needed to set the dates for the events she's come up with. When she wouldn't give me an answer, I confronted her." He'd resumed pacing while he spoke, but stopped to ask, "Did you know she doesn't plan ahead?"

Ashley looked thoughtful. "I've noticed a time or two that she's been leery of accepting invitations until right before the date. Why?"

"It's more than that. It's…it's *why* she does it. Melissa doesn't accept invitations because she doesn't think she'll be here or else she'll be undergoing treatment or something. She's cancer-free now and yet she lives day to day because she's *that* scared of believing in the future."

"And that angers you?"

"Of course it does!" His loud declaration startled the baby and Isabella released the bottle with a whimpering cry. "I'm sorry, I didn't mean to scare her."

"She's fine." Ashley soothed the baby and she was eating again within seconds. "Bryan, it sounds to me like Melissa is afraid and she has good reason to be. You can't argue that."

He raked his fingers through his hair. "I'm not. I understand that, but she can't— What was it you said Mac's motto was?" he asked, referring to her first husband, who'd died and left Ashley a single mother. "Something about attitude being everything? Well, that's true of cancer. Attitude *is* everything with the disease, with winning the battle. If you think you're going to die, your body feels it and it responds accordingly. Patients have to fight with everything they've got and even then it doesn't always work, but if they don't believe it from the beginning... Melissa has separated herself from life and built a wall to protect herself."

"Do you blame her?"

"No, but, Ashley, you need to talk to her. If the cancer does return, she can't go through it alone. She needs to find someone who'll help her, and with her dad marrying Ellen, Melissa's going to need someone to be with her."

"I agree," Ashley murmured, her expression shrewd. "So why not you?"

WHY NOT HIM?

Bryan pretended not to hear her. "All I'm saying is that it's a waste of her life," he said. "Anyone who can get Mr. Mason to laugh out loud has got a great sense of humor. And you wouldn't believe the fund-raising ideas she came up with. Have you heard about the argument she had here with her dad in the dining room?"

"Yeah. Dara told me."

"Well, I never thought I'd agree with the chief, but he's right. Melissa survived her cancer diagnosis physically, but emotionally she's not living. She refuses to try!" He shook his head. "What is she afraid of? It's more than just the cancer and her prognosis. Ashley, something else is going on here and I can't figure out what it is."

"Figure out what?" a low voice growled.

Bryan turned and found Joe leaning against the door frame. He looked tired, but wide-awake and angry, like a bear wakened early from hibernation.

"Why are you yelling at my wife?"

"Sorry we woke you," Ashley murmured, her smile tender. "Bryan's upset and frustrated, but not with me. He came to talk about Melissa."

Joe blinked. "Frustrated, huh?" He shoved himself away from the wall and stepped deeper into the kitchen, barely disguising a yawn, his bare feet making no noise as he padded across the floor. Standing by Ashley's chair, he palmed the tiny head of his daughter and leaned over to give Ashley a quick kiss on the lips. "You were *supposed* to wake me up and let me take care of her."

"You've fed her every night since we got home, and then gotten up and worked all day. I figured I could take this one. Besides," she added, "if I hadn't, I would've missed Bryan's revelations about Melissa."

"What kind of revelations?"

"He wants her."

"Now wait a min—"

"He's finally admitting it?" Joe smirked at him. "After that speech you gave me about never marrying?"

"Joe," Ashley murmured, her tone chiding. "Bryan wasn't serious about that."

Once again Bryan pretended he didn't hear her and tried not to wonder how many other private conversations Joe had shared.

"So why are you here," Joe asked bluntly, "and not with Melissa, talking about whatever is wrong?"

"I'm here because I'm so damned confused I don't know

what to do." He pointed a finger at Joe. "And if you laugh, so help me I'll kick your sorry butt to the pond and back."

"*Boys,* keep your voices down so you don't wake the whole house. And, Bryan? The swear jar is on the counter behind you. As to what you do about Melissa—you kiss her senseless and show her what she's missing. Make her want more from life than what she has now."

"I can't."

"Can't?" Ashley's surprise showed. "Why not?"

"She doesn't want me to." They didn't have to know he was just as afraid of Melissa's cancer as she was.

"You're *Bang 'em Booker.* Surely you know how to make a woman forget her common sense?"

Joe snickered, his hands caressing Ashley's neck in slow, soothing motions. "Didn't work with you."

"That was because I was already in love with you," she told her husband. "But we all know how women are around Bryan, and Melissa's no different. He's had to do something right at some point."

"Thanks for sparing my ego." Bryan shook his head at them. "But I'm not kissing her again."

"Again?" Joe asked.

"Why not?" Ashley demanded. "If you feel this strongly about her—so much that you come knocking on our door at midnight—why wouldn't you kiss her? Make her forget about *everything,* Bryan. Her fears, her upset and especially about the scars that make her so self-conscious. She likes you but she'll never admit it. She's afraid to."

His body ached at the thought, the visions in his head so erotic he stalked over to the door and stared outside until he got himself under control, all the reasons they shouldn't be together lining themselves up in his head. "What does her being scarred have to do with anything?" They didn't answer, and Bryan glanced over his shoulder to find Ashley openly gaping at him.

"You can't be serious." She glanced up at Joe, then back at him. "You're serious?"

Joe chuckled but raised his hand to his mouth, coughing weakly.

"Please tell me men really aren't so oblivious," Ashley continued. "You're a *doctor,* for pity's sake. Didn't you take a class on relating to your patients? Women's perceptions and emotions? Using your sixth sense to see beyond their words or something?"

"I have a feeling I'm not going to like this," he muttered to no one in particular.

"I'd say you're right," Joe readily agreed.

Ashley pulled the bottle out of Issy's mouth and set it aside before sitting the baby up on her lap to burp. "Melissa is scared because of the cancer and her past, yes, but it's also because she's *scarred* while you, on the other hand, are perfectly gorgeous."

Joe scowled down at his wife. "Hey."

"Not as gorgeous as you," she corrected without removing her eyes from Bryan. "But in Melissa's eyes your looks are a definite *disadvantage,* not an asset."

"Because she doesn't feel she's…" He slowed to a halt, finally beginning to understand and getting angry because Melissa didn't see herself the way he saw her. He squeezed the muscles of his neck and grimaced. She was beautiful, but how could he show her that, counter that without—

"Attractive," Ashley confirmed. "Bryan, she'll probably never tell you this and I'm not sure I should, but…Melissa didn't have reconstructive surgery."

He stared at Ashley in surprise. She hadn't? "Why not?"

Now she looked away, her focus on burping her baby girl. "She felt she was too small chested for implants to look natural and...you need to ask her, but before you go spouting this back to Melissa, I'm *not* telling you any of this," she instructed firmly. "I just want to help you both, but she's probably too embarrassed to tell you and you're too—"

"Arrogant?" Joe supplied with a grin.

"I'm not sure what he is, but he needs to know everything Melissa is dealing with so he can understand."

"I do understand." Although at the moment Ashley's wanting him not to tell Melissa now she'd shared Melissa's secret was the only thing that made sense.

"It boils down to this—your timing sucks. Her dad is giving her a hard time about moving on because he's decided to marry again, and Melissa's started a new job with a boss who's...well, *you*. She's stressed and trying to adjust."

"If the job is too much for her—"

"Bryan, it's not the job! It's life. It's the busybodies here who can't keep their mouths shut and talk in front of her like she's invisible. It's seeing gorgeous models on every magazine in the grocery aisles and being bombarded with cleavage when she turns on the TV or walks down the hallway at work."

Ashley stated that last bit with a glare, leaving no doubt in his mind that Melissa had told her about the incident with Amanda Warner. He squeezed his neck harder and hoped they didn't see the uncomfortable heat surging up his neck.

"It's being torn between liking you, but believing she can't compete with the women you've boi—uh, *dated*. That should her interest in a man become more, they'll leave the moment they get a look at her naked."

"A decent guy wouldn't—"

"Exactly. But, Bryan, the job at your practice is so important to her *because* of that. Melissa doesn't think she'll ever have anything else. She believes she isn't attractive enough for a man to want her, scars and all, and that's why she's afraid. But if you can get her to think—to *believe*—in a future, maybe her other fears will be conquered, too."

His thoughts raced, too confusing and contradictory to fathom.

"I've already told you things I shouldn't have, so I'm going to tell you something else. You screw this up and you not only screw up your office, you mess with Melissa's self-esteem forever."

"Which means," Joe added, his tone low and barbed, "don't mess with Melissa *at all* unless you can handle the consequences."

Bryan's gut formed into a knot of unease. Through the years he'd seen plenty of examples of patients who'd made the same decision as Melissa, but they *weren't* Melissa. Did it matter that she didn't have breasts?

Remembering her impassioned speech that day in the office about how every man was obsessed with breasts made sense. He wanted to go to her house right now and tell her what other attributes he found attractive. The things he liked about her.

"Put yourself in her shoes," Ashley continued softly. "I'm quite sure she feels torn between having a good working relationship with you, and how it made her feel when you kissed her. Did she like it? Did you?"

"Yeah." And he wanted to kiss her again. Wanted more. But Joe was right. Could he handle the consequences of hooking up with her? He wasn't sure. Being with Melissa…

The thought of making love to her had him shaking with anticipation. When the time came, arousal wouldn't be a problem. He wanted her—scars and all. Wanted the woman she'd become because of them. But what if something happened to her in the future? Maybe Melissa was right in that aspect; maybe things should be handled on a day-to-day basis. Futures left to happen as they happened, not to be planned. Casual. But did he want casual with Melissa? Would she want a casual relationship with him?

"Then make her feel beautiful, Bryan. Every woman out there wants to be beautiful. Melissa is no different."

He wanted to. For her sake if nothing else. He wanted to prove to her what a beautiful, passionate woman she was. Show her.

And he could. If he kept things light, sex only, he could build her confidence and then—

"I've got to go." He stalked for the door, his hand on the knob. "I'll think about everything you've said, but I'd appreciate it if you wouldn't mention this."

"We won't say a word about how you showed up here wanting to talk about her," Ashley reassured him with a grin that didn't last. "But, Bryan…whatever you decide, take it slow. For both your sakes. You are both special to us and we don't want either of you hurt."

Bryan nodded dazedly before crossing the threshold onto the porch. "Thanks for the talk. And for listening."

Outside, he moved to the steps but paused long enough to look back. Through the window he watched Joe wrap one arm around the back of the chair where Ashley sat, then proceed to tilt the chair backward and kiss her.

Bryan chuckled when the kiss ended with Joe's smiling triumph at Ashley's dazed expression. He'd seen the same look on Melissa's face. Once. But did he have the courage to kiss her senseless and be the first to make love to her since her illness?

Only one way to find out.

HAL SLID HIS KEY into the lock of Ellen's house, more tired than he had been in years. The investigation into the break-ins and beatings of elderly citizens was going nowhere, and between Ellen's upset and Melissa's silent treatment, he wanted nothing more than to crawl into a cave for some solitude.

Inside the house, he'd just set his hat on the table when he heard a low moan. He listened intently, heard another moan and then the sound of gagging. What the—

He ran through the house and took the stairs two at a time. Through the bedroom, into the bathroom. "Ellen? Sweet-heart, what's wrong?" He dropped to his knees on the linoleum beside her. She barely moved, and didn't acknowl-edge his presence at all. He checked her pulse and found it faint, but rapid. Her skin was clammy and lax. She'd been sick for a while.

Hal slipped his arms around her and picked her up. Ellen groaned when he turned to carry her into the bedroom and, despite his urge to rush, he made sure not to jostle her too much.

"Hal? G-go away. Oh, please. I don't want you to see me…like this."

"In sickness and health, Ellie." He laid her on the bed and grabbed a tissue from the nightstand to wipe her face. "How long have you been like this?"

"Since this afternoon."

Anger overtook his fear. "Why didn't you call me? You've been lying on the bathroom floor all this time?"

A low groan was his answer. Lights flashed from nearby, drawing his attention, and he left the bed long enough to spot Booker's car pulling in next door.

Out carousing and just getting in for the night, no doubt. He opened the window, hoping the fresh air would get rid of the smell of vomit and make Ellen feel better.

"Booker! Get up here! Ellen's sick!"

CHAPTER FOURTEEN

THE DOC LIFTED a hand to acknowledge his words. "Be right there!"

Hal left the window open and pulled the throw off a nearby chair so her sweat-dampened body wouldn't chill. He brushed her hair back from her forehead, praying hard. Was it the baby? A virus? Food poisoning?

He left her long enough to wet a washcloth to bathe her forehead and face, pleased to see a little color return to her pale cheeks.

"What's going on?" Booker asked, coming into the bedroom with a black bag in his hand.

Hal stood, reluctant to let go of her again. "I found her on the bathroom floor a few minutes ago. She's been there all evening."

"Ellen, did you throw up a lot today?"

She gave him a weak nod.

"You look dehydrated. Let me listen to your heart and get some readings, and see what's going on. Did you eat anything today?"

"Some. I had lunch with Hal, but felt nauseous all day."

"What about yesterday? The last few days? Eat anything different or unusual?" Another no. "Anything going on that I need to know about? Medications? Problems you've been having?"

"She's pregnant."

With two words he'd rendered the doc speechless. Booker sat there, his eyebrows high on his forehead, shock evident on his face.

"Uh...congratulations. She's had this confirmed?"

Hal nodded. "Is it the baby?"

Booker's frown returned. "I don't know yet. Ellen, are you cramping? Bleeding?" He grabbed a pressure cuff and slipped it around her arm. "Have any unusual pain?"

"No. J-just sick. My stomach won't settle at all. I've had spells...off and on the last couple weeks."

"That's it? You're sure you're not spotting?"

"I—I checked," she whispered, her cheeks red against her pale face. "I don't hurt there or...anything."

"I'll call the squad."

"No, Hal... Bryan, please, I'm just sick—*nauseous*. That's all." Her face turned red as a beet. "Please, I don't want people to find out just yet."

The doc hesitated. "You very well could have a bad case of morning sickness that isn't limiting itself to the morning, but you need to be checked out by your OB."

"Tomorrow. Please, I'll go tomorrow. First thing."

Booker hesitated. "Tell you what, how about you let me look you over a bit more and then we'll decide if you need to go to the hospital?" Without waiting for an answer, Booker put a stethoscope into his ears and listened while he took her blood pressure. "It's a little low, but normal for the day she's had."

The doc glanced at him and stilled before looking away. "Chief, why don't you go grab a bottle of cold water for her? And some crackers or toast?" He jerked his head toward the door. "I'll finish checking her out while you get her something to replace the fluids she's lost."

Without a word, Hal stumbled from the room, his footsteps dragging like an old man's. He reached out to put his hand on the stair railing but realized he couldn't see it. Lifting the hand to his face, he rubbed, only then discovering he was crying.

An hour later, Hal watched while the doc teased a blush into Ellen's cheeks and checked her blood pressure one last time. After he'd returned with two bottles of water and a box of Saltines, Booker had gone next door and retrieved some Gatorade. While he was gone, Hal had helped Ellen clean up and change into a fresh nightgown, fussing over her and loving every minute of it.

Already she looked better and, although pale and embarrassed at Booker finding out she was a pregnant bride, she smiled and laughed at the doc's comments. And for once, he wasn't jealous. Booker treated Ellen with respect, like a sister, same as he'd done with little Anna Pritchard.

Booker got up with one last teasing remark and ordered Ellen to rest and drink as much fluid as possible. Then he grabbed his medical bag from the bedstand and headed toward him. Hal stepped back into the hall and followed the doc down the stairs to the kitchen to see him out. "Thanks for coming."

"Anytime. And congrats again on the baby."

He accepted that with a nod. "Thanks. Ellen's been worried about things lately. Stressed over what people will say once they find out and a few other things."

"There's a lot of that going around. Stress, that is."

"Meaning Mel?" He narrowed his gaze. "She's worked for you a couple weeks now. Has she talked to you about the wedding?"

"Some."

"You going to tell me what she said?"

"No," the doc countered steadily. "I talked to Melissa as a doctor and as a friend, both of which entitle her to her privacy."

"Guess I should be glad she's talking to someone." He nodded reluctantly. "You did good in there with Ellen. Thanks."

"Anytime." The doc turned to go but paused, his hand on the doorknob. "Chief? Ellen and Melissa aren't the only ones stressed. Finding out you're going to be a father again must've come as a shock."

"Watch it, Doc."

"Just giving some professional advice. You take care of yourself so you'll be around to see that baby grow up."

"I'll do that." He figured this was as good a time as any to broach what was on his mind. "But my stress level would lower quite a bit if I knew you weren't going to mess around with my little girl. I was angry that day at the B and B and desperate for help to get her to see what she's doing to herself, but I don't want you getting the wrong idea."

"I understand. I respect your daughter, Chief."

He might respect her, but Booker wasn't standing there denying he wanted her or agreeing to leave her alone, either. Hal looked closely at the doc's face, wondering how many heart-stopping surprises he could take in one night. "She's not your kind of woman."

Booker smiled. "What kind do you think I like?"

"Loose. Easy. The kind you can sleep with and never think about again because you know they've moved on to someone else, too. Mel's not like that."

An indecipherable expression crossed Booker's face before he smoothed his features. "I know that, Chief."

"She had cancer."

"I think everybody knows that."

Hal took a step and stared into the doc's eyes, searching, but not finding what he'd expected. "She's too good for you."

Booker rubbed his chin as though in deep contemplation. "For once, Chief, we agree," he murmured. "The worst person in the world she could fall for would be a guy like me, but the last thing I'd ever do is hurt her."

"Then don't. Leave her alone." When Booker didn't respond, he grabbed the doc's shirt and hauled him closer still. The man didn't protest, didn't squirm. Didn't even blink. He simply looked resigned to his fate as if he knew he deserved whatever lay in wait for him in the days ahead. Hal shook his head and started laughing.

"You sure you're okay, Chief? You've had a stressful night."

"And it just got worse," he muttered, still chuckling, shaking his head and wondering how on earth he could laugh at a time like this. "Heaven help me, you're in love with her."

Booker shook his head in denial. "We're just friends."

Hal let him go. "Then I guess that means I can give Nathan my blessing to try again?"

"No."

"Why not? He's been sniffing around lately, and they were a couple once."

"Until he didn't have the balls to stick around when it mattered most," Booker growled. "You really want that for her? For Nathan to bail out should she need him?"

"I suppose you think you'd see the worst through?"

"Damn right I would, I'd—" The doc broke off, looking confused and disgruntled.

Hal laughed. "Life's funny, don't you think?" Bang 'em

Booker looked at him as if he was crazy, and maybe he was.
He'd experienced enough to drive five men crazy, but for the
first time in a long time he saw hope—for Mel—in the last
person he'd expected to find it. Yeah, life was funny. God was
playing a big joke on him right now, too, reminding him who
was boss.

"What do you mean?"

"Well, here I am getting ready to start a new family at my
age, but there you are—Taylorsville's Most Eligible Bachelor—trying to deny you've finally been caught. And by a
woman who has more than enough reasons to send you
packing when *you* try something with her. My daughter ain't
gonna make it easy for you, Doc. She'll shoot you down, but
don't let that stop you," he ordered. "She's scared out of her
mind at the thought of having a man in her life. Just like you
are at the thought of being that man. But regardless of my
thoughts on the matter, my gut says you're as smart as your
medical degree proclaims, and you've been around enough
to see the woman Mel is inside and not just the illness or the
damage it caused."

"I'd like to think so. But that doesn't change how she feels."

"Look me in the eyes and tell me you don't want her. That
if Nathan tries again, you wouldn't be willing to fight for her."

Booker opened his mouth but no words came out, and
when the truth hit, the doc looked like a man sucker punched.
Oh yeah, the boy had it bad.

Amazing. The last thing he'd thought he'd ever feel was
sorry for the doc, but he acknowledged the emotion just the
same. Booker was scared and it showed. Hal had felt the
same way when Melissa's mother had gotten the news, and
that's why he could sympathize. The doc had a lot to think
about, a lot to handle, but love was love and he was in deep.

"Let me tell you something I've learned over the years. Good or bad, we don't get to choose who we love. It just happens. Mel's mom was the love of the first half of my life, and Ellen is the love I want to end my life with. But regardless of what I want, what will be will be. I know it because I've lived it. And while apparently I'm not the only one who has to get used to the idea of you and Mel together, it looks to me like nature has already taken care of things where you're concerned. If you treat Mel badly, I'll turn in my badge and hunt you down," he said, meaning every word. "But if you treat her with the same respect you've shown Ellen and Anna, if you get my daughter to live again," he said, his voice emerging gruff, "I'll owe you until the day I die."

BRYAN STARED into the chief's eyes a long moment, then turned and left, walking the distance back to his house in a daze. Hal York, protective father extraordinaire, the chief of police who kept Taylorsville on a short leash, had given him the go-ahead. A smile crossed his face and he laughed softly. "Unbelievable."

It *was* unbelievable—because the chief was right. Ashley was right. Even Joe was right, but he'd buy Joe box seats for the next five years before he'd admit it and have to watch Joe gloat.

He would, however, admit that he'd wasted precious time mulling over the past and worrying over what could happen to Melissa should her cancer return, instead of treasuring the time he could spend with her here and now.

Hal was right—what would be would be. Melissa was well. She was cancer-free. It was time *he* dealt with the fact that life would happen whether he was prepared for it or not. Instead of condemning their relationship by assuming it was short-term or slotting it conveniently on his calendar because he planned to cut and run—*an act that would put him in a class with Nathan*—he needed to plan a future.

Rachel's words had a deeper meaning than the obvious. Well, he knew what he wanted. Whom he wanted. But convincing Melissa wouldn't be easy, and whatever the future brought—*please, God, keep her healthy*—he'd face it knowing the consequences.

He leaned against the door and exhaled in a rush, then grinned again as he fumbled to let himself into his house. He laughed as he jogged up the stairs to the second floor, whistled a lively tune when he yanked his shirt over his head and groaned when he imagined Melissa's long legs wrapped around his waist while he made love to her in his bed. *Oh yeah.*

Why waste years chasing women he didn't care for when the one he loved was right in front of him?

All he had to do was convince her.

He'd told Joe he wanted a challenge. Now he definitely had one.

MELISSA COVERED the mouthpiece of the phone and glared at Bryan. *What?* she mouthed, uncomfortable with the way he stared at her now that the patients had gone for the day.

He moved into the reception area where she sat and leaned close. Her eyes widened, taking in his every move, and she thought she saw a smile curl his lips before he dropped the file he held onto the desk in front of her and reached out to gently snag the pen from her fingers. Standing where he was, retreat was impossible. She was stuck. Stuck sitting there with her nose practically in his chest, stuck inhaling and breathing in Bryan's all-male scent and wanting to taste his skin.

She fought the tantalizing images in her head and closed her eyes briefly. The memory of last night's dream returned in sensual detail. She'd learned that if she dreamed of Bryan stripped while she wore a T-shirt, things could progress fairly far.

"Melissa?"

Bryan's breath hit her mouth, and the moist heat made her look away and wet her lips with her tongue. Was that a groan? Was he leaning closer?

"I'm outta here!" Janice Reynolds, Bryan's registered nurse, headed down the hall toward them with ever-increasing speed. "This first day back has been enough to convince me I should retire."

Bryan slowly straightened, but instead of moving away, he turned and leaned against the desk, his long legs blocking the only escape Melissa had.

"You can't retire. You'd lose your Longaberger money and have to end the madness," he teased, referring to the specially made baskets and products. Janice collected them like kids collected trading cards. A basket here, a liner there. Pottery, accessories, even the purse she carried was Longaberger.

The older woman sighed dramatically. "I 'spose you're right. Guess that means you'll see me again tomorrow. But for now, I'm going to go play with my granddaughter and pretend Mrs. McCleary didn't tell me I gained at least ten pounds while I was off work. That woman…" She shook her head and rolled her eyes before she smiled at Melissa. "Melissa, sweetie, it's so good to have you in here. You've worked wonders!"

"Thank you. Although now that I've seen the difference in how things run with you here, I don't know how we made it through without you, so make *sure* you come back tomorrow," she begged with a laugh.

Janice smiled and waved and continued on her way toward the front door. "Bryan, you let that child go home as soon as she's done on the phone."

"Don't worry about Melissa," Bryan drawled. "I'll take good care of her."

Melissa stilled. Why did he make that sound enticing?

Bryan pushed himself up from the desk and followed Janice to the front door, staying long enough to watch her cross the street and drive away. He locked the door and retraced his steps. "Who are you on hold with?"

"One of the insurance companies. They're looking into something for— Bryan, no—" She tried to keep his finger from pressing the button to end the call but it was too late. Her hand landed on top of his. "Why did you do that? Now I'll have to call them back and wade through all the voice mail again. I *hate* voice mail."

"Don't we all. But forget that for now." With a quick move, he rotated his palm and grasped her hand, pulling her out of her chair and very close. "Come on, I'm in the mood…"

She blinked up at him. "Ex-excuse me?"

"For a run." His smile widened in slow, teasing degrees. "What'd you think I meant?"

A run, of course. She hadn't actually thought he was flirting with her. Not on a serious, get-her-into-bed level, anyway. Melissa tugged her hand free. She was in the mood for a run, too, but alone. Why tempt herself and wind up aching from a Bryan dream in the middle of the night. *Again*. "I need to work on the fund-raiser. You know, call the businesses on the sponsorship list?"

"It's after five. The businesses will be closed."

"Yes, but…"

"We'll put together a master list you can work on tomorrow—after our run."

"But—"

"Come with me. You know you want to."

He couldn't really have said that with enough emphasis to make her think—

Bryan grinned when she remained speechless. His gaze lowered, swept over her body and lingered on her legs. "I'll see you around Oak Street in fifteen minutes."

BRYAN ENJOYED running with Melissa. With her long legs, she could easily keep up with his pace and generate some speed when they inevitably wound up racing. But after hanging back to watch the sway of her hips one too many times and getting aroused by the sight of her bent over to stretch, he realized he hadn't thought his plan through by asking her to run with him.

They were in a public setting, and he couldn't make a move without everyone in town hearing about it. Like before, they jogged alongside the river, circled the statue in the park and slowed to a cool-down walk.

"The wedding is Saturday." The moment the words left his mouth he regretted them. They hadn't talked much during the run, but reminding her of her father's upcoming nuptials wasn't the way to go.

"Yeah, it—it is."

"Anyway, I, uh, checked on Ellen this morning before work and she's feeling better so that's good." He'd never felt so awkward talking to a woman, not since his pubescent teenage years.

Melissa blinked in surprise. "She was sick?"

"Your dad didn't tell you?"

Her head lowered. "We haven't seen much of each other lately. He goes to work while I'm getting ready, comes home after I'm in bed." She shot him a questioning glance. "What happened with Ellen? Is she okay?"

Melissa might not like the situation with her dad and Ellen, but she wasn't unkind. Quite the opposite. "She's fine now. She was just feeling a little under the weather." Bryan spotted a bench up ahead, the same one they'd shared before. "Hey, you hungry?"

"Not much."

"How about a cone, then? Come on, what flavor? Chocolate?"

She shook her head. "I'm really not—"

"You're not going to make me eat alone, are you?"

Three more steps, the corners of her mouth twitched with the makings of a smile. "Strawberry."

Like before, Melissa walked over to hold their spot while he ordered a strawberry ice-cream cone for her and a chicken sandwich and bottle of water for himself. He carried the lot of it over to where she sat and had just unwrapped his sandwich to take a bite when Melissa's tongue swept up the side of the cone and curled delicately back into her mouth.

He was hard in an instant.

"Something wrong with your sandwich?"

Bryan lowered the sandwich back onto the white bag he'd dug it out of and hoped the paper sack in his lap covered his lack of control. "It's fine. Just, uh, decided I needed a drink first." He drank half the bottle and stared at the Ohio River flowing by, imagining himself plunging into the cold depths. Under control once again, he forced himself to eat the sandwich without looking at her, not until he heard her biting into the crunchy cone. It was gone with a minimum of fuss and before he could stop it, his mind focused on how she'd taste.

"Melissa..." He glanced around them, noted far too many people and shot to his feet. "Come on."

"What? Where?"

He took her elbow in hand and urged her to her feet, down a path and into a wooded area closer to the water.

"Bryan? What's wrong?"

"I want to talk to you and I don't want an audience while I do it."

"Oh. Then maybe we should go back to the office?"

He couldn't take her there. It was too close to his bed. That thought brought with it another image and he groaned softly. Now that he'd made up his mind about Melissa, his body responded accordingly despite the need to get other business out of the way first. "Down there," he said, pointing. A large rock approximately four feet high and flat on top was up ahead of them. "Sit down. We need to get some things straight."

Her shoulders dropped. "Are you letting me go now that Janice is back?"

The trial period. He'd forgotten he'd told her they'd reevaluate things after a few weeks. "No. I'm good with you working there. Aren't you?"

"Yeah, but if it's not that..." Wide blue eyes stared up at him, infinitely wary.

"Stop worrying about the job, Melissa. You're doing fantastic." He ran a hand over his hair and caught her watching him before her gaze darted away and a blush stained her cheeks. He liked it that she still blushed. "I just wanted to tell you that...men don't require breasts to think a woman beautiful."

Melissa gasped and tried to hop off the rock. He stepped

close, crowding her until he pressed her against the rock. Leaning low, he placed both hands on the sun-warmed surface by her hips and stopped by sheer will when her succulent lips were a breath away. Now that he'd started, he couldn't turn back.

"Bryan, don't."

"Don't what?"

"Don't. Just *don't*. Don't play with me, don't humor me, don't treat me like a—a—"

"Woman?" he drawled huskily. "Melissa, you are a woman in every sense of the word."

"Don't play games. You think you know everything there is to know about me, but you *don't*. You've no idea what you're saying, no idea how—how *untrue* that is."

He leaned forward until she dropped down onto her elbows to maintain distance between them. Seated there on the rock, her legs stretched down to the ground, thighs pressed against his, Bryan let her feel his arousal. "This isn't a game, Melissa. You said all men are obsessed with breasts and I told you that wasn't true, but I didn't finish," he clarified, his focus dropping to her mouth. "Men like other things, as well." He shifted, balanced his weight on one hand, and relished the gasp she released. Slowly so as not to scare her, he cradled her jaw, getting her used to his touch before he pushed his fingers into her short hair. "They like hair so soft it feels like silk, and imagine how it would feel against their skin."

"B-Bryan."

He curled his fingers and smoothed his knuckles down her high cheekbone, over her mouth. "Full lips made to be kissed, that make them ache thinking about them." He leaned even closer, his mouth parting, his eyes holding hers when he dropped his head and licked the flesh he craved.

CHAPTER FIFTEEN

THE MOMENT Melissa opened her mouth, Bryan pulled away, slid his knuckles down her neck to her arm, careful to avoid all contact with her chest just yet. At her hips, he paused. "They *like* a heart-shaped rear that's tight and firm and just like—" he squeezed "—this."

Melissa's lashes lowered over her desire-laden eyes, her breathing deep and measured. He felt a surge of primal excitement because he knew the signs. Knew he turned her on and wasn't alone in how he felt.

"They like," he continued, sliding his open hand down her muscled thigh to grip and raise it until she cradled his hip perfectly, fit him perfectly, "long, beautiful legs, so they can imagine what their woman's legs will feel like wrapped around them."

He kissed her then, Ashley's reminder to make Melissa forget everything but him loud in his head. He stroked her tongue with his, slipped his arms beneath her back to protect her from the rock, and nudged her hips in a poor imitation of what he craved. He laid his soul bare, let her feel every inch of the erection she'd given him and hoped she understood he wanted so much more.

Bryan smothered her moan with his mouth and didn't let Melissa come up for air. He kissed her again and again. He wanted her hot and bothered and clinging to him, wanted her to forget her scars and think only of him and the pleasure they could achieve.

Her hands found his head and gripped his hair tight. She seemed torn between trying to pull him away and hold him close, all of it done with a strength he savored, a passion he craved. Her hands slid to his jaw, down his neck and shoulders, fingers splayed as though she wanted to touch every bit of skin she could. He had to concentrate to stay focused on her, block out her touch to keep from allowing her to distract him too much. Through it all, he never took his mouth from hers other than to repeatedly tease her by changing the angle of the kisses, slow strokes, gentle nudges, breath-altering explorations she not only met, but countered until he was counting backward in his head, struggling to maintain control.

She was the very essence of his dreams. So much so his legs shook with the effort of supporting himself. Groaning, he wrapped an arm around her and lifted her from the rock. He pivoted and sat down, arranging her so she was straddling him. He pressed her body close, glad the shorts they both wore provided little barrier.

Melissa whimpered in need and tore her mouth from his. Her eyes were closed, her chest rising and falling while she dragged in breaths she couldn't fully benefit from because he didn't stop his assault. Gently, he bit a tender spot in the crook of her neck and earned a mind-blowing squeeze when she tightened her thighs.

Just like he'd imagined.

"Bryan?"

"Shh…let me." Groaning roughly, he slid his hand from her back to her thigh, slid his fingers beneath the hem of her shorts and found the heat of her a moment later. She was ready for him. Aroused and needy and everything he could've possibly wanted. "Melissa…sweetheart. You feel so good. Let me make love to you. Let me see you—"

She flinched. "No. No, Bryan, let me—let me go!"

MELISSA CAME to awareness with a flash of unmitigated humiliation. A few kisses, a few touches, and she'd nearly let Bryan make love to her? In broad daylight? The buzzing sound located somewhere behind her became the low hum of a motorboat, probably within sight of them and able to— *What had she done?*

She untangled her legs from around his waist—how had they gotten *there?*—her body burning hot with embarrassment and cold with fear.

Her wobbly legs found the riverbank a split second before Bryan pulled her back and held her close. He ignored her squirming and muttering, his arms looped around her firmly enough that she couldn't break free.

"Shh, calm down and let's talk about this."

"No. You—how could you—*ooh!*"

"Keep your voice down. We're out of sight, but if someone hears you scream we'll have an audience."

She shut her mouth immediately. The last thing she wanted was for someone to find her like *this*. One look and they'd know what she'd—what had she done? Was she so desperate for comfort, for release, that she—

Melissa lowered her head in shame, tears stinging her eyes. A few strokes of Bryan's hand and she would've done just that; even now her body quivered and ached. All for a man she didn't have a chance of keeping.

He kissed her shoulder. "Don't. I can practically hear your mind churning, but it isn't going to work. You can't escape what just happened."

"What *shouldn't* have happened."

He kissed the same spot again, his five-o'clock shadow rasping over her skin and drawing a shiver she couldn't suppress.

"Do you have any idea how sexy you are? How sexy it is that I almost made you—"

"Shut *up!*" Melissa elbowed him hard in the ribs and her jab earned her blessed release. She scrambled away from him. Thankfully, Bryan stayed where he was, an amused expression on his too-gorgeous face. "What? Is Bang 'em Booker so desperate he's resorted to banging his—"

"You say one word to put yourself down and I'll show you desperate."

Meaning what? Given the look on his face, she wasn't sure she wanted to find out what retribution would entail, but at the same time, her pulse jumped at the thought.

"I'm not that man anymore, Melissa. I haven't been for quite a while now."

"So you're saying your reputation is all fictitious?" She snorted. "Don't lie about it, Bryan. If a female had your reputation she'd be called all sorts of nasty names."

"It's not all a lie," he admitted. "I took advantage of some of the offers made because I could. Because I felt the need for control. I'd lost someone I cared about, that I'd fought to help save but couldn't, and it hit me hard. I could control the other, the sex. Then the paper came out declaring me the so-called winner and the offers increased. But once I realized there was nothing more unsatisfying than meaningless sex, I stopped taking advantage but by then the damage was done."

"Oh, poor baby," she drawled. "That doesn't explain why you— Why didn't you leave me alone?" Melissa clenched her hands into fists, the urge to hit something strong. "You had no right to kiss me! To *touch* me!" *To make me want you!*

"You enjoyed it. Deny it and I'll show you differently."
Bryan shoved himself off the rock and stalked toward her. "I
want you, and you need to know that. I want to prove to you
what an incredibly sexy, desirable woman you are and—
Melissa, we're not finished with this. *Stop!*"

She swung around, her mad dash to escape temporarily
halted. "Why? You want to screw me against a tree? Back on
the rock? Guess it might work." Her chin raised and she
played her last ace, desperate enough, scared enough, to want
him to feel the same way. "So long as I didn't take my shirt
off. But if I did, what would you do then? *Huh?* I'll tell you
what. *That*—" she waved a hand at his still obvious erection
"—will fizzle fast. You'd look away in horror and be sick with
disgust because I…I…"

"You didn't have reconstructive surgery."

Shock rippled through her. "How do you know that? You
asked someone that about me?"

"Does it matter?" He moved closer slowly, one step at a
time. "I knew it when I kissed you. I knew it when I listed all
the things I think are beautiful about you. Had you not pulled
away, I wouldn't have stopped." His voice lowered. "And if
you take your top off right now, if you let me see you, I'll tell
you the same things, *do* the same things, all over again."

She swallowed tightly, the lump in her throat too big.
Maybe he wanted her, maybe he even thought he could handle
her body, but what then? She couldn't handle Bryan. His
looks. The women. She'd had two boyfriends in her whole
life because she didn't date unless she *really* liked a guy.

She couldn't *be* with Bryan and not— "I'll help you with
the fund-raiser," she whispered, her voice taut, hoarse. "And
I'll keep working for you. But if you ever t-touch me like that
again, I'll—"

"Run away? It's what you're doing with every step backward you take. You want to know if I have the guts to make love to you?" he asked, following her, drawing ever closer. Too close. "Come here and I'll show you. If not here, let me take you somewhere. Back to my house, a hotel. Let me show you what you're afraid of, Melissa. Prove to you there's no reason for you to be afraid, not with me."

His words had her curiosity aroused again, wondering. Could he? "Your ego is amazing."

"It's not ego that makes me want you."

"I refuse to be another Bang 'em Booker *conquest!*"

"Then be more."

Fear tore at her, unquenchable hope. Why would he say something like that? He couldn't mean it. It was a ploy, a line guys like him used to get women into their beds. Her evil conscience snickered in her head. *Other women, maybe, but her?*

Havoc-wreaking doubts made her shake, but it was the need in Bryan's eyes that shot pure terror through her. She wanted him, too. Liked him. Had grown close to him working side by side, running with him. Laughing with him. But she couldn't. Of all the people she couldn't stand to have leave her when he couldn't follow through on his words, it would be Bryan.

Beautiful, perfect Bryan.

Without a word, Melissa turned on her heel and ran back to the path. She continued running out of the park, all the way back to the house. Away from him, away from temptation. Away from everything. Especially the mocking voice in her head that said she was the coward her father accused her of being.

"I'M GLAD YOU'RE HOME." Hal stared at his daughter's tear-pinched features and figured Booker had made a move on her.

One she apparently hadn't been receptive to. Problem was, he didn't know if he should be glad or sad that she'd turned the doc down.

Now there was a dilemma for a father to be in.

After her mother's surgery it had taken a while to convince his wife he loved more than her breasts. But they'd fallen back on their years spent together, the child they shared. Experiences Mel didn't have.

"I'm going to work here tonight," she murmured huskily.

"Booker got a woman at his place?"

"No, he—no." Mel added a tea bag to the mug on the counter and drummed her fingers impatiently at the kettle heating on the stove. "Bryan, um, mentioned Ellen has been sick?"

He pulled out a chair and sat down at the table, hoping she'd do the same. They'd avoided each other long enough. They needed to talk, get things sorted out. "Morning sickness, a really bad case of it. Her doc gave her something to help today and she says she's already feeling better, but she's still weak and pale. She took a few days off work." He rested his arms on the table and clasped his hands, hating that he seemed to want the impossible. "Mel...I'm leaving tonight." He looked up in time to see her lose what little color she had in her cheeks and shoved himself to his feet in case he needed to catch her. "Sit down. Please?"

The kettle began to whistle. It took her a second to move, but she poured the steaming water into the cup and then crossed the room. He had a feeling her slow, deliberate steps were to buy time, adjust to what he'd said. He couldn't blame her. It would take him some time to adjust to all the changes taking place, as well.

"Why are you leaving tonight? I mean, you're not getting

arried until Saturday. Won't it look badly if the chief and
is girlfriend are living together?"

"I think it would look worse if people thought I didn't care
nough about my future wife and child that I let them stay
lone knowing she's having such a hard time."

"You said she was feeling better."

"She isn't throwing up every few minutes, but she's still
izzy. What if she falls down the stairs? I found her lying on
he bathroom floor last night, too sick to even call for help. You
now what that's like. Could you leave her there?" He sat down
vhen she did, taking in her bleak expression and hardening his
eart out of sheer will. Mel was okay. Of the two women in his
ife, his daughter didn't need him as much as Ellen did right now.

"I'm…I'm going to miss you." She didn't look up from
ner mug, but her lower lip trembled the way it had when she
was little.

That trembling lip had ripped his heart out more than once.
"Mel, this isn't— Sweetheart, I *love* you. I'll always love you
and I only want what's best for you. You know that, right?"
A weak nod was his answer. "So listen to me. If you *ever* need
any help with the bills or projects around here, ever need to
talk or just want some company, you are to call me. Come see
me. Understand?" She didn't respond. "Melissa Ann, you
will always be my little girl. Always be the best example of
the love I held for your mother."

"But that's over now."

"My love for her will never be over, but I can love more
than one person, Mel. Just like I can love more than one
child. I love you, and the baby Ellen carries."

Her nose turned red at the tip and a tear trickled down her
cheek. "I just wish…"

"What?"

She sniffled, shaking her head mutely. Her hand trembled visibly when she lifted it to wipe away the tears, and a raw laugh escaped her chest.

"Wishes can come true, Mel. So can dreams. It's all in what you believe, all in your faith."

"Maybe."

"No, not maybe. God's proved that to both of us by healing you."

She blinked once and sniffled. "Then why not heal Mom?"

Hal hesitated a long moment. How many times had he asked himself that question. "Maybe God thought the angels needed a new soprano. Your mama did love to sing."

She tried to smile and the effort was painful to watch. A sad attempt at pride he recognized too well.

"I've never thought of it that way...Dad." She shoved herself up from the table. "I'll help you p-pack."

"It's done."

"Oh." She sat down in the chair again. "Oh, well...okay."

He raked a hand through his hair. "Mel, about Saturday. Please come. I can't imagine getting married without my daughter there. And I know it's unusual, and probably not something you want to do under the circumstances, but instead of a best man, I'd like you to be my witness, to stand up with me and...show your support."

"I can't do that." She pressed her fingers to her mouth as though to hold back a sob and inhaled deeply. "I couldn't do that to M-Mom."

"What about what you're doing to me?" Hal sat there a long moment. "Never mind," he murmured finally. "You and your mother were very close, and after everything you've been through with your cancer, you feel even closer. I understand that. But would you have wanted her to deny love?"

He got to his feet and scooted the chair back into position beneath the table, closing the distance between them. He leaned over and kissed her head, rubbing her shoulder gently. "Mel, this isn't goodbye. It's a new beginning. And whether you realize it or not, Ellen, the baby and I want you along for the ride."

Melissa didn't respond. Couldn't with the lump clogging her throat.

"I love you, sweetheart." Silent, her father walked out of the kitchen, the door swinging back and forth behind him the way it always had.

Only this time it *was* different. The problem with beginnings was that there was an ending preceding them. She heard the front door shut, her dad's cruiser start, its powerful engine roar as it pulled away. The house was silent; she was alone. And she didn't want to be.

"Oh, *Mom…*" The sobs she'd held back tore out of her chest. She wanted to feel again and hated Bryan because he made her feel too much. Made her want more than was possible. "Mom, *please…*" She wrapped her arms around her stomach, hugging herself tight because there wasn't anyone else there to do it. "I need you *so much*. I miss you so much. Sing a song for me."

BRYAN GLARED down at the file in front of him, unseeing.

"What's got your shorts in a knot?" Janice entered his office and dropped two files on his desk. "Mrs. Case is here. She just peed on a stick and it's positive. Want me to go over the basics and refer her to Dr. Amos?"

"Sure…thanks, Janice."

"Uh-huh. Now tell me what a foot doctor is going to do to help a pregnant woman?"

Pulled from his brooding, he blinked. "Huh?"

"You just told me to send a pregnant woman to a foot doctor."

He sat forward in his chair and rubbed his hands over his face roughly. "Sorry. I didn't sleep much last night and it's catching up with me."

Janice helped herself to one of the seats across from his desk. "Looks like Melissa is having the same problem today." She glared at him. "You mess up the best office help in here since your grandfather retired, and I'll kick your butt from here to his house so he can ream you out himself." She wagged a finger at him. "Are you messin' with that sweet girl?"

"No." He glared right back. "Melissa has made it perfectly clear she wants nothing to do with me."

"So you *tried?* What am I asking? Of course you did." Janice's disgust changed to a snicker. "Well, now ain't that a first. Don't think I've ever heard a single story about a woman turning you *down*. We need to mark this on the calendar. Where's a pen?"

"Did you need something?" His tone must have been a good indication of his mood because Janice got to her feet and ambled over to the door.

"You know, maybe I do have one more thing to say."

He bit back a groan. "What?"

"Heard a little while ago that Hal York moved in next door. Saw him carrying a box myself. Must be hard for Melissa to be alone all of a sudden after twenty-some years in that house there together."

"And your point is?"

"Melissa's not happy about her daddy surprising her with his marriage. Told me she wasn't going to the wedding. I think a date by her side would change her mind. Boost her confidence."

He leaned back in the chair and rubbed the bristle he'd forgotten to shave from his jaw. "Didn't you just tell me to leave her alone?"

"Yes, but I also didn't indicate you should be her date. You got any friends?"

"Janice."

"I suppose you could escort her to her daddy's wedding and *then* leave her alone. If anything would set her daddy on end, it would be seeing you beside his little girl."

Ah, now the truth came out. "And you want the chief set on end because…?"

Janice lifted her chin with a sniff. "The chief of police is gettin' married, has attended our church for years and he doesn't ask my Roger to officiate the ceremony? That's not nice."

He grinned, pretty sure the chief hadn't asked because of Ellen's delicate circumstances. "I'd say Hal's been friends with the judge a long time, too. Maybe he asked because of that?"

The older woman crossed her arms over her ample chest. "I'm just saying he should've asked Roger to officiate or else given him a reason why not. And if I were you, I wouldn't be making fun and teasing me when your ego looks to have taken a blow. You haven't said two words to Melissa all day."

"I haven't exactly heard her saying two words to me."

She shook her head at him. "But you're a man, and everyone knows men are typically at fault."

Bryan shook his head and waited until the R.N. left his office before he gave in and laughed. Maybe Janice had a point. Melissa might bluster up to the last second about not attending, but she'd go to the wedding. No way would she miss it. It wasn't in her to hurt her father that way.

But like Janice said, it didn't mean Melissa wouldn't want to ruffle her father's feathers. After all, who wanted to attend a wedding alone?

THE REST OF THE WEEK crawled by at a snail's pace, and September arrived with blessedly cooler temps.

Melissa went about her business and endured Bryan's questioning stares as best she could, attempting to do the same with the women parading through the office, but not succeeding. Bryan was a good doctor, but she and Janice both rolled their eyes at the number of women entering the reception area for their appointments dressed in skimpy outfits, full makeup and healthy smiles—all to gain Bryan's handsome, doctorly attention.

Attention she didn't want. So why was she sick every time one of those women came in? And why did she come up with excuses to walk by the exam rooms and make sure Janice was present and accounted for?

Five o'clock rolled around, the last of Bryan's fan club was gone, and she couldn't wait to go home even though she had nothing to go home to. Maybe she should check into getting a pet?

"Can you stay tonight? We need to finalize things for the kickoff next week."

Melissa kept her back to Bryan and scrunched her face up in a grimace. "I, um, can't. Stay here, that is. I have to… I'll work on it at home."

"Melissa—" Bryan stepped into the small area on her side of the counter, his large frame taking up all the extra space. "Stay. I won't kiss you unless you want me to."

Want him to? "That won't happen."

"Then you have nothing to worry about, do you?"

"YOU LOOK LIKE a woman with a secret," Ashley murmured in her ear when Melissa bent close to kiss Issy's head. "Give it up."

"Sorry, no secret."

"Then why the red face?" her friend pressed.

"It's anxiety over…today."

"Hmm. About the wedding or what your dad's going to say when he stops hovering over Ellen long enough to realize Bryan is your *date?*"

"It's not a date. We were both coming to the wedding and since we left the office at the same time, we decided to ride together."

"Is that what they're calling it these days? Then just why did I have to loan you a dress?"

Despite her willing it away, heat suffused her face. How on earth could she have fallen asleep in Bryan's arms? She didn't even remember him sitting on the couch beside her! "I, um, didn't have time to shop." She glanced at Ashley and quickly away. "Besides, I've always wanted an excuse to borrow this dress."

"It's two sizes too big for you."

"But she still looks gorgeous in it, doesn't she, Joe?" Bryan moved to her side and smiled down at her, the grin predatory.

Melissa looked away, flushing, her body's instant response making her want to groan. "I think I'm going to go see—"

"Absolutely," Joe agreed with a nod, sliding his arm around his wife's shoulder and pulling her close. "You made your old man proud, Mel. He was barking orders left and right, worrying you wouldn't show."

"What changed your mind?" Ashley asked softly. "When you didn't come to the rehearsal last night I wondered if you'd show up this morning."

Melissa lifted her shoulder in a self-conscious shrug, ignoring Bryan's sparkling eyes and the fact Ashley's comment about him being her date had hit home. Had she hoped by arriving with Bryan her dad would call things off? "I realized it was something my mom would've wanted me to do, that's all."

On the patio her dad held Ellen close, the small wedding cake in front of them ready to be cut and the photographer hovering nearby.

"So," Joe murmured when silence followed her words, "what's this I hear about you spending the night with Bryan?"

CHAPTER SIXTEEN

ASHLEY'S HEAD SWUNG around with the speed of a rocket, her mouth agape. "*That's* why you needed a dress? You spent the night with Bryan?"

Melissa glared at Joe, still refusing to look at the man next to her or acknowledge Bryan's datelike behavior. "I fell asleep on Bryan's *couch* after working on the fund-raiser, which you are expected to attend."

"Don't even attempt to change the subject." Ashley looked at Bryan, her stare hard and unflinching. "And *you* just remember what I said."

"What did you say?" Melissa questioned. "What are you talking about?"

"May I have your attention, please? The bride and groom are going to have their first dance, and then at the bride's request, there will be a special dance for the groom and his daughter."

A special *what?* Her stomach fell to her knees. Sitting behind her father with her back to the crowd while he promised to love another woman besides her mother was one thing, but dancing with him with everyone watching? Pretending she was here because she wanted to be?

Music began to play and Melissa turned in her seat, intending to leave while she could. A firm hand grasped her arm and held her in place. Bryan. She knew his touch. *A little too well now.*

"Don't embarrass your father by stalking out. Lift your chin, smile and do whatever you have to do to get through the dance. Then I'll take you home."

Her dad and Ellen danced for the photographer and the small crowd of invited guests. Then it was her turn. Bryan escorted her onto the patio and placed her hand in her dad's, then gallantly asked Ellen to dance. Bryan led the woman in a modified waltz, but Ellen's gaze stayed on her, worried, when she and her father stood there unmoving.

"Remember when you used to put your feet on top of mine and we'd dance?"

Like it was yesterday. "Vaguely."

"Come on, Mel. For old time's sake?"

She allowed him to pull her close and give her a hug. Melissa closed her eyes and relished the moment, heard the photographer snapping away. Melissa concentrated on putting her feet in the proper place, tried to make peace with herself and her feelings and enjoyed the feel of her father's protective arms.

This would probably be the last dance she ever got to share with him. She'd best enjoy it while it lasted.

THE BASKETBALL SHOOT-OUT, cook-off and festival would've ended on a good note if not for her father and his on-duty officers being called away for yet another break-in. The fall weather was perfect and cooperative, the deep rich colors of the decorations vibrant and beautiful amid the oranges and reds and yellows of the maples planted throughout the park.

Melissa smiled wearily at Nathan when he moseyed over to where she sat beneath a shade tree that repeatedly pelted her with falling leaves, and tried to squelch the awareness she felt when Bryan noticed Nathan's presence.

"Looks like another winner for you, Mel."

"Not for me, for all of us. The clinic is definitely needed."

Nathan grabbed a chair from nearby and twisted it around to straddle it, leaning his arms across the back. "Hey, I've been giving this a lot of thought and—"

"Looks like you're up at the dunking booth, Nate." Bryan smiled. "Better not be late or Mrs. H. will give you grief about being tardy."

Nathan didn't look pleased by the interruption—or Bryan's shortened version of his name. Obviously reluctant, he got to his feet. "Mel, can we talk later? Maybe grab some coffee?"

"Um…"

"She'll be busy."

She rolled her eyes at Bryan before smiling at Nathan. "Sure." Ignoring Bryan's glare, she watched Nathan walk away, her mind comparing the officer's dark coloring to Bryan's. Rubbing her head, she studiously marked Nathan's name off the list in front of her and noted a volunteer switch was due at the concession stand where the food from this morning's cook-off was being sold.

Solid hands landed on her tense shoulders and began to rub. "Bryan…" That was all she could get past her lips because she had to clamp them closed to hold in a moan.

"The look on your face," Bryan drawled huskily. His breath hit her ear and made a shiver race down her spine. "That's a look I could easily get addicted to." His lips brushed her temple. "I liked holding you last night."

She couldn't believe she'd done it again. "I'm so sorry I fell asleep on your couch. I guess the late hours are getting to me." She knew better than to ask why he hadn't woken her up.

"I didn't mind."

Uh-huh. "Still i-it won't happen again."

"I hope it does."

"Bryan."

"Have you dreamed of us yet, Melissa? Thought about what would've happened if you'd let me keep touching you that day by the river?"

She lost the ability to breathe, her lashes too heavy to hold up. "No. Now go away. I'm working."

A rich, masculine chuckle rumbled out of his chest. "So you'll sleep in my arms, accept my massage but shoot down my questions?"

"Hush, Bryan, please? And you shouldn't touch me like that," she said, shrugging her shoulders ineffectively to loosen his hold. "People will talk even more."

"I've dreamed about us. Actually, I think about that day and what could've happened all the time. When I bit your neck right here—" his fingers pressed a particular area, his touch equivalent to a lightning strike "—you tightened your legs around me and almost made me—"

"Bryan!"

"I backed off to give you time to adjust to being on your own, but I haven't given up. Have you figured that out yet?"

She had. But she still didn't know what to do about it. If she gave in to Bryan and they made love—then what? He'd move on, that much she knew for sure. It was inevitable. But part of her, the part practically panting at the mere touch of his hands on her shoulders, begged to see if Bryan could get her through her first experience with sex postmastectomy. Wanted to know, just once, if it would be as unbelievable as it was in her dreams, as amazing as it had been in the park.

Bryan's hands slowed and, unbidden, she leaned her head back and looked up at him, her head brushing against him where he stood behind her. His jaw clenched tight, his eyes broadcasting his need and making no effort to hide it from her, as though—

As though she was the only one to turn him on?

A grim smile crossed his face. "This isn't the place for me to do what I want to you, but I promise you, Melissa, one day soon you're going to look at me like that and I'm going to kiss you until you forget everything—*everything*—but me. Got that?"

She swallowed, her blood heated at the thought, but even though she wanted so badly to open her mouth and protest, she didn't. She couldn't. Because she wanted it, too.

LATER THAT EVENING, Melissa left the shower, glad the successful day was over, and dreading the other events taking place tomorrow. She dried off, then wrapped the towel around her before leaving the bathroom and entering her bedroom. The first thing she noticed was the picture of her mother on her bedside table, the one her father had left in his bedroom when he'd moved out.

She'd talked to him once since the wedding, the conversation short and uncomfortable. He'd always worked long hours, but she'd still seen a lot of him when they'd lived together. She missed those casual moments they'd had.

Melissa picked up the photograph and stared at her mother's face, tracing her fingers over her features and remembering Bryan's breath-stealing promise. "How'd you do it, Mom? Even married to Dad, how did you let him?"

She set the frame back beside her alarm clock and walked to her dresser to pull out pajamas. Another hard, early day awaited her tomorrow. She reached for the drawer and the towel came untucked. Before she could catch it, the length of damp cotton fell to her feet. She looked up, frozen at the sight of herself in the mirror.

She squeezed her eyes shut, incapable of looking directly at her chest. She'd looked right after her surgery.

Turning so that her back was to the mirror, she searched for her favorite pj set but couldn't find it, and exhausted tears seeped into her eyes. Grabbing another pair, she shut the drawer with her foot, her gaze winding up on the mirror again. Biting her lip, she stared at the length of her back, her rear. Heart shaped?

She wrinkled her nose and eyed her butt again, frowning, critiquing. Her legs were long and toned, her hips dipping in at her waist and giving it good definition. She twisted, turning to face the mirror a little more though not too far, her arms protectively shielding.

A decently flat stomach. The scar from her cesarean ran horizontal rather than vertical and was mostly invisible thanks to time. Josie had been a small baby, a preemie. The only stretch marks she'd had were on her—

Do it. Look. She'd learned early on to close her eyes while bathing, and trained herself to shave her legs without once looking there because if she did—

She raised her hands to where her breasts would have been, *should* have been, and touched lightly. She always kept a washcloth and soap between her hand and skin. Always. But now…

"Nothing," she whispered, sliding her fingertips down her flat chest, over the tiny pinpoints marking her radiation spots.

Marks she'd have forever. Her breasts were gone, the nerve endings severed. Her body mutilated by surgery but saved from a cancer running rampant. Nothing left, but what had she gained? In the end would it really help her? *Save* her?

"Don't buy into it. You know better than to listen. They're *wrong*." So why was it getting harder and harder to turn Bryan down? To resist his teasing, his touch? The way he made her feel? When she'd woken up in his arms—

Dear Lord, why? *Why* her, why—

Why did she suddenly want to believe she could have more?

CHAPTER SEVENTEEN

HAL WAS GETTING tired of fielding complaints from Taylorsville's citizens and city officials because he and his men had been unable to catch the druggie breaking in and abusing the elderly before stealing their medications.

October had ended with cold temperatures, and now bits of snow flew through the November air and dusted the ground. Maybe they'd have a white Christmas. In this part of southern Ohio, Christmas could be snowy and cold, or balmy and warm.

He spotted a flash of light at the side of a house a ways off the road. Slowing, he waited patiently and sure enough, the light came again. Near a window. Calling for backup, he drove up the grass-spotted asphalt driveway. The moment he opened the door, he heard screams and shouting from inside.

Hal pulled his gun from his holster and ran for the door. "Police, open up!" He paused for a split second when the screams turned into terrified sobs, and it took four kicks to the well- made door before it finally flew inward with a crash.

He moved inside cautiously, listening, trying to stay shielded. Hands grabbed hold of his legs, startling him, and he swore when he realized he'd nearly stepped on the homeowner lying on the floor.

"Help me," Mrs. McCleary begged. "Please. He hurt Richard. He hurt my Richard." Sobs ripped through the woman clinging to him. "Don't leave us. Please don't leave."

Tires squealed from somewhere outside the house, and Hal bit back a curse. So close. He holstered his weapon and bent. "Where's Richard?"

"QUIT WORRYING."

"I *can't*," Ashley murmured in response to her husband's order. "I'm nervous for her. The fund-raisers have covered the basics, but it's going to take a lot more money to complete the clinic and Melissa's worked hard getting donations to auction. What if people don't bid? She'll be so disappointed if tonight isn't a success. Bryan, too."

Bryan closed the distance between him and his friends, humbled that Ashley cared so much about him and Melissa, and entertained by Joe's tie-strangled appearance.

"Ashley won, huh?"

Ashley turned with a smile. "Hi, Bryan. Don't get him started again, please? I told Joe I had to see him in a tux at least once, and after discovering there was a band, I insisted it be tonight."

"Yeah, thanks for doing this," Joe drawled with sarcasm, but the look in Joe's eyes when he looked at his wife said he didn't mind as much as he let on. Possibly because Ashley wore a bright red, cleavage-baring dress that showed off her lush figure and dark hair to perfection. Melissa's comment about a woman's chest being the first thing men notice rang in his head, and Bryan made a conscious effort not to look.

"Everything looks so romantic." She tilted her head to one side, her expression thoughtful. "Who are you here with?"

Joe turned his head as though scanning the crowd, mur
muring, "Subtle," near his wife's ear. He couldn't blame her
The past month had been a steady ebb and flow, trying to ear
Melissa's trust only to have her shy away.

"I'm not here with a date."

After months of working with Melissa, teasing her, flirtin
with her and having her falling asleep on his couch twice only
to wake up and bolt for the door, he was starting to believ
he *was* losing his touch. He'd become a recluse who rarel
left the office except to visit his granddad. Offers he wasn
interested in continued to come his way, but in the mood he'
been in of late, they were fewer and farther between. Not tha
he minded. Only one woman appealed.

"Looks like someone else is dateless. Imagine that."

Prodded by Ashley's announcement, Bryan turned. Stand
ing in the doorway of the Baxter Grand Marquis Hotel'
ballroom stood Melissa. She wore a shimmery ice-blue gow
held in place with thin straps at her shoulders. From there th
gown draped over her chest in long layers, a slit dipping low
nearly to her stomach, revealing a kiss-provoking V of ski
between her—

Bryan scowled. The draped front was enough to mak
Melissa's lack of breasts a nonissue, at least where her attir
was concerned, but it also made a man want to tug the stra
from her shoulder and feel her skin.

"Wow. Doesn't she look wonderful?"

Wow was right. Melissa turned to say something to
member of the hotel staff, and Bryan fought the urge t
remove his jacket and place it over her shoulders. Like th
front, the V dipped low in back, this time all the way to th
small of her back.

"Where did she get that dress?"

Ashley laughed at his tone. "That little ol' thing? I helped her find it online. Gorgeous, isn't it?"

"Nathan thinks so," Joe added.

Bryan focused on the officer moving toward Melissa. Uncaring about the gossip it would incite, he crossed the room in hurried strides and reached Melissa first, but only because Nathan had been held up by Melissa's father.

The chief caught his eye and Bryan nodded once in thanks. Then he grasped her arm in a light grip and brushed her mouth with a kiss. Let Nathan, Hal and the rest of the town interpret that. He was staking a public claim for all to see and see it they did. Melissa's wasn't the only gasp he heard.

"Bryan, what are you *doing?*"

He smiled into her upturned face. "Saying hello. You look absolutely amazing."

"Thank you." The silvery shadow on her eyelids sparkled when she looked down. "But you've got to stop saying things like that—and doing...*that.*"

"I mean it, why not say it?" He lifted her face with a hand under her chin. "And do it? You're beautiful and I want you. *All* of you. And if you'll let me, I'll take you upstairs and prove it. So...will you?"

"Will she what?" Hal asked from nearby, his voice a low grumble.

Melissa jerked away from him and backed up a step. "Um...nothing. Bryan was just—just..."

"I was just telling Melissa how amazing she looks."

"The doc's right about that," her father agreed. "You look great, Mel."

She kept her attention focused on her father and tried to breathe. "Thank you. You're looking pretty handsome yourself all dressed up."

Her dad patted Ellen's hand and the two exchanged a look. "Mel, you've got the week off with the groundbreaking coming up, and Ellen and I would like to invite you over for lunch or dinner. Will you come?"

She'd concentrated so hard on getting ready for the auction, scheduling the event so that the gala kicked off Baxter's Winter Festival of Lights, she'd almost forgotten about being off all next week. Bryan closed his practice for a week every spring and summer, and since he'd missed his summer vacation due to the problems at the office, he'd planned a winter break instead to coincide with the ground-breaking.

"Oh...well, thanks, but—"

"Don't say no. Just think about it."

"We would both like to see you." Ellen's smile appeared strained. "I'd like to get to know you better, Melissa, and...um—oh, no. Please excuse me!"

Melissa watched as Ellen turned and ran toward the exit behind her, a hand over her mouth. Bryan, her dad and she followed Ellen, but all of them came to an abrupt stop outside the well-marked ladies' room.

Her father began to pace, his expression anxious. "She gets sick when she gets nervous," he muttered darkly. He looked at her, at Bryan. Glanced at his watch and then at the door once more.

"I'm sure she's fine, Chief."

"The doc says it's all the hormones, but she gets dizzy sometimes and..." He stared at Melissa, but when she didn't move, her father headed purposefully toward the door.

A woman emerged, her shock at seeing a man about to enter apparent. "That's the ladies' room."

"I can read."

The woman sniffed and stuck her nose in the air. "Then you know you *can't* go in there," she said before tottering away. Every few seconds she looked back to make sure he hadn't budged.

"I'll go," Melissa murmured reluctantly.

His shoulders sagged with relief. "Thank God. Get in there, and let me know if she's okay."

Bryan smiled at her. "I'll take the chief and go find Ellen some water. We'll be right back if you need us."

She nodded and watched their broad shoulders head back toward the ballroom. "Traitors." Inhaling, she entered the restroom and wrinkled her nose at the unmistakable sound of retching. She spied a stack of paper towels and grabbed a bunch, dampening them with cold water before locating the only closed stall. "Ellen?"

By then the retching had stopped, and she heard a few quiet gasps, sniffles. The toilet flushed, and moments later an extremely pale Ellen opened the stall door. She flushed when she saw Melissa standing there, the color in her cheeks stark against her sickly white skin.

"Here, I thought maybe they'd help." She waited until Ellen accepted the towels before she put her arm around the woman's shoulders and led her over to the lounge area. She could feel Ellen trembling. "Sit down. Bryan and Dad went to get you some water, but they'll be here soon."

Ellen's lips lifted up at the corners. "Your father will probably barge in here and scare someone off."

"Actually, he already tried. Don't be surprised if security is outside when we leave," she joked.

Ellen's rueful chuckle sounded hoarse and weak. "Melissa—"

"Ellen—"

"Wait. Me, first," Ellen insisted. "I'm feeling better, but I don't know how long it'll last before…" She waved a hand toward the stalls.

Melissa nodded, praying this talk would go better than their last, and knowing she had to do something to end the tension among all of them. It was time to grow up and face the decision her father had made. Past time. She wasn't a child anymore and she couldn't view her father's marriage from that perspective. She had to face it like an adult, see it like an adult. "Okay."

"I—I can't *stand* the thought of you hating me or my baby," Ellen murmured, lowering her eyes when they flooded with tears. "I don't want that at all."

"Ellen, I don't hate you, or my little brother or sister." The rush to reassure her father's wife was there, automatic, but not insincere. "It's just been a surprise, the suddenness of it, but I'm—" she sighed "—getting used to it."

"I understand that." Ellen's expression turned sheepish. "Believe me, I understand. I'd long ago given up hope of ever having my own family and contented myself with my work. Now I have a—a stepdaughter and a baby on the way. It's very overwhelming." She folded the unused towels and placed them on the back of her neck.

"Guess Dad hovering around all the time probably isn't helping much, huh? I mean, he's great, but he defines stubborn."

Ellen laughed softly, nodding. "Oh, most definitely. That man, when he decided we were going to date, I couldn't turn him down. Although I tried at first." She leaned against the overstuffed cushions with a dreamy smile, her eyes closed. "He made me forget all about my protests."

"My dad?"

She nodded, raising her lids to look at her. "Your dad. Then I couldn't imagine myself with anyone else, much less alone."

"What changed your mind?" she asked, thinking of Bryan and the way he looked at her.

Ellen blushed and lowered her lashes again, her expression turning so winsome and revealing, Melissa couldn't look away despite her shock.

"I was in his office one day going over a few things and he kissed me. It was a surprise to say the least. I think for him, too. But he took my breath away, and I knew then and there he—he meant what he said. He didn't look at me like some men view a widow—" she scrunched her face up in a telling grimace "—but like a woman. I couldn't say no and he knew it, the devil. I didn't stand a chance after that."

A knock sounded at the door followed by her father's urgent, worried call from the other side. Melissa rose and opened the door. Her dad saw Ellen and stalked inside without hesitating. Melissa held the door and watched the tender concern her dad showed Ellen. The way he fussed until he knew she was okay, then teased her about upchucking in a fancy hotel.

"Come on," Bryan murmured, his lips close to her ear. "Let's leave them alone. The auction is about to start."

She nodded, not looking at him, her thoughts buffeted by a sea of emotions that threatened to drag her under. Emotions that made her think Bryan could keep her afloat.

Had he meant what he'd said earlier? Would he really take her upstairs and make love to her? More important—did she have the courage to find out?

THREE HOURS LATER the local auctioneer left the stage, grinning from ear to ear at a job well done. The man had vol-

unteered his services and auctioned off everything from denta
visits and landscaping, to restaurant dinners, gift baskets
golf-club memberships and a car from a local dealership. I
typical auction style, the per-plate attendees laughed at the
auctioneer's not-so-funny jokes and outbid each other with
competitive glee.

Before that, Bryan and Melissa had stood onstage and
given out awards for the generous donations of some of the
businesses. Then, to honor the man of the evening, Melissa
had surprised him and his granddad both with a photo pre-
sentation using the many pictures displayed throughout his
grandfather's home. Only a handful had been used for advertising, but Bryan had watched the show with everyone else,
his gut tight, hand clenched on the untouched drink he held
because so many of the pictures included him and his
granddad together.

And then he realized what Melissa had done. Three
hundred of Taylorsville and Baxter's citizens watched him
grow up on screen. Most of the pictures had been taken during
the three consecutive summers he'd spent there, others from
visits made over the years, summers and holidays and special
occasions. Melissa had showcased Granddad's travels and ad-
ventures during the lack of photos of Bryan's teenaged years,
but no one seemed to notice. All they saw was that he was
one of them, not an outsider, but the next generation of Taylorsville's family physician.

Going onstage to give his speech about why establishing
the clinic was so important to him was easy to do after that
because Melissa had done the groundwork and gained the
audience's support with images of the good it would do all
of them. She'd watched with tears sparkling in her eyes while
he revealed his hopes for the future, that of following in his

grandfather's footsteps and growing old in a town that cared for its own.

Bryan thought he saw a look of longing on Melissa's expressive face when he talked of the years ahead. But was it real? Had she realized the emptiness in her life because of her attitude?

The auctioneer returned and asked for everyone's attention. Bryan got choked up watching Meg wheel his grandfather onstage to hear the grand total announced. Added to what Bryan had already saved and the sum his grandfather himself had donated, the urgent-care clinic was funded in full.

Thunderous applause roared through the room. Bryan hugged his granddad a long time, neither of them wanting or able to let go.

Later Meg and Tilly drove his granddad home. The band played a slow, jazzy tune and Bryan searched the rapidly thinning crowd and assorted hotel staff for Melissa. When he spotted her, he swallowed the last of his drink and slowly approached.

"Thank you so much for coming," Melissa said, shaking Carl Detaill's hand. "I appreciate the compliments and hope you've had a fun evening."

"Oh, we did, we did. And I insist you think about what I said. I meant every word." The man winked at her and nodded.

Suddenly aware of his presence, Melissa shot Bryan a look, her smile faltering. "I will," she murmured, her lashes falling low over her eyes. "I'll be in touch."

The hospital board member held out his hand. "Dr. Booker, congratulations on a *very* successful event. I'm impressed with the turnout and all your hard work. When the hospital said our support was limited, well—let's just say I imagine there are a few board members wishing now we'd helped you get the ball rolling so we could've been more involved. Regardless, I wish you much success."

"Thank you. I hope you enjoyed yourself."

They exchanged a few more pleasantries before Detail and his wife walked away. Studying Melissa, Bryan noticed she continued to avoid eye contact. "What was that about?"

"Oh, nothing. Just chitchatting. You know."

"Is something wrong?"

She inhaled and blinked up at him. "No. But before I forget, I want to let you know how great you were tonight. Your speech was wonderful and quite moving. I spotted quite a few audience members crying and several donations were upped after you spoke."

He shoved aside the doubts he had for a later time and grinned. "That's great. I'm glad to know people aren't as unfeeling as they sometimes seem. Not when it comes down to the good of a community. But now, it's our turn to celebrate. Dance with me?"

Melissa glanced around them. "Bryan, it's late—"

"All the better." His gut tightened when she surprised him by laughing, the sound nervous, a little strained, but playful. *Playful* on Melissa was unexpected.

She glanced at the ornate clock on the wall. "The band is only going to be here for another fifteen minutes or so."

He held out his hand. "Then what are we waiting for?"

Ignoring the noise of the staff bustling about cleaning up the dirty dishes, he pulled the unprotesting Melissa into his arms and twirled her onto the dance floor. Tiny white lights twinkled over their heads, candles burned low in their glass holders. The ambience was romantic and seductive, the perfect end to a perfect evening of giving.

Melissa looked up at him, her lips parted and tempting.

Bryan pressed her closer with a hand on the small of her back, his fingers stroking her satiny-smooth skin and eliciting a shiver in response. Smiling, he kissed her temple and swayed to the music, the feel of her body rubbing against his sending desire flooding into his groin. One song blended into two...three.

Melissa's hand gripped his, trembling, the other resting on his shoulder, every now and again sliding down his chest or up to his neck as though she forgot herself long enough to enjoy the feel of him. He didn't speak, didn't want to do anything to bring her to awareness of what she did. Didn't want the night to end.

The band paused and, without stopping the slow, swaying motion, he glanced at them and saw them staring back, the room virtually empty, the auction guests gone. Lightly, Bryan lifted his hand from her back and rubbed his fingers together, indicating he'd pay them to play longer.

A couple of the band members shook their heads with expressions of regret, but the saxophone player nodded. Almost immediately rich notes filled the air, a popular love song.

Bryan returned his hand to her back, gently smoothing it down the length of her spine, dipping beneath the low-cut material to touch and tease. A sound left her, a shuddering, revealing moan, her breath moist and hot on his neck. Slowly, the act drawing on every ounce of restraint he managed to maintain, he kissed her temple, trailed his lips down her cheek. He waited, hoping. Aching. And then her mouth lifted to his.

Bryan took what Melissa offered, plunging his tongue into her sweetness, but keeping the caress light. Wanting her to want more, want him, as much as he wanted her. He didn't know how long they stayed like that, kissing, dancing. Their bodies barely moved, but they put out enough heat to set the room aflame. Finally, unable to withstand any more and praying she'd follow, he raised his head and let her see everything. His desire, his need. His love. Hoping she'd give him a chance. Maintaining eye contact, Bryan cradled her face and kissed her again. "Come upstairs with me," he murmured against her lips. "Melissa, let me show you how beautiful you are."

Amazingly, a shy nod was his answer. Bryan kissed her again, hard and fast, then took her trembling hand in his. He pulled some bills from his pocket and dropped them onto the table closest to the dance floor, lifting a hand to the sax player in thanks while leading her to his room.

CHAPTER EIGHTEEN

SILENT AND BREATHLESS, Melissa allowed Bryan to guide her through the plush hotel and into an elevator. She expected the trip upstairs to be awkward, but Bryan didn't wait for the doors to close. He hauled her close and kissed her again. Made her forget about the people in the reception area, the maid sweeping the lobby floor and the reservation clerk eyeing her enviously.

Bryan kissed her hungrily, licking her lips and sucking her tongue, sending her heart rate soaring. How did he do that? Make her feel sexy and warm and beautiful?

When he lifted his head, she realized the elevator had chimed, indicating they'd arrived at their destination. She didn't remember him pressing a button. Bryan captured her hand again and led her down the hall to the ornate door of a suite. Had he expected her to—

"I'd hoped tonight would end like this, Melissa. With *you*, no one else." His husky tone revealed his sincerity.

Inside the suite, she swallowed nervously and waited while he locked the door. The light-headed feeling she'd come to associate with Bryan's kisses turned into a fight-or-flight instinct born of fear. She wanted this. Wanted him. *But could she?*

He drew her into his arms and even though she raised her

head for a kiss, hoping he'd make her forget, Bryan simply held her close and she opened herself to him a little more although she warned herself against it. This one night... This could only be *one* night. She couldn't handle more than that. Couldn't handle more of Bryan or—

"I want more, Melissa."

She lifted her head and stared up at him, only now aware she'd spoken aloud. Wetting her lips, she fingered the black silk tie he wore. "If you can...if *I* can... Bryan, it's just tonight. One night, and only one night, and then we'll never talk about it or—"

"Why set limitations? I want *you*, Melissa, not a fling. Not a one-night stand." He cupped her face in his hands, his expression fierce. "I want to make love to you. I want...I want to be with you—"

"You can. *Tonight*."

"Melissa—"

"I can't give you more. I *can't*. If this isn't enough then...I'll go."

"No."

"Bryan—"

Bryan smothered her protest and gasp of surprise when he swept her into his arms. She gripped him tight and broke the kiss after a long moment, unable to breathe due to the panic surging through her.

His mouth nibbled her neck as he carried her through the sitting room and to the bedroom. The bed had been folded down in preparation and an ornate lamp cast a soft glow.

Bryan sat on the edge of the bed with her in his lap and smoothed his hand up her arm, fingering the strap of her gown. "You're going to hyperventilate. Breathe with me. In and out. Nice and easy."

She tried to follow the pattern he set, but when he stroked

his knuckles along her chest and followed the deeply plunging V, she faltered. *Could she do this?*

Bryan stopped touching her and took off his tuxedo jacket. Watching him was heady, every woman's fantasy come to life. A breathtakingly gorgeous man undressing for her, looking at her as if she were the only woman he had ever wanted. Soon her breathing was under control because her thoughts shifted to him instead of herself.

She followed his movements with her hands, balanced herself on his lap while she fingered his tie, then pulled it loose. Bryan sat still, letting her unbutton and pull and tug and stroke to her heart's content. Discovering, learning him the way she had in her dreams.

"You're…perfect." She hadn't meant to say the words aloud, but his response surprised her. Bryan's hands shook. They actually *shook*. And one glance at his face said it wasn't in nervousness but need. He wanted *her*. His expression was both tender and fierce.

Bryan nudged her chin up until she met his gaze. "So are you. To me, you are perfect, Melissa. My beautiful, perfect, amazing woman…kiss me."

Instead of giving in and doing what they both wanted, Melissa got to her feet. She avoided his gaze but noted the stillness in him, knew he thought she was leaving and relished the rough growl that rumbled from deep within him when she kicked off her heels and curled her toes into the thick carpet.

She held out her hands and pulled him up to stand in front of her. Her fingertips traveled down, over his pecs, the desire-hardened expanse of his stomach, paused at the cummerbund he still wore. Smiling, she followed the bank of material around his waist to where it fastened and unhooked it, letting it drop to the floor. That done, she pressed a kiss to the center of his chest and unfastened the last of the shirt buttons.

Bryan stroked her arms and back while she worked. More than once she found herself smiling, loving it when his nipping distracted her and she had to regroup and begin her various tasks again. He didn't rush her, didn't push. No, Bryan let her look her fill and ground his teeth when she tested his restraint. Tentatively, teasingly, she unfastened his slacks and let them drop to his ankles, the sight of him standing in his underwear at odds with his sexy reputation.

Several seconds passed before Bryan gave her a playful scowl and stepped out of the pants, toed off his socks, and used the act as an excuse to kiss her with a seductive stroke of his tongue. "What?" he demanded, his voice strained.

Her cheeks heated even more. "It's… I would've…um, thought you a briefs or commando guy. That's all."

His hands slid down her back to her hips, squeezed her rump and pressed her to the ever-expanding bulge beneath his boxers. "Um, B-Bryan…" She frowned, barely noticing when he smoothed his hand over her shoulder to trace the crease with a fingertip.

"I know what to expect, Melissa. Don't be afraid. Never be afraid with me."

"But…the lights." She shook her head, her gulping swallow audible and thoroughly embarrassing. "I can't…not with the lights on. Please."

Bryan bent and grasped the switch, then hesitated. "This is for you, Melissa, not me." A twist of his fingers plunged the room into darkness. That done, Bryan returned his hand to her waist, found the short zipper of her dress.

She pressed him backward onto the bed to keep him from touching her. "Not yet."

He caught her hips with his hands. "Then lie down with me, let me feel you. Let me touch you the way I want to touch you. The way I *need* to touch you."

Bryan's husky plea removed the last of her reservations. She put her knee on the bed, allowed him to guide her down, press her against him. She shifted closer to his seeking hands and felt his fingers wrap around her ankle where they slid with agonizing slowness up her calf, stroking the ticklish back of her knee before moving to her thigh. His knuckles smoothed over her skin, teasing, higher and higher until—

He growled long and low. "A *thong?* Sweetheart, you could've warned me."

The all-male comment drew a throaty laugh from her. "I couldn't wear anything else with this dress."

"Thank God."

Smiling, she wished she could see his face, his expression, but knew to see him, he'd be able to see her. Unless— "Bryan, can…could I wear your shirt?"

His hand tightened on the tiny string at her hip and pulled. "No."

Melissa shivered as Bryan uttered the word, the sound low and amazingly sensual.

"I want to feel you, all of you," he continued. "I want nothing between us but skin." Her panties gone, his hand returned to her thigh. "Roll over."

Inhaling shakily, she hesitated a long moment, then rolled away from him. She felt Bryan shift on the king-size bed, felt him find her skirt and lift it out of the way. He straddled her legs then and tugged the dress upward, the cut allowing him to pull it over her head easily.

Melissa pressed her chest to the cool sheets, and moaned when Bryan's hands dropped to her shoulders and proceeded to massage her back. He seemed in no hurry, but she felt the tension rising in him, the way his hands weren't quite steady, the way his body felt hot and hard and heavy. Just like her own.

His hands stroked lower, the base of her back, over her hips, where he stopped and squeezed. "You have the most beautiful behind."

She gasped, unable to lie still when he cupped the flesh, his thumbs dipping inward, between her thighs.

"And your legs," he murmured, dropping a kiss to one hip before sliding lower. "Do you know how many times I've fantasized about your legs? I'd hang back to watch you run, the way your muscles bunch—" his fingers gently tightened "—and release."

She buried her face in the soft mattress with a moan, but she wasn't so oblivious she didn't catch Bryan's low murmur of praise. In an instant he turned her over before she could voice a protest, then covered her with his body.

"Say you want me, Melissa."

He doubted that? Bryan kissed her, hard and rough. The room spun, but Bryan was her anchor. Her gift to herself and the first step toward the future.

"Say I'm not the only one so turned on right now that all I can think about is being with you, inside you, forever."

He kissed her again before she could protest the forever part, then tore his mouth from hers and nibbled on her neck. His teeth sank into the muscle at the base with just enough pressure to have her curling her legs around him, sliding the hardest part of him against her. She whimpered, a part of her shocked she could make such a sound. Part of her thrilled that she could, after everything she'd been through.

"That's it. Melissa...sweetheart."

He kissed his way lower, but she was in such a dazed state it took her a moment to realize his destination.

"B-Bryan, no. *No*."

He caught her hands in his when she tried to push him away, secured them above her head with one hand and freed the other to stroke her chest. Slow, tender caresses that left nothing hidden.

Tears stung her eyes and she turned her face away, tried to roll over. How could she have thought she could do this? "*Don't*. Bryan, please don't ruin this."

Bryan ignored her, murmuring words of comfort and praise, searching out her scars with his fingertips and lips. Lying beneath him, trapped by his hips and the hand holding hers, she waited for his body to react. For his erection to dwindle. For her magical night to stop.

"Can you feel me touching you?"

She didn't answer, wouldn't. Some nerves had been damaged or destroyed by the surgery, some not. What did it matter though? He wouldn't be able to make love to her. Not now.

"Melissa?" Bryan raised his head and even in the darkness she felt his stare. He hesitated, then pinched her lightly.

She jumped.

"You can feel me," he murmured, a smile in his voice. "Good."

Good? That was all he said before she felt him shift into her, felt the warm, wet slide of his tongue over her skin, over her scars. She strained against him in a feeble attempt to get away, but it was more to hide her sobs than to escape his touch. She couldn't—he *couldn't*—

"Beautiful." *Kiss.* "Brave." *Kiss.* "Melissa…ah, honey, you are so beautiful. Smooth and sleek and *strong*. So strong."

Another chuckle. "Proud. We're going to clash, you and I, but I can't wait. You're a woman to be reckoned with. A fighter."

She bit her lip, tried to hold them back.

"Shh. Don't cry. Ah, honey, don't cry." Bryan placed one last lingering kiss right over her heart before lifting his head and taking her lip into his mouth, smoothing his tongue over the hurt she'd caused and cradling her face in his palm.

The warmth he'd shown her, the tenderness, set her free. Instead of being angry over his high-handedness, she turned ferocious, her tears forgotten, and kissed him with every ounce of desire and pain and want inside her. She arched her back, needing to feel him, needing him to touch her even though she knew come morning, when she had to leave, her heart would be broken just like her father had warned. But she had tonight. Hours and hours until—

She shoved that worry aside, her fingers clinging to the hand holding hers. Having no way of touching him otherwise, she raised her knees and encircled his hips with her legs.

Another rough chuckle left him. "Not yet. You in a hurry?"

"Yes."

Bryan kissed her again before he rolled to the side of the bed and fumbled, mumbling under his breath. A moment later he mumbled again. "You've got me so crazy I can't— Melissa, I need to turn on the light."

She rolled onto her stomach and grabbed a pillow from the headboard, holding it to cover her chest. "Um, okay."

The lamp came on. She blinked at the sudden brightness, then watched him search for the condoms in the drawer. He kept his back to her, his focus on what he was doing, and for that she was grateful. He knew how she felt, knew why she felt it and yet—

A thought registered and, before she could squelch it,

Melissa bent her knees, crossed her ankles, lying in what she hoped would pass as a seductive pose. She might not have a future with Bryan, but she wanted one moment in the light when she could see him. When he could see her and…like what he saw? "Bryan?"

All movement stilled. Bryan looked at her, his mouth parting to draw in more air as his hot, heavy-lidded gaze slid down her body lying propped atop the pillow and lingered on her butt, her legs. He tossed the condom onto the bed by her hand and shucked his boxers before climbing back onto the bed beside her.

"Th-the light."

"What about it?"

She blinked at him. Why hadn't she thought that far ahead? Fear swamped her. "Bryan…"

He rolled the condom on in an efficient motion she didn't want to overthink, and then slid an arm around her waist, pulling her close, pillow clutched in front of her included. A slight smile curled the corners of his mouth. She watched him, waiting, while he lowered his head and kissed her, the barest brush of his lips over hers. Time stopped. Need rose. He held her face, cradling it tenderly, his thumb stroking her cheek before he pulled away again. Staring into her eyes, he smoothed a finger over her eyebrows, palmed her head and murmured something about the softness of her hair.

Sighing, she shivered as Bryan pressed kisses to every freckle he found, whispering his thoughts, his need, into her skin, all the things he wanted to do with her. The surprise of him making love to her in the light faded and desire built again until she welcomed the feel of his hand sliding up her knee and thigh.

"So sweet," he murmured, dropping another kiss onto her

shoulder while his fingers teased, eliciting gasps from her she couldn't control.

Bryan positioned himself between her legs and took her mouth in a kiss that stole all thoughts from her head. She couldn't think, couldn't breathe. All she could do was feel and moan and arch toward him as he joined them with a smooth, easy movement.

"Open your eyes, Melissa. That's it. Do you trust me?"

How could she not? A heartbeat later the truth slammed into her. How could she not? Here she was in a hotel room, Bryan's body joined with hers. Of course she trusted him. But when had it happened?

"Hold on to me, sweetheart."

She gasped when he kept them joined, but sat up and pulled her with him, the pillow still held to her chest. The natural move was to curl her legs around him, and she did, shivering when Bryan's rough appreciation blew hot in her ear. She picked up the pace, her tongue entwining with his in rhythm with their powerful thrusts.

Every stroke took her deeper into the moment, until she lost herself in the feel of him and her hands shifted from the pillow to his back, loving the strength of him, the sensations. Loving him.

She whimpered at her thoughts and tried to hold back, to pull away and regain a semblance of control, but Bryan wouldn't let her.

Her head fell back in ecstasy and her body tightened. Tightened and tightened until she lost herself completely to him, crying out her release. Bryan's moan followed hers and a smile formed on her lips when she realized she'd brought him to such a state.

Limp, more thoroughly sated than she'd ever been in her

life, she kept her eyes closed as Bryan lowered her onto the mattress. She struggled to regain her equilibrium while he disposed of the condom, but it was Bryan's husky chuckle that had her opening her eyes the very moment he climbed back into bed and turned off the light.

"What?"

He pulled her close, still smiling when he kissed her, his hand sliding with ease over her hip. Then she identified the tone of Bryan's chuckle. Satisfaction. Triumph. Pleasure and pride alike.

At some point while they'd made love, he'd removed the pillow from between them—with the lights on—*and she hadn't even noticed.*

THE NEXT MORNING Melissa woke with a start, unused to having a big, hairy body behind her in the bed. Her movement must have disturbed Bryan because he rolled onto his back. The tangled sheet pulled low on his stomach as a result and despite having wakened hours before to the feel of Bryan stroking her and entering her from behind, her body instantly warmed.

If someone had told her she'd ever feel this way after having both breasts removed, she'd have called it a cruel lie. But now that she'd had her one magical night, she knew there could be no more. She had to protect her heart.

Last night's job offer from the hospital administrator had been a godsend. The success of the fund-raising events had drawn their notice and they wanted a go-getter like her to work for them on building their PR, not only with the local community, but with larger hospitals, as well.

Getting away from Bryan would be good for both of them. Her feelings for him had grown throughout the past few months, dangerously so. Bryan might be a player, but he had a heart. One that had already been broken by one woman's passing. The last thing she wanted was for him to think her life—or death—was his responsibility. To fall back into the void where he went from woman to woman in an attempt to escape what he saw as a failure in himself. He might have recovered once, but could he do it again? What if he completely gave up medicine this time?

Silent, she got to her feet and grabbed her dress from the floor. It was early yet, and thanks to her many trips into and out of the hotel preparing for the gala, she knew a back way that would allow her to leave undetected. She tiptoed across the floor and retrieved her shoes, smoothed her sleep-crushed hair as best she could. Then she spared one last look over her shoulder at Bryan, his big body relaxed and beautiful in sleep.

Trembling, she left, determined to go home before he woke up and had to decide whether or not he agreed to her terms.

FORTY MINUTES LATER, Melissa entered Taylorsville's outskirts and prepared herself to pass Bryan's practice. The long drive had given her time to think, but she still wasn't sure what to do. As a policeman, her dad had often said the best place to hide was right out in the open. She doubted Bryan would brag about sleeping with her, and her dad and Ellen were so into each other they wouldn't miss her for days. She could call them later, when she got to wherever the money she'd saved would take her.

Rounding the curve in the road, she glanced at Bryan's house and slowed. "Oh, no." Anna Pritchard was back. Heart thumping at the sight of the bruised, pitiful creature outside Bryan's door, she pulled into the parking area and hurried out of the car. The girl stumbled into her arms.

"He did it *again!* He s-said he wouldn't," Anna cried, the words torn from her chest. "He *promised!*"

"I'm sorry, sweetheart. I'm so sorry. Anna, come on. Let's get you in the car and—"

"What happened—"

She looked at Ellen and wished the ground would open up and swallow her. One glance at her wrinkled gown and appearance and Ellen knew.

"Anna's hurt," Melissa informed her quickly, praying with all her heart her father wouldn't come storming over next. "Would you call an ambulance?"

For once the girl didn't protest. Anna simply clutched at her, crying, mumbling words she couldn't make out about promises and love and hate.

"It would be quicker to drive her."

She acknowledged that with a nod, but no way was she going to go to the hospital in her gown.

"I'll take her. You go home and get changed."

"What if you get sick?"

Ellen smoothed Anna's hair back, her expression concerned. "I'll…I'll call Hal. He had an errand to run out to the mayor's house. If you leave now, you'll miss him on his way here."

"O-okay. Thank you."

The other woman stepped back and crossed her arms over her front to ward off the cold air. "Where's Bryan? I can't imagine he'd simply—"

"I left," she muttered. "Stay with her. I'll run and grab the phone and bring it to you."

Apparently sensing she wouldn't discuss Bryan or what happened, Ellen nodded. "It's on the base right by the door."

Minutes later, Melissa was on her way, Ellen's expression

burned into her memory. She'd asked the woman not to say anything to her dad and Melissa knew Ellen hated being placed in that kind of situation.

At home, Melissa showered and changed, tossed some clothes into a suitcase and zipped it tight. She hurried through the living room, grabbed her purse and pulled the door open—gasping sharply when she saw someone standing on the other side.

CHAPTER NINETEEN

THE SOUND OF THE PHONE woke Bryan. He jerked upright, knowing instantly Melissa was gone. He grabbed the phone and prayed it was her. "Hello?"

"Bryan? It's Ellen. I'm at the hospital—"

"What's wrong? Is it the baby? Is your OB there?"

"I'm fine, it's not me."

"Did something happen to Melissa?" Bryan heard Ellen speaking to someone, her voice muffled, and fought his impatience, keeping his fear at bay by sheer will. Had Melissa had an accident? *"Ellen?"*

"Just a moment—yes, water is fine, just something cold, Hal, please. Thank you." A moment passed, but he thought he heard the deep rumble of the chief's voice. "Bryan, I'm sorry—it's Anna again. We—I found her this morning outside your house. They gave her something to calm her because she was hysterical, but I wanted to let you know."

"Thanks. I appreciate the call. I'll—"

"Bryan, I saw Melissa this morning. She found Anna."

He bit back a curse and shot out of the bed, paced as far as the phone cord would allow. "Was she all right?"

"You've made some mistakes since you've moved here and treated women abominably, but, Bryan, if you hurt that girl after I urged you to hire her—" A frustrated sound traveled through the phone. "How dare you put me in the middle of this given the circumstances of how you and Melissa began working together?"

"I love her, Ellen." Bryan chuckled at her silence, used to seeing Ellen happy, sad or flustered, but never angry or speechless.

"What?"

"She's the one you warned me about," he murmured drily. "The woman I want, the one I love who wants nothing to do with me."

"Oh. Oh, Bryan...I don't... Are you *sure?*"

"I obviously didn't have to shake her out of my mattress this morning, did I? Yeah, I'm sure. Actually, she told me. Said she only wanted one night, last night."

"And you agreed? Feeling the way you do about her?"

"Guess my ego was bigger than I thought. I agreed, but only because I'd convinced myself I could change her mind."

"Hal's heading my way so I have to hurry. Bryan, if you love her, *do* something. Don't give up."

"I don't plan to," he murmured, hanging up and hurrying to dress, knowing whichever doctor had admitted Anna would probably keep the girl on medication for a while. He'd drive back and see her later; he hoped with Melissa in tow.

It was only a matter of time before the whole town found out he'd spent the night at the hotel with Melissa. Her wish for secrecy was a product of the night, part of the fantasy he'd allowed her to create. A town as small as Taylorsville didn't have a true secret. Everyone knew everything or made up what they didn't. But if he had to, he planned to use that to his advantage. He was desperate. Desperate enough to brave Melissa's anger if the end result meant getting her to see the truth.

Bryan cut the drive time to Melissa's house by fifteen minutes. He drove around to the back and parked by her car, nervous and yet looking forward to the encounter.

It wasn't until he headed for the door that he lifted his head and froze. The screen door was broken, hanging from its hinges, the back door open. Her comment about him being like her father when he'd told her to keep the door locked hit him and sent fear straight to his gut. She always locked the door. Always.

"Melissa!"

HAL STARED at the trashed house and tried to get a grip on his terror. He had to hold it together because the doc sure wasn't. Booker paced, growled out curses and practically ripped his hair out by the roots every time he ran his fingers through it.

The bathroom floor was covered in shards of glass and blood, the bottles of Mel's leftover cancer and pain meds scattered throughout the house like whoever found them had grabbed them all to take with him, then wound up popping the pills and tossing the bottles aside as he ransacked the place.

Staring at the red splatters of blood and smears on the floor, he prayed hard. *God, please.* Whose blood was it? And where was his little girl?

"DON'T MESS with Bryan's head."

Ashley snickered from where she stood at the kitchen sink, washing the breakfast dishes too big to be placed in the dishwasher. "I think it's a bit late for that warning."

Melissa blushed. *"Ashley."*

"I meant his *brain*," Joe countered, sending an unamused look toward his wife.

Melissa sat at the Brodys' kitchen table, an untouched plate of food in front of her. Seeing Ashley on the other side of her back door an hour ago had given her a start, but that was nothing compared to how surprised she'd been to find out the couple had seen her and Bryan outside the hotel suite, and Ashley had insisted Joe let her check on Melissa on their way home.

"So…you slept with Bryan, enjoyed yourself, but now you want to end things?" Ashley's shook her head. "Have to tell you, sweetie, that's usually not the way things work with him."

She rolled her eyes. "Believe me, I know."

"You could do worse."

"What a recommendation," Melissa muttered. "Look, Joe, I know you're trying to help, but—"

"Why don't you let us girls have a talk?" Ashley asked pointedly, softening her words with a grin. "Maybe go give Wilson and your dad a break and take Max out for that ice cream you promised him?"

"You won't get away from him easily, Mel. Bryan's not like that with you." With that warning, Joe shoved himself off the counter where he leaned and headed for the rooms his dad and Wilson shared.

"He's right, you know. Bryan looks at you and heats up like a flash fire. Now, what's this really about?" Ashley demanded.

Giving in, Melissa told Ashley about Bryan's past. "So even if he wants a relationship, I can't. Bryan deserves more than to go through that again."

"Who says he'd have to? I'm going to agree with your dad and Bryan here, hon. You have to think positive. What good will it do you to prepare for something that might never happen?" Ashley smiled at her, her eyes searching. "Melissa, you told me that you couldn't be with Bryan because of your scars. Well, obviously that isn't a factor for him. Now you've come up with another excuse—"

"It's a legitimate *reason*."

"You're splitting hairs."

"Even if I could ignore the women throwing themselves at him on a daily basis—"

"He hasn't been with anyone except you in quite a while now. He's lost interest. Think there isn't a reason for *that?*"

"But—"

"Ashley?" Dara entered the kitchen carrying a fussing Isabella. "I hate to do this to you after telling you I could work today, but I just called home to check on Mom and she's not answering. I need to go see about her, but I promise I'll be right back if she's okay."

"No problem. I slept in this morning so I'm feeling much better today. Joe's surprise was just what I needed. Thank you for staying last night and keeping Issy and Max."

"My pleasure. They were both little angels and I was glad to help out." A smile replaced her harried frown. "How romantic that Joe took you away like that. Oh, what I wouldn't give for a man to plan a romantic night for me."

Ashley shot Melissa a knowing look before she took Isabella from Dara. "Come'ere, baby girl. Oh, time to eat, huh?"

"I've gotta run. Mom fell last month and she's pretty unsteady, and the home-care nurse won't come again until tomorrow."

"Keep us posted?" Ashley urged.

"Sure. Thanks again." With a final wave and nod, Dara exited the kitchen.

"It is a romantic gesture for a man to make, isn't it?" Ashley asked once they were alone.

"I need to get moving," Melissa said, pushing the plate

away before getting to her feet. "I'll use your car to drive myself back to the house and lock the keys inside so you and Joe can pick it up later."

"You're not going anywhere." Ashley donned her most maternal expression and pointed toward the ceiling. "Melissa, you're upset. *Scared*. And there are nine bedrooms up there in the guest section. If you need a place to hide out and think, at least do it where we know you're safe. We're the only ones here right now. Pick a room and lock the door if it makes you feel better, but no one will even know you're there unless you tell them. Who knows, maybe while you're here you can think of all the reasons you and Bryan would make the perfect couple."

Melissa smiled sadly. "Or all the reasons we wouldn't?"

BRYAN WAS STANDING outside Melissa's house when he saw Wilson's battered old pickup truck crawl through the four-way stop at the corner and then turn at the last minute and head their way.

He left the yard and jogged over to the truck.

"What happened?" Joe asked, leaning forward to see overtop his son's car seat.

"Someone broke in and tore the place up," he explained hurriedly. "Melissa's gone and there's blood all through the house. Joe, if something's happened to—"

"She's fine. Mel's with Ash at the— Bryan, wait!"

MELISSA STARED at the ceiling and ignored the tears trickling into her ears. What a mess. Bryan had to be awake by now, would know she'd sneaked out. Would he be angry? Or would he even care at all? She ran a hand under her nose and moaned. What to do?

Step one was to take the job at the hospital, but step two?

Anna's image entered her head and Melissa shut her eyes in pain. How could anyone stand to be abused like that? Why didn't she leave? Why didn't Anna believe in herself enough to know love wasn't ugly?

Ashley's raised voice reached her ears, followed by a ruckus. Her name? She sat up and had just touched her toes to the floor when she heard someone running down the hall toward her bedroom.

"Melissa? Open up or I'll break it down." Bryan's voice was so loud he might as well have been in the room with her.

"Bryan, calm down," Ashley ordered. "She's fine, I told you that."

"I want to see her myself. There was blood on the floor."

"*Not* hers! Joe and I picked her up before the break-in. Once we saw how upset she was, we made her come with us."

Break-in? Melissa jumped off the bed and fumbled with the old-fashioned latch, barely getting out of the way before Bryan pushed his way inside and wrapped his arms around her in a bear hug.

"Thank you, God. Sweetheart—thank God you're all right."

She breathed deeply, closed her eyes and let herself enjoy the feel of him one last time. "I'm fine," she murmured, her voice muffled against his shirt. "Bryan, what—"

His mouth settled over hers, the kiss one of desperation and hunger. "Never do that again," he ordered against her lips. "Do you hear me? Melissa, when I woke up and you were gone—then at the house. Don't leave me like that. When I saw the blood—"

"What blood? What break-in?"

"Someone broke into your house and cleaned out the medicine cabinet."

"Oh, *no.*" She tried to get free. "I need to—"

"Your dad's there now, and you're not going anywhere except with me." His expression changed before her eyes, turned from one of relief to anger to— "I love you, Melissa." He palmed her face in his hands, holding her still. "I *love* you. I love your body—"

"B-Bryan, please. There's no comparison to yours or other women's and I know it."

"You're right, there's not."

Her mouth parted at his bluntness.

"I'm surrounded by women, and I've had more than my share, but none of them have ever made me feel what you do. I've never looked at them from across a crowded ballroom and gotten weak at the knees, or watched them run and—"

Melissa pulled away from him. "No. *No*. It was one night. *One night,* you promised."

He shook his head. "I never agreed to that. And I'm determined to make you see how good we could be together."

"You'd grow bored with me and run around and—"

"Weren't you listening? Melissa, I don't want them, I want you! No one else ties me up in knots or makes me crazy the way you do."

She wasn't sure that was a compliment. "And my cancer?"

"You don't have cancer."

"But I did," she said, establishing more distance between them. "And the odds are I will again."

"You don't know that, but if it happens, then we'll—"

"What are you doing, Bryan? Huh? Think! Do you know what you're saying?" She stared at him, incredulous. "One night is all you ever wanted with those other women. Why isn't that enough now?"

His smile turned her stomach to mush. "Because you're not them. Because I want more—*a lot more*—from you."

She shook her head slowly, unable to handle the responsibility his assertion brought with it. "I can't give you that."

"Yes, you can." He stepped closer but stopped when she backed away. "Melissa, I want to marry you, to spend my life with y—"

"*What* life? A life of tests and MRIs? Cancer scans? A life with no *children?*"

"All I need is a life with you."

Her laugh lacked humor. "Bryan, it wouldn't *be* a life! When are you and everyone else going to get it? A life with me isn't worth the burden you'd carry with you on a daily basis!"

"*Why* do you think that?"

"Because you don't deserve to bury another woman you—" She broke off, unwilling to admit she saw the naked truth in his eyes, his expression. A truth she couldn't allow herself to see or feel because if she did, if she dared hope...

"Love? That's right, come on, say it," he dared. "Believe it, Melissa, because it's true. I love you. I love you. *Say it.*"

She shook her head, mute. How could he possibly love her?

"Afraid?" Bryan moved toward her, following her as she retreated into a corner of the pretty bedroom, her back to the wall, and Bryan looking hard as the proverbial rock in front of her. "I understand that, sweetheart. But listen to me and listen good, okay? Because *I say* loving you is worth whatever trials and tests we face. I'll gladly, *thankfully,* take a life with someone I love, over a safe one without you in it. I've been without, Melissa. I've tried to pretend being with those women was enough, but it wasn't. And none of us are safe. Sometimes life isn't pretty and neither is what we'll face if your cancer returns. I realize that."

"Then you shouldn't want—"

"You? But I do. I want you. I want whatever I can have with you. Why would you choose being alone when you know that you could have love with someone who loves you in return?"

"I never said I loved you."

"But you do, don't you? Otherwise you'd be laughing at me instead of looking at me like you are."

She lifted her chin, emotion swelling inside her chest, making her fight for each breath. "I'm taking a j-job at the hospital. Mr.—they asked me last night. I'm q-quitting."

"You're running away, but it won't work. It won't stop how you feel, sweetheart. I tried to deny my feelings for you, but it didn't work."

"Make it work. I'm leaving."

His expression softened. "There's no need to be afraid anymore. Together, we can face anything."

"No. *No*, because you'll get tired of fighting the inevitable and want someone else. Someone *not* like *me*. Someone who looks like a woman and—"

"Try me," he dared, stepping closer. "Take a chance at living, Melissa. With me. Who else has the guts to keep me in line? Who else can match my stride?" He nudged her chin up with his hand. "I love you. I *need* you. Be with me, stay with me. Marry me."

Tears flooded her, uncontrollable, a bottomless pit rushing up from the depths of her and swallowing her whole. Bryan's words were the sweetest, most amazing words anyone had ever said to her. The most loving. She saw his sincerity, his passion. But it contained *too much love*. And if it was true, real, then how could she let him risk so much? She had to protect Bryan because he wasn't protecting himself. She loved him enough to do that.

"Melissa—"

"No." The word emerged on a gasp, not strong enough to be heard. Lifting her chin, she forced herself to look him in the eyes and say it again. "No, I won't marry you. I want you to leave. I've had my n-night with *Bang 'em Booker*—" she forced a snideness into her tone she didn't feel "—and I don't want any more."

"Melissa—"

"Don't ask me again. I said no, my answer is *no*."

Bryan's expression turned to stone, but before it did she saw the hurt. The pain. Pain she'd caused, but less pain now than there would be later. He should know that. Why didn't he *know* that?

He stood for a long moment, his chest rising and falling with angry breaths, his eyes searching hers. It took all her strength and courage not to look away. She had to make it clear she meant what she said. She did mean it. And after minutes passed Bryan realized it. She saw the understanding dawn, the hurt and pain, and the agony. Saw it because she felt it, too, inside where it cut the deepest.

Without a word, Bryan turned and left. She watched him, holding her breath until her knees gave out and she slid to the floor, curling in on herself.

Less pain now than it would be later. She wouldn't leave Bryan behind, reeling and damning himself for her death. She couldn't. She loved him too much for that.

BRYAN HAD DRIVEN to the construction site on automatic pilot. He didn't remember making the drive itself, only that one minute he'd dropped into his car and started it, and then he had arrived. Now he stared at the construction equipment that had been left in preparation, and dreaded the public groundbreaking scheduled for tomorrow. How would he get through it knowing Melissa's hard work was the only reason the funding had come through? Knowing that she should be there but wouldn't be?

He closed his eyes and remembered her smiling challenges during their runs together, the way she nibbled her lip when she filled in the little squares on the organizational chart. He sat a long time, imagining he smelled the scent of Melissa's hair on the leather seats. The sound of Joe's laughter and Hal's, in his head. Building, growing. Ellen's words about payback for loving a woman who didn't love him. So this was what that felt like. To love someone, care for them, need them, want them with every breath, and not have them want you back. To finally find the balls to admit it aloud and risk a once-broken heart on an iffy future.

Love sucked. But love her he did. Now what?

Straightening in the seat, he turned the key in the ignition and started the vehicle, not knowing where he was going but determined to drive until he got there.

MELISSA IGNORED Ashley's attempts to change her mind and borrowed Ashley's car to drive herself home after crying until she had no tears left. She'd called her dad from the B and B to say she was okay, somehow managing to get through the conversation without him realizing what bad shape she was really in.

He'd reluctantly agreed that since all her cancer meds and leftover pain patches were now gone, the guy probably wouldn't be back. It was little comfort after the day she'd had, but she was desperate enough to take what she could. She needed peace and quiet, and after Bryan's visit, Ashley's hovering had made her too nervous to stay.

Her dad had invited her to spend the night with him and Ellen, but she couldn't, not with Bryan right next door. Inside her house, Melissa stared at the mess and began the cleanup, the chores occupying her hands and thoughts. She carried out a bag of broken glass and trash and a person approached, silhouetted by the setting sun. Melissa jumped and sucked in a startled breath.

"I'm sorry! I didn't mean to scare you." Anna stepped closer, her movements slow and obviously painful.

"What are you doing here? You should be in the hospital."

"I checked myself out."

"Anna, you shouldn't have done that."

"I—I had to." She toed the ground with her worn sneaker, her fat lip trembling. "If I tell you something…will you help me?"

Melissa dropped the bags into the covered bins. "If I can. Why don't you come in? I'll make us some tea." She led the way into the kitchen, Anna's unmistakable groan easy to hear.

"Are you in pain?" It was easier to think about someone else's pain than her own.

Anna shook her head slowly, taking in the damage done to the house. "He did it. I'm too late."

"You know who did this?"

Anna lifted her bruised hand, splints on two fingers this time, and indicated the mess. "His mom mentioned seeing you and I told him how you— He said you'd have some left, that people like you always had some left."

"People like me? Anna, what are you talking about?" It came to her then, the puzzle clicking together. "Tilly's son? Tilly's son is your boyfriend?"

Anna sniffled, her head jerking in a nod.

"He's the one breaking into the houses? Hurting those people?"

"He gets the n-names from her, from her files when she's not around. Melissa, you've got to help me."

"Of course I will. Anna, you don't have to be afraid. My father's the police chief. He'll protect you, and I'll stand by you when you help prosecute him."

"No!" the girl cried harshly, her words slurring together a bit because of her swollen cheek and mouth. "I...I want help for *him*. A lesser sentence or—or rehab or something. Please, Melissa? You said you'd help me."

"Why on earth—"

"He needs *help*," Anna insisted. "It's not his fault he needs the medicine. He got hurt and the doctors gave it to him, and his mom gave him some, too, because she's a nurse and he was still in pain, but then he wasn't better and he still *hurts!*"

"So he breaks into people's homes to steal it and beats you up when he's high? Anna, it's not just you, he hurt those people! Why would you help him after that?"

The girl lowered her head, tears sliding down her cheeks. "I didn't want him to do this. I begged him not to! Not after you've been so nice to us and gave us the medicine."

"He's a drug addict, of course he— What do you mean 'us'?" Melissa gaped at her. "He beat you up to *get* the drugs?"

Anna wouldn't look at her. "I asked him not to come here and he got m-mad. He said I didn't love him, but I do!"

Anna needed help as much as the boyfriend did, as much as— Melissa froze for a split second and then raced for the phone. She called Bryan's apartment but no one answered. Next she dialed the practice. Busy? "He's working on the construction project," she mumbled. "That's all." But her instincts screamed and she had to know that Bryan was okay.

Frantic, she grabbed her purse and keys and made one last call. "Dad, it's me. Where are you?" Explaining the situation, she hung up on her father as he was ordering her to stay home and let him handle it, but her father was too far away, on a rural road on the outskirts of town. If something was wrong, he wouldn't make it in time. Bryan—she had to get to Bryan.

Melissa raced out to the car, biting back her impatience when Anna moved too slowly due to her broken ribs and injuries. The drive to Bryan's practice took her full concentration since she drove with the sole purpose of reaching him. Finally she pulled to a stop by the back door and sagged in the seat, relieved to see Bryan's car parked where it always was, the neighborhood quiet.

"He's here."

What?

Melissa looked to where Anna stared and saw an older model S-10 pickup parked in the narrow alleyway between Bryan's practice and the house on the other side of his and Ellen's. She jumped out and ran, vaguely aware that Anna followed. If anything happened to Bryan—

The back door was unlocked, partially open, Bryan's keys still in the lock. She pushed it open.

"No, stay out! Melissa, *run!*"

Everything happened in slow motion. She skidded to a halt, reeling at the sight of a man holding a gun on Bryan. The addict swung the pistol toward her, and Bryan lunged.

Melissa screamed. The gun went off. And both men went down.

CHAPTER TWENTY

"BRYAN!" Melissa ran up the hall, ignoring Anna's boyfriend as he rolled on the ground. She fell to her knees beside Bryan, gasping at the blood soaking his shirt. "Bryan? Bryan, talk to me. Oh, God, please, no. *Bryan?*"

"D-don't move, Scottie! *Don't move!*"

Melissa looked up and saw Bryan's attacker on his feet and struggling to escape, one hand holding his head.

"I'll *shoot* you! *Scottie!*"

Hoping Anna meant what she said, Melissa grabbed some towels from the bottom of the open drug closet and held them on Bryan's stomach, trying desperately to stanch the blood.

"Anna...babe, come on. We gotta get out of here." Tilly's son flashed Anna a cocky grin, his eyes glazed over from the drugs in his system. "Come on, baby, put it down. You know you won't do it. You won't shoot me."

"She might not, but I would. You're under arrest."

Melissa felt dizzying relief at the sound of Nathan's voice. Within seconds, Scott was cuffed and Anna relieved of the gun. Another of her father's officers arrived and took them both outside.

"How bad is he?" Nathan asked, kneeling beside her on the floor.

"Bad."

"The EMTs will be here soon, Mel. And the chief's on his way. Press that tight and stay calm."

Stay calm? "He said he loved me. He asked me to m-marry him but I said n-no. Why did I say no? *Why* didn't I say yes?"

Nathan didn't hide his surprise well. After several seconds, he lifted his hand and ran a callused fingertip down her cheek. "You didn't say yes because you needed to be sure. Because you were afraid and you didn't understand how much he cares for you. Now you know."

She closed her eyes, careful not to move her hands or the compress against Bryan's stomach. "But...Nathan, you couldn't. How can he want me? Why?"

"Look at me. Hey...Mel?"

She raised her eyes to his, fighting the urge to look away. To curl up in a ball and cry. Fighting, always fighting.

"Sweetheart, don't let my being a jerk about your illness keep you from being with a guy, even Booker if he's the one you want. God, much as I hate to say it, he's got it bad for you. Last night... Hell, Mel, it's obvious."

"But I didn't...I didn't believe him."

He stroked her hair. "And that's probably my fault, because of the way I treated you, but any man willing to put himself in front of a gun to keep you safe loves you. Just like you love him. Otherwise you wouldn't be crying all over him."

She shook her head. "I'm not crying."

Nathan's smile was tender. "You will be once he's okay."

Her laugh was choked with tears she couldn't release yet because Bryan *wasn't* okay.

Nathan put his hand on top of hers. "Take things one at a time. Right now, getting him stable is the first hurdle. Then you get him through surgery. Then you talk. Hear me? Keep your head up and talk to him, Mel. Tell him you love him. And tell him if he doesn't treat you right your old man isn't the only one who's going to set him straight."

Once again Melissa fought to contain her tears. She lowered her head and closed her eyes and prayed hard, vaguely conscious of Nathan getting up. Blinking, she studied every line of Bryan's face, memorized every detail. "Is he right?" she whispered hoarsely. "B-Bryan, is he right? Please be okay. Please, Bryan, for me. Because you said—because you said you love me and—I love you, too."

MELISSA STARED at her hands and wondered if there was anything more frightening than blood. Blood meant so many things. It was the difference between living and dying, the difference in believing in heaven and hell or nothing at all. Blood had built kingdoms, covered battlefields, destroyed families and people and now it had the potential to destroy the man she loved.

"I'm sorry, miss. You're not the only one asking about Dr. Booker. Since you came in with him in the ambulance, I consulted with the doctor, but he said rules are rules. We can't give you any information about his status because you're not family."

Numb, Melissa returned to the chair she'd vacated and sat down. Back to blood again. She drew some curious looks from the others waiting and supposed she should go to the bathroom and wash up as best she could, but she didn't care. She couldn't leave. Wouldn't risk not being there if something went wrong.

"We got here as fast as we could," Ashley said, sliding into a seat beside her. "Any news?"

She blinked and struggled to focus, her brain function sluggish. "Where's Joe?"

"He's coming. He dropped me off so you wouldn't be here alone any longer than you had to be."

"Ashley, I ruined everything." She lowered her head and looked at her hands once more. "If I'd stayed at the hotel or...said yes to Bryan's proposal, he wouldn't be here. None of this would've happened."

"Stop it, Melissa. You didn't pull that trigger, and for all you know, you and Bryan might have been at his practice today anyway. This isn't your fault."

"But if Bryan—"

"He'll be fine," Joe stated forcefully, joining them. He squatted in front of her and Ashley, leaning against Ashley's legs for balance but covering her hand with one of his. "Bryan loves you, Mel. Turning him down will just bring out the stubborn side in him." That said, Joe squeezed her hand and then sat down in the empty chair on the other side of her, his big body giving her comfort but nothing else.

Amazing how time changed things. She'd thought herself in love with Joe once, but when she compared that to how she felt for Bryan...well, there was no comparison. Why hadn't she figured that out before? Why hadn't she been able to say the words before Bryan got hurt? She loved Bryan. She'd admit it, but did it really matter? Even now, with Bryan on an operating table, she was torn. There was still a chance she could get sick.

"Mel?"

Melissa stood at the sound of her name. Her dad and Ellen hurried toward her but she didn't wait. Seconds later, she was in her father's arms. *"Dad."*

"Shh...it'll be all right."

She tried to believe that, but she hadn't had a happy ending yet. Her mom, Josie. Her cancer. Melissa hugged him tighter and pressed her nose into his chest. "They won't tell me anything because I'm not related."

He gently untangled her arms. "They'll tell me. You sit down while I go find something out."

Ashley stood. "Joe will make sure Bryan's grandfather has been called and I'll get Melissa something to drink. We'll be right back."

Her father put his hands on her shoulders and walked her to the chair. "I'll be back with some answers as fast as I can."

When he left, Melissa found herself alone with Ellen. The other woman remained quiet a long moment, then reached over and pressed something into her hand. "Take this. My first husband gave me this the Christmas before he died. I keep it with me for times like these."

"It's beautiful," she whispered, staring at the cross charm.

"I think so, too," Ellen murmured. "I'd like it if you hold it for me, Melissa. As long as you need it, all right?"

Her fingers closed over the charm and squeezed. "Bryan was so weak. He lost so much blood."

"He's in good hands," Ellen murmured. "The doctors will take good care of him."

"Bryan's grandfather is on his way," Ashley informed them, rejoining them and sitting across from her. "The nurse said he was listed as Bryan's contact person so he was called first thing."

"Good." Melissa nodded. "That's good."

Awkward silence fell over the three women.

"The gala was a great success," Ashley murmured. "Bryan was so proud of you for pulling it off. He strutted around like a peacock telling everyone what a great job you did."

Next to her, Ellen laughed softly. "Did you see the way he watched her all night? Bryan didn't take his eyes off her."

"Because he's in love," Joe stated firmly, coming over to seat himself beside his wife. He wrapped an arm around Ashley and pulled her close, pressing a kiss to her temple. "And he didn't care who saw it."

Melissa didn't acknowledge Joe's words. She couldn't because if she did she just might— "Where's Dad?"

Joe inclined his head, and she noted her father spoke with Bryan's grandfather and Meg, the housekeeper, who'd just arrived.

"I should go say something but…what?" she whispered dully.

"Let your father fill him in and then they'll come join us," Ellen reassured her. "It's fine."

"Your dad said the nurse will tell him as soon as she gets word from the O.R.," Joe added. "We'll know as soon as the desk knows something."

She nodded again, feeling like a puppet, only going through the motions. Before long, her dad, Randall and Meg came to join the vigil. She gave Randall and a teary-eyed Meg hugs. And then they waited. And waited. A half hour passed but still no news. All of them either stared at the floor or paced, talking in whispers and asking the same questions over and over again because they were so distracted they couldn't retain the answers.

"Drink this." Ashley pressed a cold soda into Melissa's hand. "I found a machine working upstairs and you barely touched the water I gave you."

Melissa hesitated, but took a sip thinking she'd humor Ashley and that was all she wanted. Before long the can was empty. "Thank you."

"You know, I've been thinking," Ashley murmured. "I understand why you turned Bryan down, but…I have to tell you, despite the devastation I felt at losing Mac, I wouldn't trade the time we had together for anything. Bryan loves you and he has every right to. Just like you have every right to love him. I just…thought you should know."

"My years with Peter are priceless to me," Ellen murmured, "and I'm quite sure your father feels the same about your mother. Loving once doesn't mean you can't love again."

Melissa squirmed in the chair, uncomfortable with the fact that all of them stared at her. "If it were you, wouldn't you both have protected them from all the anguish and hurt if you could?" she asked, her voice emerging hoarse from strain. "Kept them from suffering the way you did when they—" She couldn't say the word. Not with Bryan's life at stake. "It doesn't matter what I want. Working for him wasn't supposed to be like this."

"Because you never expected to love him?"

The question took her aback. She might've expected Ashley to ask it, maybe Ellen. But not her dad. She gave a tired smile. "You warned me, didn't you? I know it would never work. Never last. You don't have to say it."

"Why wouldn't it last? Because of the cancer?" Ashley questioned before her dad could speak. "Are you really going to argue that after what happened today? Bryan was *shot,* Melissa."

"I *know.* I was there."

"But you're still fighting how you feel and for what reason?" Ashley argued. "You couldn't keep Bryan from getting shot, and you can't control your future and whether or not your cancer returns."

"We're all going to die one day, Mel," Joe murmured.

"That we are," her father agreed. "It's not how long we live, it's how we live that's important. How we love."

"Melissa." Ashley sat forward. "You're scared, and you should be. Loving a man like Bryan won't be easy. I only know what I've lived, but I can honestly tell you I wouldn't change the course of things. Losing Mac *hurt,* and at the time I didn't know what I'd do without him. But he taught me how to love, and if I hadn't known him, hadn't loved him *and* lost him, I wouldn't have known how to love Joe."

"But that's not the same thing. Mac's death was an accident. A tragedy in a time of war. He didn't already have a deadly disease waiting to spring up again."

Her dad shot out of his chair and walked away from them.

"You don't *have* a disease, either," Ashley countered. "You had one, past tense. I could be diagnosed with cancer tomorrow where yours might never come back. And, Melissa, being sick once doesn't mean you aren't worthy of being loved. Maybe…maybe like Mac, the girl Bryan lost taught him how to love you, and all this—*today*—is meant to prove to you how much you really love him. Look at us," she said, waving her hand at the gathering surrounding her. "Would you ever in a million years have imagined all of us sitting here like this talking about *love?*"

Gruff chuckles followed Ashley's comment. Joe's, her father's, even Randall's odd-sounding rumble.

"Maybe this is to make you fight for Bryan and not the other way around," Joe suggested. "Once Pretty Boy is released, he'll not be lacking offers of comfort from women."

"They'd better not—" She broke off, her cheeks heating.

"Love and jealousy go hand in hand, Mel. Don't think they don't." Her father scowled as he took his seat again.

"Think about it," Ashley continued softly. "What if your situation were reversed, and Bryan had had cancer?"

"Ashley, please." She was so confused. She couldn't think,

couldn't do anything beyond worry about whether Bryan would be all right. All the talk about life and death and love—she just wanted Bryan to be okay.

"Hey, what else have you got to do while we wait? Come on, Melissa, what if? What if you loved Bryan and he pushed you away because he'd been sick a while ago? Would you let him do it or would you love him anyway?"

"It's not the same."

"It is-s." Randall lifted and lowered his hand on the arm of his wheelchair with a *thump*. "It is-s."

Ashley smiled at the old man before turning her attention back to Melissa. "See? Tonight proved that, yeah, your cancer could return, but Bryan is in just as much danger. He was shot by a drug addict, but it could've just as easily been a car accident or a multitude of other things. Dying can happen at any time. It's up to us if we're ready for it. Every moment we have with our loved ones is precious. And to Bryan and the rest of us, that means you're precious, too. We love you and we're going to love you whether you like it or not. It's up to you whether or not you love us back."

Of course she loved them. She loved all of them. Every one of them. Even…even Ellen. Because she'd made her dad happy. Because Ellen cared enough to give Melissa a treasured keepsake to make her feel better and because Ellen carried Melissa's little sister or brother. That was a start, a wonderful start. Overwhelmed, Melissa lowered her head. Her heart ached with wanting to believe Ashley's words. "What about children? He's so good with kids and I can't give him any."

Her father's thick brows lowered in a scowl. "That boy doesn't strike me as the type of man who'd only love a child if it were his own flesh and blood."

He was right. Bryan would love any child, no matter what. She thought of him stitching up the little boy's head the night of the barbecue. Remembered the look on his face.

"Dr. Booker? Would you and Chief York come this way? The surgery is complete and Dr. Ackerman would like to speak to you."

Melissa jerked at the sound of the nurse's voice. The woman didn't look at anyone other than Randall and her dad, but even though the old man hadn't said more than a few words the entire time he'd been there, one glance told Melissa he understood her fears.

Pulling his gaze from hers, Randall raised his hand toward the nurse. "Have him c-come here. We're his-s f-f-family."

The nurse hesitated only a moment. "Yes, sir."

"Thank you," she whispered.

Randall nodded. "Families s-stick together." He tapped his heart. "F-faith, M-Melissa."

"Chief York? Dr. Booker?" A scrub-clad doctor sauntered toward the group but stopped in front of Randall. "I'm Dr. Ackerman. Dr. Booker, the surgery on your grandson was touch and go, but we removed the bullet and repaired the damage. He's stable and should make a full recovery. He won't wake up for several hours yet, but if you'd like to go back and sit with him, you can."

Randall shook his head. "T-take her." He pointed toward Melissa and she stepped forward, unable to remember when she'd stood up.

The doctor's eyes flicked toward her with interest then back to Randall again. "It's family only, sir."

Randall dipped his head in a nod. "His f-fiancée."

"I didn't realize," the doctor murmured, dipping his head once and smiling at her now. "Nurse Collins will take you back."

Melissa couldn't wait to get to Bryan's side, but she stopped long enough to hug Randall. *"Thank you."*

The old man's eyes sparkled with warmth and understanding. So much like Bryan's. "T-tell 'im you l-love him. Best m-medicine."

She tried to smile. Maybe it was the best medicine. And maybe they were all right.

But did she have the courage to take that ultimate leap of faith?

BRYAN STRUGGLED to find his way through the fog. His side hurt, his throat hurt and he felt like he'd been slammed by a semi. Then it came back in an instant and he tensed, groaning when pain followed.

"Bryan? *Bryan?*"

Icy-cold fingers framed his face, the shock of it bringing him fully awake.

"Oh, thank God," he heard Melissa rasp huskily. "Thank you, thank you, thank you."

Something hit his mouth, salty and warm. "Don't…cry," he whispered, opening his eyes.

Melissa sniffled, her nose runny, her eyes red rimmed. She looked beautiful. Scared out of her mind, but beautiful.

"Heard you after…I got shot." Most of it was fuzzy, and maybe it had been a dream, but he didn't think he'd dreamed hearing the words he'd waited so long to hear her say. "You said…you love me." Saying the words out loud made him smile. "Say it again."

Melissa released a husky laugh. "I love you," she whispered, her hands trembling against his cheeks. "I love you."

"That mean…you'll marry me?"

Her expression softened even more, the face of a woman

torn. His heart rate increased and the monitor behind him bleeped more quickly as a result.

"Oh, Bryan. Just rest. We'll talk and sort things through once you're out of here. I'll be here, though. I won't—"

He shook his head and tried to wet his lips with a tongue drier than desert sand. "Now. Tell me now."

She stared down at him, searching. Hopeful? "You're taking advantage of being hurt."

"Is it working?"

Her laugh was choked with tears. "You're sure about *everything*? Bryan, you have to be sure. The cancer and...and children. I won't risk passing the gene on and watching the cycle continue. I won't and you need to know that won't change."

"I know."

Her eyes sparkled with tears. "And my scars? How I d-don't have any breasts?" She whispered the word *breasts*.

"Look at me." His eyes narrowed on hers when she finally managed to meet his stare. "I'm scarred now. You going to...hold it against me?"

She laughed softly again, doubt tinged but happy, too. He wanted her happy. She deserved happy.

"Never."

"Good." He mustered up the energy to smile, relieved. "Because now you've got to...get to work. Lots to plan."

Melissa wiped her eyes and sniffled. "We just finished a huge fund-raiser and have a medical facility to build. What are we working on now?"

"A wedding. You've got...six months. I'm going to teach you to...plan ahead."

EPILOGUE

Four years later…

MELISSA PACKED AWAY the last of the quotes she'd pulled from the corkboard lining her dry-erase board, then straightened to survey her classroom. How could another school year be over?

She and Bryan, their family and friends, had celebrated her five-year milestone weeks ago at Randall's large home—now their home since they'd moved in with him—and she had a whole summer to play with her daughter.

"Mommy, mommy! They're chasing me!"

Brianna, adopted a year before, ran into her classroom and flung herself at Melissa, wrapping her chubby little arms around her legs. She giggled excitedly, gazing over her shoulder expectantly until her aunt Madeline raced into the room behind her.

Four years old, Maddy had the same blond hair and blue eyes that Melissa shared with her dad, and once she'd held her baby sister in her arms, Melissa had known she couldn't spend her life mourning her lost daughter or withholding the love she had to give.

"Pick me up, pick me up! They'll get me!"

Melissa laughed and placed a loud, smacking kiss on her daughter's forehead before swinging her up in her arms. "Now you're safe."

Bryan entered the room behind the kids and she shared a smile with him, one of love and life and instant awareness. His gaze slid over her in a knee-weakening sweep blatantly full of promises to be carried out later, and the sight made her want to call Ellen and see if she was up to babysitting Brianna for a couple hours. Maybe all night.

"You ready to go?" Bryan asked, his smiling knowing.

"We got a surprise!"

"You do?" She eyed the girls, wondering which one would spill the news first. "What is it?"

"A—"

"Not s'pose to tell!" Maddy called.

"—picnic!"

Bryan winced. "So much for that."

She pulled him close and gave him a searing kiss. Bryan might have been a player once, but marriage had changed him. Even Joe said so. Their love life was the stuff of trendy magazine articles, and for the past four years she and Bryan had won a different award in the *Taylorsville Tribune*—that of Taylorsville's Most Romantic Couple. Not even Joe and Ashley had beaten them yet.

"A picnic, huh? Any special reason?" she asked.

"You'll have to wait and see."

"What's the occasion?"

Holding her and Brianna both in his arms, her husband grinned. "A celebration."

She drew in a sharp breath, the clues falling into place. "Because...*because...?*"

Bryan nodded, his smile tender. "I just got the call. The paperwork will be completed tomorrow and then you will be a mommy again very soon."

"A little boy. Oh, Bryan!"

His lips met hers and held. Tears prickled behind her lids, but they were happy tears. Tears full of joy and thankfulness and life.

She still had doubts and fears of what the future might bring, but they were fleeting since she'd finally placed the worry over her future in God's control and decided to enjoy the man she loved, the family she'd always wanted. Life was for living, and she planned to live every second of it. It was all in what a person believed—and she believed without a doubt that she'd finally gotten her happy ending.

* * * * *

THE ROYAL HOUSE OF NIROLI
Always passionate, always proud

The richest royal family in the world—united by blood and passion, torn apart by deceit and desire.

Nestled in the azure blue of the Mediterranean Sea, the majestic island of Niroli has prospered for centuries. The Fierezza men have worn the crown with passion and pride since ancient times. But now, as the king's health declines, and his two sons have been tragically killed, the crown is in jeopardy.

The clock is ticking—a new heir must be found before the king is forced to abdicate. By royal decree the internationally scattered members of the Fierezza family are summoned to claim their destiny. But any person who takes the throne must do so according to The Rules of the Royal House of Niroli. Soon secrets and rivalries emerge as the descendents of this ancient royal line vie for position and power. Only a true Fierezza can become ruler—a person dedicated to their country, their people...and their eternal love!

Each month starting in July 2007,
Harlequin Presents is delighted to bring you
an exciting installment from
THE ROYAL HOUSE OF NIROLI,
in which you can follow the epic search
for the true Nirolian king.
Eight heirs, eight romances, eight fantastic stories!

Here's your chance to enjoy a sneak preview of the first book delivered to you by royal decree...

FIVE minutes later she was standing immobile in front of the study's window, her original purpose of coming in forgotten, as she stared in shocked horror at the envelope she was holding. Waves of heat followed by icy chill surged through her body. She could hardly see the address now through her blurred vision, but the crest on its left-hand front corner stood out, its *royal* crest, followed by the address: *HRH Prince Marco of Niroli...*

She didn't hear Marco's key in the apartment door, she didn't even hear him calling out her name. Her shock was so great that nothing could penetrate it. It encased her in a kind of bubble, which only concentrated the torment of what she was suffering and branded it on her brain so that it could never be forgotten. It was only finally pierced by the sudden opening of the study door as Marco walked in.

"Welcome home, *Your Highness*. I suppose I ought to curtsy." She waited, praying that he would laugh and tell her that she had got it all wrong, that the envelope she was holding, addressing him as Prince Marco of Niroli, was some silly mistake. But like a tiny candle flame shivering vulnerably in the dark, her hope trembled fearfully. And then the look in Marco's eyes extinguished it as cruelly as a hand placed callously over a dying person's face to stem their last breath.

"Give that to me," he demanded, taking the envelope from her.

"It's too late, Marco," Emily told him brokenly. "I know the truth now…." She dug her teeth in her lower lip to try to force back her own pain.

"You had no right to go through my desk," Marco shot back at her furiously, full of loathing at being caught off-guard and forced into a position in which he was in the wrong, making him determined to find something he could accuse Emily of. "I trusted you…."

Emily could hardly believe what she was hearing. "No, you didn't trust me, Marco, and you didn't trust me because you knew that I couldn't trust you. And you knew that because you're a liar, and liars don't trust people because they know that they themselves cannot be trusted." She not only felt sick, she also felt as though she could hardly breathe. "You are Prince Marco of Niroli…. How could you not tell me who you are and still live with me as intimately as we have lived together?" she demanded brokenly.

"Stop being so ridiculously dramatic," Marco demanded fiercely. "You are making too much of the situation."

"*Too much?*" Emily almost screamed the words at him. "When were you going to tell me, Marco? Perhaps you just planned to walk away without telling me anything? After all, what do my feelings matter to you?"

"Of course they matter." Marco stopped her sharply. "And it was in part to protect them, and you, that I decided not to inform you when my grandfather first announced that he intended to step down from the throne and hand it on to me."

"To protect me?" Emily nearly choked on her fury. "Hand

on the throne? No wonder you told me when you first took me to bed that all you wanted was sex. You *knew* that was the only kind of relationship there could ever be between us! You *knew* that one day you would be Niroli's king. No doubt you are expected to marry a princess. Is she picked out for you already, your *royal* bride?"

* * * * *

Look for
THE FUTURE KING'S PREGNANT MISTRESS
by Penny Jordan in July 2007,
from Harlequin Presents,
available wherever books are sold.

HARLEQUIN®

Mediterranean
N I G H T S™

*Experience the glamour and elegance of cruising the
high seas with a new 12-book series....*

MEDITERRANEAN NIGHTS

Coming in July 2007...

SCENT OF A WOMAN

by

Joanne Rock

When Danielle Chevalier is invited to an exclusive
conference aboard *Alexandra's Dream,* she knows it
will mean good things for her struggling fragrance
company. But her dreams get a setback when she
meets Adam Burns, a representative from a large
American conglomerate.

Danielle is charmed by the brusque American—
until she finds out he means to compete with her bid
for the opportunity that will save her family business!

www.eHarlequin.com

HM38961

Romantic
SUSPENSE

Sparked by Danger,
Fueled by Passion.

Mission: Impassioned

A brand-new miniseries begins with

My Spy

By *USA TODAY* bestselling author

Marie Ferrarella

She had to trust him with his life....
It was the most daring mission of Joshua Lazlo's
career: rescuing the prime minister of England's
daughter from a gang of cold-blooded kidnappers.
But nothing prepared the shadowy secret agent
for a fiery woman whose touch ignited something
far more dangerous.

My Spy
#1472

Available July 2007 wherever you buy books!

n o c t u r n e™

**DON'T MISS THE RIVETING CONCLUSION
TO THE RAINTREE TRILOGY**

RAINTREE: SANCTUARY

by *New York Times* bestselling author

BEVERLY BARTON

Mercy, guardian of the Raintree
homeplace, takes a stand against
the Ansara wizards to battle for
the Clan's future.

*On sale July,
wherever books are sold.*

THE GARRISONS

A brand-new family saga begins with

THE CEO'S SCANDALOUS AFFAIR

BY ROXANNE ST. CLAIRE

Eldest son Parker Garrison is preoccupied running his Miami hotel empire and dealing with his recently deceased father's secret second family. Since he has little time to date, taking his superefficient assistant to a charity event should have been a simple plan. Until passion takes them beyond business.

Don't miss any of the six exciting titles in THE GARRISONS continuity, beginning in July. Only from Silhouette Desire.

THE CEO'S SCANDALOUS AFFAIR

#1807

Available July 2007.

REQUEST YOUR FREE BOOKS!
2 FREE NOVELS PLUS 2 FREE GIFTS!

HARLEQUIN®

Super Romance®

Exciting, emotional, unexpected!

YES! Please send me 2 FREE Harlequin Superromance® novels and my 2 FREE gifts. After receiving them, if I don't wish to receive any more books, I can return the shipping statement marked "cancel." If I don't cancel, I will receive 6 brand-new novels every month and be billed just $4.69 per book in the U.S., or $5.24 per book in Canada, plus 25¢ shipping and handling per book and applicable taxes, if any*. That's a savings of close to 15% off the cover price! I understand that accepting the 2 free books and gifts places me under no obligation to buy anything. I can always return a shipment and cancel at any time. Even if I never buy another book from Harlequin, the two free books and gifts are mine to keep forever.   135 HDN EEX7   336 HDN EEYK

Name _____ (PLEASE PRINT)

Address _____ Apt. _____

City _____ State/Prov. _____ Zip/Postal Code _____

Signature (if under 18, a parent or guardian must sign)

Mail to the **Harlequin Reader Service®:**
IN U.S.A.: P.O. Box 1867, Buffalo, NY 14240-1867
IN CANADA: P.O. Box 609, Fort Erie, Ontario L2A 5X3

Not valid to current Harlequin Superromance subscribers.

Want to try two free books from another line?
Call 1-800-873-8635 or visit www.morefreebooks.com.

* Terms and prices subject to change without notice. NY residents add applicable sales tax. Canadian residents will be charged applicable provincial taxes and GST. This offer is limited to one order per household. All orders subject to approval. Credit or debit balances in a customer's account(s) may be offset by any other outstanding balance owed by or to the customer. Please allow 4 to 6 weeks for delivery.

Your Privacy: Harlequin is committed to protecting your privacy. Our Privacy Policy is available online at www.eHarlequin.com or upon request from the Reader Service. From time to time we make our lists of customers available to reputable firms who may have a product or service of interest to you. If you would prefer we not share your name and address, please check here. ☐

HSR07

Do you know
a real-life heroine?

Nominate her for the Harlequin
More Than Words award.

_____

Each year Harlequin Enterprises honors five
ordinary women for their extraordinary
commitment to their community.

Each recipient of the Harlequin More Than Words
award receives a $10,000 donation from Harlequin
to advance the work of her chosen charity. And five
of Harlequin's most acclaimed authors donate their
time and creative talents to writing a novella inspired
by the award recipients. The More Than Words
anthology is published annually in October and all
proceeds benefit causes of concern to women.

HARLEQUIN

**For more details or to nominate
a woman you know please visit**
www.HarlequinMoreThanWords.com

COMING NEXT MONTH

#1428 SARA'S SON • Tara Taylor Quinn
One morning, a young man knocks at Sara Calhoun's door—the son she gave up for adoption twenty-one years ago. The son she hasn't seen since the day of his birth. This meeting leads to the unraveling of other long-hidden secrets and...maybe...to the love Sara's always wanted to find.

#1429 STAR-CROSSED PARENTS • C.J. Carmichael
You, Me & the Kids
What if Romeo and Juliet had been children of single parents? And what if those parents had fallen in love, as well? Leigh Hartwell can't believe her daughter Taylor has run off to be with a boy she met on the Internet. Which is why she drives several hundred miles to drag the girl home. But Taylor has other ideas...and so does the father of the boy she's gone to meet.

#1430 THE SHERIFF OF SAGE BEND • Brenda Mott
Count on a Cop
Lucas Blaylock, sheriff of Sage Bend, Montana, can't ever forget that he's the man who broke Miranda Ward's heart when he jilted her at the altar. He won't let himself forget it, because someday he might prove just as bad as his criminal father and abusive brother. But for now, he'll do anything he can to help the woman he loves find her missing sister....

#1431 THE OTHER WOMAN'S SON • Darlene Gardner
Jenna Wright can't say no when a handsome stranger hires her rhythm and blues duo to a long-term gig on Beale Street. But she soon finds out that Clay Dillon is keeping a secret from her and that his offer really is too good to be true. Seems she and Clay have something in common—his half sister, a young woman who desperately needs what only Jenna can give her.

#1432 UNDERCOVER PROTECTOR • Molly O'Keefe
FBI agent Maggie Fitzgerald has never had a problem being undercover...until she's assigned to investigate journalist Caleb Gomez. She needs to focus on extracting his information about a drug dealer. But Caleb's charm is reminding her she's a woman first and an agent second.

#1433 FATHER MATERIAL • Kimberley Van Meter
9 Months Later
Natalie Simmons books a rafting trip hoping to reconnect with her ex-fiancé, but instead she has one night with river guide Evan Murphy—and leaves with more than just memories. When he finds out she's pregnant, Evan is determined to show her he could be a good dad. Too bad Natalie is convinced he's not father material.